D0352501

QUANTUM

In 1948, a German scientist discovered a blueprint for the construction of the universe that could surpass the theories of Einstein. But his secret past caught up with him and his work was seemingly lost forever. Now, buried knowledge has been rediscovered. America and Russia are in a ruthless fight for the ultimate power of the new millennium – and – ex-Navy SEAL Nolan Kilkenny finds himself caught in the crossfire. He races to solve a decades-old mystery – that's if the solution doesn't kill him first...

QUANTUM

QUANTUM

by

Tom Grace

Magna Large Print Books
Long Preston, North Yorkshire,
BD23 4ND, England.

British Library Cataloguing in Publication Data.

Grace, Tom
    Quantum.

    A catalogue record of this book is
    available from the British Library

    ISBN   978-0-7505-3441-3

First published in Great Britain 2000 by Pocket Books

Copyright © 2000 The Kilkenny Group, LLC

Cover illustration © Roy Bishop by arrangement with
Arcangel Images

Tom Grace asserts the moral right to be identified as the author of
this work.

Published in Large Print 2011 by arrangement with
HarperCollins Publishers

Magna Large Print is an imprint of Library Magna Books Ltd.

Printed and bound in Great Britain by
T.J. (International) Ltd., Cornwall, PL28 8RW

Acknowledgements

My thanks to John Van der Velde, Yukio Kamazara, and Lawrence Jones – professors of Physics at the University of Michigan – for their insights into the challenges and promise of physics research in the near future; to Fred Mayer, University Planner at the University of Michigan, for helping me dig up the past; to Shannon Zachary and Kathleen Dow of the University Library for an education in the preservation of books; to Stuart Cohen of the University of Michigan Marine Hydrodynamics Laboratory for the tour of Martin Kilkenny's old workshop; to Prof. Wolfgang Porad for giving me the lay of the land regarding research and Notre Dame; to B. J. Keepers and Scott Gochis for their generous advice on the Special Forces; to Barbara Jones for her understanding of the transportation industry; to the Ann Arbor Police Department; and to Nathan Jacobson , my friend and guide to Russia.

Thanks also to my editor Rob McMahon for his sound advice and sense of humor; to my agent Esther Margolis for her wise counsel; and to Larry Kirshbaum, Maureen Egen, Jamie Raab, Harvey-Jane Kowal, Jimmy Franco, Stephen Lamont, and their talented and able colleagues at Warner Books for their support and encouragement.

A special thanks to my wife, Kathy, and our children for their love and support as I write late into the night.

For John Steven Rosowki
A friend, classmate, and a true renaissance man
One of the brightest minds I have had the
privilege to know.
1962-1984

Prologue

DECEMBER 10, 1948

Ann Arbor, Michigan

In the shadows of a small white building near the center of the University of Michigan campus, a young man stood motionless as he watched and waited. He was tall and wiry with harshly chiseled features, as if he'd been carved rather than born.

From his concealed vantage point near the eastern end of the L-shaped Economics Building, the man-made canyon formed by the four-story masonry bulk of the Randall Physics Laboratory and the equally massive West Engineering building lay open before him. The two buildings defined one corner of a large campus quadrangle. A pair of diagonal walkways crisscrossed the formal lawn from opposite corners of the square, intersecting at a large concrete plaza in front of the Graduate Library. The plaza and campus green surrounding it were known as the Diag.

A wide flat hole surrounded by mounds of earth and debris lay to his right, just beyond the concrete walkway that extended out from an alley toward the center of the campus. A few days earlier a demolition crew had brought the aging boiler house and its attendant smokestack to the ground. The scene around him vaguely resembled many towns and villages of Europe he'd prowled as the Allied forces fought their way into Germany.

He put aside those thoughts and, instead, focused on the two men who stood in the illumination of a street-lamp not one hundred feet away. From this distance, he struggled to hear the men speak as a steady wind out of the north swallowed the sound of their conversation. Snow swirled into vortices around them as they shuffled and stamped their feet, trying to stay warm.

A few minutes later the older of the pair, a woodworker who built large model ships in a shop in West Engineering, shook his friend's hand and walked off at a brisk pace. The snow barked under his boots, echoing off the surrounding buildings. The woodworker quickly rounded the far side of the Economics Building and disappeared from view as the other man then climbed up the stone steps that led to the rear entrance of the Physics Lab.

A light flickered and then illuminated a small third-floor office, and from the shadows the hunter watched as Johann Wolff hung up his hat and coat and sat down at his desk.

Might as well settle in, the hunter thought as he crouched down atop his duffel, behind the thick evergreen shrub.

He shrugged off the cold and discomfort – conditions he'd been hardened against long ago – and instead focused on his mission. If Wolff

14

followed his usual routine, like a typical German, then he could expect the young physicist to work late into the night before returning to his rented room a few blocks away.

Johann Wolff pulled six notebooks out of his battered leather briefcase and set them carefully on the desk. He'd started the oldest of the slim volumes in Germany after the war, and each marked his painstaking progress in the pursuit of a scientific vision.

He opened the newest of the notebooks and carefully ran through the calculations again, following the flow of numbers through his complex mathematics. This was new territory. The methods he'd developed to describe what he saw as the next logical step after Einstein and Heisenberg were as radical as the calculus created by Isaac Newton to describe gravity.

Wolff's formulas allowed him to move fluidly back and forth in time. The nearly musical cadence of the variables described an evolving universe of heretofore unimagined elegance and sophistication. The notion that the universe was static and unchanging had died nineteen years earlier when Edwin Hubble discovered that the cosmos was indeed expanding, as was predicted by Einstein's theories.

'Mein Gott!' Wolff cried out as an image of the delicate, multidimensional structures that define both matter and energy clearly formed in his mind.

Wolff flipped to a blank page in his notebook and quickly began to sketch the mental picture before it faded. His skilled hand produced the image of a coiled loop that twisted and wound into itself like a knotted ball – an image that attempted to represent a subatomic-sized chunk of the universe possessing seven additional dimensions beyond the readily apparent three dimensions of space and one of time.

Smiling with childlike wonder, Wolff stared at the drawing and realized that, at twenty-nine years of age, he now stood ready to overthrow everything in the realm of theoretical physics that had preceded him.

'I've got to let Raphaele know about this,' he said excitedly as he rummaged through his briefcase.

Wolff extracted the pages of a letter he'd started earlier that day while riding the train back from Chicago. The words and formulas flowed rapidly from his pen as he briefly laid out the framework of a theory that would describe the structure of everything from the tiniest bits of matter to the entirety of the universe. The letter quickly grew from a few pages of personal news to a thick sheaf filled with concise fragments of his blossoming theory. The six notebooks on his desk were the seeds of a larger work he knew lay ahead of him, one whose publication would shake the world.

Shortly before midnight Wolff shut off the light in his office. Bundled against the evening chill, he exited through the building's side door and began walking toward the center of campus.

'Excuse me,' a voice called out.

'*Ja?*' Wolff answered cautiously, still unable to see whom the voice belonged to.

'I'm down here.' A hand waved furiously at him from the excavation behind West Engineering.

Wolff stepped over the barricade and peered into the void left by the demolition of the boiler house. He saw a dark-haired young man in a soiled gray coat standing in the pit below.

'Be careful near the edge, it might give out on you. That's how I ended up down here. Think you could give me a hand getting out?'

'Sure,' Wolff replied. Judging by the smears of dirt on the man, it looked as though he had already made a few unsuccessful attempts to climb out on his own.

Wolff set his briefcase on the ground and knelt in the snow close to the edge of the pit. The young man moved toward him, and Wolff reached down to grasp his hand.

'I'll start climbing on three. Ready?'

Wolff nodded.

'One, two...'

Before the count of three came, the young man yanked hard and pulled Wolff headfirst into the pit. Wolff felt his shoulder burn, his arm rotating behind him as he fell. Deftly, the man bent Wolff's forearm upward, pressing the physicist's hand between his shoulder blades as he drove his face into the ground. Wolff's forehead plowed through two inches of freezing mud before slamming into the hardened earth. A crack of bone resonated inside his head, followed by a sudden rush of warm fluid into his sinus cavity – the bridge of Wolff's nose crumbled as it impacted a large stone.

The man crouched over Wolff, pinning him to the ground. The weight of the attacker's body bore down on the point where the man's knee met Wolff's spine.

'Why? Why are you doing this?' Wolff shouted with globs of dirty snow and mud spraying from his lips. 'Let me go!'

Wolff struggled to pull free, but the young man had the advantage of strength and leverage.

'You are Johann Wolff. From 1939 until 1945 you were a research scientist with the Reichsforschungsrat. Your job was to devise more efficient ways of killing people.' The man spoke deliberately, each word carrying the weight of a pronouncement. 'Under your supervision, over two thousand men, women, and children lost their lives as test subjects and slave laborers. The Nokmim, the avengers of your victims, have found you guilty of crimes against humanity and have sentenced you to death.'

'Lies! I did not help the Nazis! I am a scientist. I killed no one!' Wolff countered, vainly trying to face his accuser.

The man shifted his weight and drove Wolff deeper into the mire. With his free hand, the man pulled a long serrated knife from the sheath strapped to his thigh and plunged it into the side of Wolff's neck. The stainless-steel blade sliced Wolff's carotid artery, several muscles, and the jugular vein. Wolff blacked out as the blood pressure in his brain, temporarily heightened by adrenaline, abruptly dropped. The sharpened edge passed effortlessly through Wolff's throat, nearly decapitating the physicist. The breath in Wolff's lungs escaped with a gurgling hiss, the warm moist air mixing with the steam already rising from the expanding pool of blood. The tension in Wolff's body waned as he slowly descended from unconsciousness into death.

The assassin quickly dragged Wolff's body to the far end of the excavation and placed it in a partially buried maintenance tunnel at the base of the demolished smokestack. He then retrieved the physicist's briefcase and placed it with the body.

As the winter storm increased, he opened his duffel bag and took out a folding shovel. Without a glance, he expertly flipped the folding shovel head open and tightened the neck to lock it in place. Quickly and quietly, as the cold wind howled above him, the assassin entombed Wolff in the tunnel and removed any evidence of the murder. Within a week, according to what the workmen had told him, the entire site would be filled and leveled with the surrounding lawn.

'Vengeance has been served,' the young man said softly as snow began to blanket the final resting place of the war criminal Johann Wolff. 'May God have mercy on your soul – and mine.'

1

JUNE 5, PRESENT DAY

Ann Arbor, Michigan

Nolan Kilkenny punched the accelerator of the Mercedes ML 320 and piloted the black SUV into a sharp right turn onto the Huron Parkway. The yellow signal switched to red as he passed beneath.

In the passenger seat, Kelsey Newton stripped the towel from her head and began brushing out her shoulder-length mane of blond hair. The still-damp strands clumped together, and beads of water sprang off Kelsey's brush with each flick of her wrist.

'Hey, watch it,' Nolan said as a few errant drops struck his face.

'You want me beautiful, don't you?' Kelsey replied, her face hidden behind a veil of hair.

'You always are.'

'Well, thank you, but it doesn't just happen, you know.'

Kelsey set the brush down on her lap and quickly wove her hair into a French braid. She then put the brush back in her purse and pulled out her mobile phone and began dialing.

The SUV's speedometer edged over fifty as they passed the large blue-and-white sign that announced their entry onto the grounds of the University of Michigan's North Campus. A smaller road sign set the speed limit at twenty-five miles per hour.

'We'll be there in a few minutes,' Kelsey said reassuringly as Nolan sped down the winding road that led to the Michigan Applied Research Consortium.

Kelsey set her phone back in her purse. Ahead, nestled deep within a wooded site, stood a glistening ribbon of glass and stainless steel that defined the curvilinear form of the MARC building. The ultramodern structure was the physical embodiment of a vision that Nolan's father had nurtured throughout his career in international finance: the idea that a bridge needed to be built between cutting-edge academic research and the businesses that fueled the nation's economy. In operation for less than three years, Sean Kilkenny's bridge carried a steadily growing flow of valuable technology from the university's research labs into the world, and an equally impressive flow of money back into the university's coffers.

Nolan parked in the first spot he found. Kelsey was already out her door and moving at a near run toward the building's main entry by the time he pulled his briefcase out of the backseat and locked the SUV. After a short sprint, he caught up with her just as she passed through the door. In the lobby, Sean Kilkenny stood waiting for them.

'Glad you two could make it.'

'Sorry we cut it so close, Dad. Traffic on US Twenty-three was a bear.'

21

Kelsey gave Sean a peck on the cheek. 'Thanks again for letting me borrow Nolan. I really doubt I could have replaced the entire tube array in only two days.'

'You're welcome, Kelsey. Anything to advance the cause of science.'

'Dad, you should see this proton detector experiment. Imagine a sixty-foot cube of water hidden in a salt mine under Lake Erie. It's pitch black down there, and the walls are lined with a couple of thousand jumbo-sized flood lamps.'

'Photomultiplier tubes,' Kelsey corrected.

'Whatever. Strangest underwater job I've ever been on.'

'I'm just glad I had an experienced diver down there with me,' Kelsey said as she squeezed Nolan's hand. 'The PDE tank can be a little disorienting.'

'I wouldn't let anyone dive alone in that thing, especially you,' Nolan said lovingly.

'I assume that this project has been put to bed?' Sean questioned.

Kelsey shot a furtive glance at Nolan, who reddened slightly. 'We finished our part. The physics department can now handle the rest of the upgrade.'

'Good, because after Sandstrom makes his pitch to the board, I have a feeling that MARC's newest project director is going to have his hands full.'

Kelsey brushed a fleck off Nolan's tweed jacket, causing Sean's mood to relax slightly as he watched her evaluate his son's appearance. It reminded him of how his late wife used to fuss over him before an important meeting, and it pleased him to know that his son had someone who cared for him in that same way.

Kelsey and Nolan had known each other since the earliest days of their childhood, when her family moved in to a home just a few doors up the street. They had attended school together, and both had distinguished themselves academically and athletically. They'd been best friends for years, sharing the strong bond of kindred spirits.

At eighteen, their ambitions took them on separate journeys. Kelsey attended the University of Michigan, where she pursued her passion for physics through to a doctorate and a faculty position. Nolan embraced the challenges of the United States Naval Academy, deferred his entry into the navy two years for a graduate degree from MIT, and then surprised his family and friends by joining the Navy SEALs.

Their friendship survived the twelve years of separation through a steady stream of phone calls, letters, and holiday visits. Eighteen months ago, when Nolan left the navy and returned to Ann Arbor, they resumed the comfortable pattern of their platonic relationship.

Both were ready for something more, but neither was willing to risk the security of what they had for the unknown – until they were nearly killed by a group of industrial spies. In the year following that brutal attempt on their lives, the two began enjoying an increasingly amorous relationship.

'Okay?' Nolan asked as she straightened his tie.

'Handsome as ever, dear.'

'You both look fine,' Sean said impatiently, checking his watch. 'The break's about over. Let's get inside. Nolan, Sandstrom and Paramo are waiting for you.'

Nolan followed his father and Kelsey into the conference room.

'Excuse me while I go make sure everything's ready for Sandstrom's dog and pony show,' Sean said before making a beeline for the podium.

From the doorway Nolan and Kelsey surveyed the crowd. The attendees had broken into several small groups, enjoying both the refreshments and the conversation.

'I see them, Kelsey. Look by the windows. The blond guy with the red beard is Sandstrom. Next to him – the older man, about a foot shorter with white hair and tortoiseshell glasses – that's Paramo.'

Beside the curved wall of glass that bowed outward into the woods, Kelsey spotted Ted Sandstrom and his mentor, Raphaele Paramo.

'Nolan,' Sandstrom called out as they approached, relief visible on his face. 'I was afraid you weren't going to show.'

'Wouldn't miss it, Ted,' he replied, then introduced Kelsey to the two physicists.

'Professor Newton,' Paramo said, shaking her hand enthusiastically, 'this is indeed a pleasure. I've read your paper on optical electronics. Very interesting work.'

'Thank you,' Kelsey replied, enjoying the admiration of a respected peer.

Sandstrom then clasped her hand warmly. 'I

understand we have you to thank for our being here today.'

'That may be overstating things a bit,' she demurred. 'All I did was look over the report that Notre Dame sent to MARC regarding your research. After I read it a few times – I admit it took more than one pass to really comprehend what you and Professor Paramo have accomplished – I told Nolan's father that he'd be a fool not to take a closer look.'

'Well, thank you for your vote of confidence.'

Across the room, Sean Kilkenny began to address those assembled. 'Ladies and gentlemen,' his amplified voice resonated above the murmuring conversations, 'if you'll kindly take your seats, we can move on to the next item on our agenda.'

The MARC board of directors, a mix of business executives and university regents, took their places at the conference table. Around the periphery of the room, members of the still-forming Notre Dame Applied Research Consortium (ND-ARC) and important guests of both universities returned to their seats. Sean Kilkenny waited until everyone was ready before proceeding.

'Last fall I had the pleasure of meeting our guest presenter while in South Bend for the Michigan–Notre Dame football game. While I am sure that some of us were pleased with the outcome of that game' – MARC's founder paused as a ripple of laughter followed his remark – 'I am doubly sure that others here are looking forward to the rematch this fall.' Another pause for partisan laughter. 'Be that as it may, my encounter with Ted Sandstrom, a professor of physics at Notre Dame, left a far greater impression on me than the game. Fellow board members and honored guests, I would like to introduce Professor Ted Sandstrom.'

The MARC director stood aside as Sandstrom approached the podium carrying a large Halliburton case.

'They're all yours, Ted,' Sean said quietly as he clipped a wireless microphone to Sandstrom's lapel.

Sandstrom looked over his audience. He recognized among the guests several wealthy Notre Dame alumni and a few of the regents. The presidents of both universities were seated together along the left wall. A sudden wave of nausea hit him, but it quickly subsided as he realized that this was no different from any classroom he'd ever been in. He was there to teach these people something about physics, and that was something he did very well.

'Good afternoon. As Mr Kilkenny said, I am a physicist. More precisely, I am an experimental physicist, which means I like to test ideas to see whether or not they work.'

Sandstrom pressed a button on the podium; the lights dimmed and the Asian symbol for yin and yang appeared on the large, flat wall display.

'In declaring that E equals mc squared, Einstein linked energy and matter together in such a way that the two are inseparable and, in some ways, indistinguishable. Matter is a mani-festation of energy. If you label the left side of this

26

symbol as matter' – Sandstrom pointed to the black yang –'and the right as energy, then the region that I'm interested in is here.'

Sandstrom traced the S line that defined the border between yin and yang.

'Here, in the boundary between matter and energy, resides the realm of quantum physics. This is where the classical physics of Newton and Galileo fall apart. The mathematical precision that we use to describe the motion of the planets is dethroned by an uncertainty principle that replaces absolutes with probabilities. In this thin edge, the distinction between matter and energy blurs.'

Sandstrom touched the podium keyboard again, and the image transformed into a horizontal grid, tilted slightly upward to show perspective. At random intervals two sections of the plane would distort, one spike warping upward while another went in the opposite direction. The warped areas would break free like water droplets and form gridded spheres that moved about briefly before being reabsorbed by the plane.

'The plane you see in this illustration represents a negative-energy state. This condition exists only in a vacuum in which all matter has been removed. In this state, quantum theory predicts that fluctuations in this energy allow for the spontaneous creation of both matter and antimatter.' Sandstrom pointed at the gridded spheres. 'Theory also states that these particles disappear rather quickly, and being a balanced system, the net energy is essentially zero. This just shows, even at a quantum level, that you can't get something for nothing.'

The gridded plane expanded and curled around on itself, forming a sphere.

'One theory about the origin of our universe puts it in a negative-energy state at the start of the Big Bang.'

Sandstrom zoomed in on the gridded sphere just as thousands of tiny blue and red particles appeared inside it.

'Now if matter and antimatter are created in equal amounts, then all these new particles should have collided with their opposites and annihilated each other in a burst of energy – leaving the universe a net zero.'

The red and blue particles quickly disappeared, and the gridded sphere collapsed into nothingness.

'This outcome is true only for a perfectly symmetrical universe. Suppose that our universe was asymmetrical, and at the moment of the Big Bang, there was more matter than antimatter.'

The new animation showed thousands of red and blue particles racing around, each collision giving off a brief white flash. After a few seconds the gridded sphere held only blue particles. The view panned out as the sphere expanded until it evolved into a spiraling galaxy and then gradually changed back into the yin-yang symbol.

'If this theory is valid, the question becomes: What caused the universe to be asymmetrical, allowing unequal amounts of matter and anti-matter particles to be produced?' Sandstrom paused briefly and looked over his audience. 'At this point, I suspect that more than a few of you are wondering where I'm going with this presentation. So let me backtrack a bit for you. Eleven years ago Professor Raphaele Paramo and I began to investigate the effect of strong electrical fields on totally evacuated spaces. Our experiments had some very interesting results.'

Sandstrom tapped the keyboard, and a photograph of a laboratory, scorched and in shambles, filled the screen.

'This one got away from us.' A brief laugh rose from the audience. 'Based on the theoretical calculations, the energies involved in this experiment should have been very low. As you can see, theory and reality were not in agreement. When we activated our test apparatus, an energy surge built up inside the evacuated chamber. The chamber quickly ruptured and a ball of lightning emerged. This coherent sphere of electricity floated around the lab for a few seconds before landing on an electrical panel. The explosion and resulting fire did significant damage to our lab. Fortunately, no one was hurt.'

The President of Notre Dame nodded, recalling the incident clearly.

'We rebuilt our laboratory and began to probe further into the discrepancy between theory and experiment. Here is the result of that work.'

Sandstrom switched off the projector, and the lights came back up. He then picked up the Halliburton case, set it on the conference table, and extracted what looked like a twelve-inch hexagonal nut made of matte black metal. Centered in the top face, in place of a threaded bolt, sat a six-inch-diameter hemisphere of clear Lexan. Sandstrom set the device down on one side so those in the room could see into the transparent dome. Clearly visible beneath the Lexan cover were three nested rings of a gold-tinted metal. A bluish, semitransparent sphere sat in the center of the rings like a gemstone in a jeweler's setting.

'The blue sphere, the heart of this device, contains nothing – it has been evacuated as completely as current technology allows. Surrounding it are three rings of a room-temperature superconducting material recently developed at Stanford University. The rings provide the strong electrical field I mentioned a moment ago.'

Sandstrom then pulled two small, freestanding digital devices from the case and plugged them together in series.

'These are standard watt meters that we use to measure the electric power on the input and output sides of the device. The calibration on both meters' – Sandstrom paused as he plugged a cord from the first meter into a wall receptacle – 'should be identical – which I am pleased to see is the case.'

Both meters registered identical 2200 watts. Satisfied the audience understood that both meters were operating properly, Sandstrom unplugged the cord, disconnected the meters, and reconnected them to jacks on opposite sides of the device. He then stood beside the table, holding the cord to the first meter in one hand.

'According to the first law of thermodynamics,

the total amount of energy coming out of a system must be equal to the total amount of energy going in. This phenomenon is known as conservation of energy, or the "no free lunch" law. It's a good law that has proved itself time and again – until now.'

Sandstrom plugged the cord into the wall socket. The first meter jumped to life, registering the voltage that coursed through it like before; the second meter registered zero. Inside the device, the centermost golden ring began to spin. As it accelerated, the next ring began rotating, and finally the outermost ring joined in the orbital dance. The spinning rings created the illusion that the bluish globe was floating in a golden haze; then sparks appeared within the orb. The sparks increased in number and intensity until the vacuum within the sphere held a ball of brightly glowing energy. The audience shielded their eyes from the intense glare emanating from the device until Sandstrom took an opaque black cover from the Halliburton case and placed it over the Lexan dome.

'It does get a bit bright,' Sandstrom said sympathetically as several members of the audience blinked their eyes. 'If you'll please take a look at the meter measuring the energy output.'

Several members of the MARC board stood and moved closer to get a better look at the meter.

'Is that thing registering correctly?' asked an electrical engineer who'd made his fortune in the computer industry.

'This isn't possible,' said another, straining to

believe what her eyes were showing her.

'That's exactly what I said when I first saw the numbers. The energy output from this device is approximately two thousand times what we're putting in. Now, since I firmly believe that energy can be neither created nor destroyed, the only conclusion I can draw is that this device is a faucet and the energy I'm using to create a strong asymmetrical energy field has opened the faucet, and that energy from some other source is pouring through it.'

The room buzzed with dozens of conversations as several people tried to shout questions at Sandstrom. A tidal wave of sound erupted from the normally diplomatic attendees as each tried to comprehend the impact of this discovery. Overwhelmed by the chaos that was overtaking the room, Sandstrom looked to Sean Kilkenny for help in subduing the crowd. Kilkenny, a boardroom veteran, quickly grabbed a microphone.

'And when Professor Sandstrom finally does determine exactly how his invention works,' the MARC founder said loudly, demanding the attention of the audience, 'he will likely win the Nobel Prize. In the meantime, this discovery quite literally changes everything. Quantum technology will irrevocably alter the global economic landscape. The small size and weight of quantum power cells – relative to the energy they deliver – finally give electric motors a huge power-to-weight advantage over internal-combustion motors. This advantage will cause a stampede in the transportation industry as manufacturers rush to exploit it, and a panic in the fossil-fuel industry as they look for ways to cope with this advancement. The last time a technological shift of this magnitude occurred was almost a hundred years ago when small, efficient, fuel-burning engines supplanted the horse and carriage.'

Audience members with ties to the Big Three automakers and the petroleum industry nervously nodded agreement.

'These industries are mature and established, and possess very deep pockets. While it might be possible for a maverick inventor with a better mousetrap to play David and Goliath with the likes of General Motors, the battle would be bloody and fierce. As much as I enjoy rooting for the underdog in an impossible fight, I also recognize that a young firm, one in control of a technology that promises to change how so many things in our world are done, could instigate a global economic war. The failures of the Asian and Russian financial markets in the late 1990s would pale in comparison to the sudden collapse of the industrial pillars that support our modern world.'

Sean Kilkenny let that thought hang over the now silent audience for a moment as he scanned the faces of so many people that he knew and respected.

'To his credit, Professor Sandstrom is not an ivory-tower scientist. He cares about the effect his work will have on the livelihood of millions of people, and his concern is legitimate. The manner in which this quantum technology is unleashed on the world poses a very real

33

dilemma.' Sean Kilkenny then paused dramatically, and smiled. 'It has also presented us with a unique opportunity. Those of you who know me well know that I believe in the concept of MARC, of the absolute necessity in building bridges between the worlds of academic research and industrial production. This is what I have chosen to do in my retirement, and I promote this cause with the fervor of an evangelical preacher on a crusade.'

'Amen, Brother Kilkenny,' one of the board members shouted out.

'Amen, indeed. My introduction to Professor Sandstrom was no accident.' Sean motioned to the Catholic priest seated beside the University of Michigan's President, 'Father Joseph Blake, the President of Notre Dame, is familiar with what we've accomplished with MARC and is very interested in transplanting the concept. I, of course, agreed to help in any way I could. The fruit of that initial discussion is twofold. First, the Notre Dame Applied Research Consortium officially opened for business this morning.'

Polite applause from the MARC board to their colleagues on the ND-ARC board filled the room.

'Second, as chairman of the MARC board, I have received a formal offer from Suzanne Tynan, my distinguished counterpart at ND-ARC, to enter into a joint venture, the purpose of which is to patent any technological application for Sandstrom's quantum power cell that we can think of, and to license these applications to any and all parties who believe that they can make use of them. In short, we have been asked by our colleagues from South Bend to work with them in managing an intellectual property that may well be to this new century what the electric light, the internal-combustion engine, and the microchip were to the last.'

The momentary silence that followed the announcement evaporated, along with any semblance of parliamentary procedure, as the MARC board erupted with questions.

'How's this thing going to work?'

'Sean, what kind of commitment are we looking at?'

'Do we have any projections?'

Sean turned to where Sandstrom stood with Paramo, Kelsey, and Nolan and smiled. He lived for moments such as this.

'Mrs Quinn,' he said loud enough to be heard over the din of questions being called out at him, 'would you please distribute the prospectus for this venture.'

Loretta Quinn, Kilkenny's trusted assistant for more than thirty years, nodded and made a quick circuit around the conference table, handing each of the board members a sealed and numbered packet of documents.

'Due to the nature of the information contained in these packets, I feel it is my duty to remind you that this is a confidential matter, and the premature disclosure of any of this material would invite legal action equivalent in severity to the wrath of God. To answer a few of your questions, I have signed a letter of intent with ND-ARC. We have thirty days to review our proposed arrangement and iron out any wrinkles. While we debate percentages and punctuation, I have authorized the use of some of our resources by ND-ARC. If, at the end of thirty days, we decide not to pursue this venture, all materials will be returned and we will be compensated by ND-ARC for any resources used during this period. Most of your remaining questions should be answered in the prospectus, which I request you read thoroughly. In short, this discovery' – he motioned with his hand toward Sandstrom's quietly running device – 'is the future. At this time I move that we adjourn and further discussion of this matter be added to the agenda for the closed board meeting next week.'

'I second the motion,' called out board member Diana LaPointe, a respected attorney specializing in patent law and intellectual property.

'All those in favor?' Sean asked.

'Aye,' the board unanimously responded.

'The motion is carried, and this meeting is adjourned. Thank you all for coming.'

As the meeting broke up, board members carefully placed the sealed packages they had been given into briefcases, treating the documents with the same reverence one would give an original draft of the Constitution. Nolan, Kelsey, and Paramo moved to the front of the room, where Sandstrom was carefully placing his equipment back in the Halliburton case under Sean's watchful eye.

'So, Sean,' Sandstrom asked as he flipped the latches on the case closed, 'what happens now?'

'You go back to work. Over the next week the

board will digest what we've just given them. I suspect the meeting next week will be a doozy. In the end, I doubt we'll take the entire thirty days to decide. This deal is just too interesting to pass up. By the way, Nolan,' Sean said, turning to his son, 'now it's official: You're our coordinator for the quantum project. Your first assignment will be to relocate Ted's lab off campus.'

'Something a little bigger, I hope,' Sandstrom said.

'A bit,' Nolan replied. 'But some of the space we need is for business activities related to your work. Now that you've discovered a new way to print money, you'll need some room to stack, count, and store it.'

'How's lunch next Tuesday look?' LaPointe asked as she eyed her planner.

'I'm open,' Conrad Evans replied. 'Noon at the Candy Dancer?'

'Works for me.'

Evans and LaPointe penciled the lunch meeting into their calendars.

'See you on Tuesday, Conrad,' LaPointe said with a smile as she zipped her leatherbound planner closed and walked away.

Evans slipped a thin booklet into the interior pocket of his double-breasted blazer and picked up his briefcase. He then scanned the room for a moment, and located the attractive brunette in the tailored linen suit. For Evans – a long-divorced, slightly overweight middle-aged workaholic – Dr Oksanna Zoshchenko was a breath of fresh air.

A chemist by training, Zoshchenko discovered early in her career that her true gifts lay in administration. Her native intelligence coupled with a skillful sense of diplomacy was cited as the primary reason for her rapid ascent to the highest levels of the Russian Academy of Sciences. Among those whose position in the academy she eclipsed, rumors imputed Zoshchenko's meteoric rise to her considerable physical assets and her willingness to use them to further her career.

'So, Oksanna, what did you think?' Evans asked as he approached the sultry brunette.

'It was quite illuminating.' Zoshchenko's Ukrainian accent was soft, a hint of something both foreign and exotic.

'Very diplomatic of you. Normally, these board meetings are fairly dull. At least that surprise show-and-tell we had at the end livened things up a bit. Oh, and regarding that, I'm afraid I must ask you not to mention the Sandstrom presentation to anyone, at least until after they've published their research. It's all covered in the nondisclosure agreement you signed.'

'I was a scientist long before I became a bureaucrat, so I understand discretion with regard to research. I promise I won't discuss what I've seen here.'

'Thank you, and again, I apologize. This was one meeting I couldn't bow out of, and I didn't want to abandon you in the lobby for two hours. Thank you for your patience.'

'Your apology is unnecessary, Conrad. I truly found this meeting quite educational. Our economy, our way of thinking is so different from yours. We have many brilliant scientists, like this Sandstrom, but no mechanism to transfer technology to our industries. No way to capitalize on innovation. This consortium is a very good idea, one of many that I will take back to Moscow with me.'

'Well, then, as a regent of this university, I am pleased that your visit here has been a productive one.' Evans glanced at his watch. 'If you like, we still have time for a decent meal before you leave.'

'I'd like that,' Zoshchenko replied appreciatively. 'It's a long flight back to Moscow, and the food served on airplanes is not so good.'

2

JUNE 7

Moscow, Russia

Marathon flights, even in the comfort of first class, always left Oksanna Zoshchenko feeling sore and exhausted. Upon her arrival the previous evening at Sheremetyevo-2, she returned to her apartment and immediately collapsed into bed. She slept late, then went to an exclusive spa for a massage and to have her hair and nails done, wanting to look her best for her afternoon appointment.

Revitalized, Zoshchenko guided her white BMW sedan up Kosygina Prospekt, into the wooded area of southwest Moscow known as Vorobyovie Gory – Sparrow Hills. Turning off the main road, Zoshchenko drove down an avenue lined with trees and ten-foot walls. The walls were punctuated at regular intervals by gates and guardhouses, where permission to enter the manicured grounds and approach the mansion was either granted or denied.

Though prerevolutionary in appearance, most of the magnificent *rezidences* in Sparrow Hills were actually built during the reign of Stalin for privileged members of the ruling class. During the Revolution of 1917, Communist guns bore down on the forces of the provisional government from these same hills.

The road wound through the hilly terrain, until Zoshchenko finally reached her destination: a large two-story mansion that once housed the Politburo's longest-serving member. In keeping with the new winds blowing across Russia, the imposing composition of carved stone and brick now sheltered Victor Ivanovich Orlov, founder of VIO FinProm and the nation's wealthiest *biznesmeny.*

Zoshchenko stopped at the gatehouse, where a neatly dressed and well-armed guard checked her name against a list of those permitted entry. After a quick but thorough sweep of her BMW – car bombings by business rivals were not unheard of in Moscow – the guard waved her through.

She followed the cobblestone drive until she reached the ornate, pillared entryway. A pair of well-dressed guards appeared as she parked her car. Like the man at the gate, both were armed, and a flesh-toned coil of wire sprang from ear to collar on each. One of the guards opened the door for her courteously.

'Thank you,' Zoshchenko said as she exited her BMW.

She walked a few feet away, then stopped as she had done many times before. She knew the procedure and, because it was necessary, felt neither fear nor irritation. The second guard smiled politely and quickly waved the metal-detecting wand around her body.

'Welcome back, Dr Zoshchenko,' the guard said as he switched the wand off, relieved that he'd found nothing.

Personal security was truly a matter of life and death among the men who had clawed their way out of the rubble of Soviet Russia's collapse and built business empires from the ruins. Chief among these men, the oligarchs of the new Russia, was Victor Ivanovich Orlov.

As Zoshchenko mounted the granite steps to the entryway, discreetly placed security cameras monitored her approach, and a butler opened the massive wooden door.

'Thank you, Anatoli,' she said as she entered the ornate foyer.

'He's in his office,' the butler replied. 'Shall I escort you up?'

Zoshchenko waved her hand dismissively and continued walking. 'I know the way.'

She climbed the curved staircase to the second floor; sun streamed through the beveled glass of the Palladian window at the upper landing. Turning left, she followed the wide hallway past

41

an impressive display of original masterpieces –
any of which would fetch millions at auction –
toward a pair of French doors. As she reached
the doors, she heard a faint electronic buzz and
the click of a mechanical assembly as the door
locks released. She grasped the silver lever
handles and pushed; the precisely balanced nine-
foot-tall doors swung open effortlessly.

'Dr Zoshchenko, welcome back. You had a
pleasant trip, I hope?' Irena Cherny asked
politely as Zoshchenko entered the anteroom.

Cherny was a petite woman in her early thirties
and attractive in a refined, classical sense. Orlov
had an eye for beauty, both in art and women,
and surrounded himself with the best of both.
Zoshchenko had no way of knowing whether
Cherny provided any intimate personal services
to her employer, but she hoped that a man of
Orlov's intelligence knew enough not to cross
that line with a woman positioned at the heart of
his business empire.

'My trip went well, Irena,' Zoshchenko replied
without elaboration. 'Thank you for asking. Can
he see me now?'

'Victor knows you're here, but he's on the line
with Zurich. It should only be a moment.'

Cherny glanced at the multiline phone on her
desk as one of the illuminated buttons blinked
off. 'I'll take you in now.'

Zoshchenko passed the hand-carved desk
where Cherny sat, and followed the young
woman to the pair of leaded-glass doors that led
to Orlov's office. Cherny twisted the silver
handles and stood aside to allow Zoshchenko to

enter, then drew the doors closed.

The office occupied more than fifty square meters of the second floor. Through a bank of windows that had been reglazed with Armorlite three centimeters thick, Orlov enjoyed a commanding view of the Moskva River and Luzhniky Park on the opposite bank. In the distance, off to the right, Zoshchenko saw the towers and gilded onion domes of the Kremlin.

Near the far wall, at the focus of the opulent room, sat a massive inlaid wooden desk that supported a slab of polished white marble. Behind this island of wood and stone, Orlov stood looking down at the financial information displayed on a thin flat computer screen. He wore a custom-made charcoal suit that complemented his trim physique. Orlov kept his graying, sandy brown hair close cropped and neat, more a matter of function than any overt sense of style, which further enhanced his aura of precision and discipline.

'Oksanna, my love, you have returned to me.'

Orlov walked around the marbletop desk and greeted her with a warm embrace and a kiss on the cheek.

Zoshchenko returned the embrace, and then allowed her hands to slide down Orlov's back until they reached his buttocks. She pulled his body close and kissed him with deliberate intensity. Several minutes seemed to pass before either surfaced for air.

'I missed you, Victor,' Zoshchenko declared softly.

'I noticed,' Orlov replied, a flush on his face.

At fifty-three, Victor Ivanovich Orlov was arguably one of the most powerful men in Russia. In the years since the collapse of communism, the former government trade analyst had amassed a fortune conservatively estimated at nearly fifteen billion dollars. He leveraged several of his highly placed connections in the international finance community and established the first privately held bank in Russia. With the backing of his own bank, he then stormed the Russian industrial landscape, acquiring controlling interests in more than twenty formerly state-owned enterprises. His businesses now included banking, mining, oil and gas, aircraft, shipping, telecommunications, real estate, and mass media. The ongoing crises in the Russian economy had only served to bolster his position by weeding out the lesser oligarchs.

'I still fantasize about that desk of yours, Victor.'

Orlov eyed the pristine marble surface, indulging himself in a little mental imagery. 'Ah, but sadly not today. Let's sit and have some tea while you tell me what has brought you here so urgently. Irena said you mentioned a business matter that we needed to discuss.'

They sat down on a couch near the windows over-looking Leninskiy Prospekt and the park beyond. A silver tea service rested on a low table in front of them. Orlov poured two cups while Zoshchenko composed her thoughts.

'Victor, over the past ten years I have provided you with valuable information regarding state industries and natural resources. For my part, I have been paid very well and I have no com-

44

plaints about our business arrangement.'

Orlov sipped his tea, quietly studying Zoshchenko as she spoke. From her position within the Academy of Sciences, Zoshchenko had identified a number of opportunities that Orlov had exploited in building his vast business empire. He had made Zoshchenko a millionaire several times over in compensation for her efforts.

'During my visit to the United States, I uncovered something, an opportunity unlike anything I have ever brought you before. I learned of a physicist who is about to change the world. His name is Ted Sandstrom.'

Orlov said nothing as Zoshchenko described Sandstrom's work and the quantum energy device. The gift of an eidetic memory allowed her to accurately describe even the most minute details of what she had seen at the MARC board meeting. The pace of her narrative quickened with her excitement, and after twenty almost breathless minutes, she reached the end of her story.

'So, at some point during the next month, the consortia from Michigan and Notre Dame will join forces to manage this technology?' Orlov asked.

'Yes.'

'And, as yet, no scientific papers have been published and no patents have been applied for?'

'Again, yes. Lawyers are to begin work on the patent applications later this summer. The patent filing for the original device will occur this fall, well within the time-frame in which Sandstrom will put his idea into use. Sandstrom and the consortia are maintaining a very low profile regarding this project. And with good reason.'

'So, very few people know about Sandstrom's work?'

'I would say no more than thirty, but only Sandstrom and his associate Paramo actually know how to construct one of these quantum energy devices.'

'What value would you place on Sandstrom's work? What is it worth?'

'This isn't an oil field or a diamond mine, Victor. What we're looking at is an entirely new industry in the moments just before its birth, an industry with a multibillion-dollar potential. These consortia are planning to serve as midwife and guardian of this nascent technology, but as the Americans are so fond of saying: Possession is nine-tenths of the law. If a scientist working for one of your companies announced this discovery first, then you would own this technology. I believe there is an opportunity here, if you act quickly.'

Orlov sat silent for several minutes, digesting everything Zoshchenko had said and extrapolating possible scenarios.

'This could work,' Orlov said objectively, 'but I'll need a good physicist, someone capable of understanding this quantum technology. I have a building on the outskirts of Moscow that should suit our needs for this endeavor.'

Reaching over the arm of the couch, Orlov pressed the intercom button on the phone that sat on the end table.

'Irena, I need you to cancel the rest of my appointments for the week.'

'Yes, sir,' Cherny replied.

'I also need you to contact Dmitri Leskov. Tell him to come here immediately. Have my cook prepare dinner for three and have it brought to my office; I'll be working late tonight.'

3

JUNE 23

South Bend, Indiana

'What the fuck?' the driver of the semi growled when he noticed the flashing blue lights in the mirror cluster on his door.

'Problem, Jimbo?' the skinny young man seated next to him asked.

'Yeah, a cop.'

'Shit, were ya speeding?' the third man on the bench seat asked.

'I don't think so. Potholes are so bad 'round here, I'd jar my teeth loose if I went more than five over the limit. Must be down on his ticket quota and I'm the only thing on the road right now.'

The driver carefully took the semi off to the side of the two-lane county road, put the rig in neutral, and switched on the hazard lights. A white, unmarked Chevy Blazer pulled up behind the truck. A moment later a uniformed Indiana state trooper stepped out from behind the wheel. In the mirror, the driver watched as the trooper slowly approached.

'Looks like a real hard-ass, Jimbo,' the skinny man said, craning his neck to get a view in the mirror.

'Yeah, a real tough guy,' the driver replied anxiously, his heart racing.

'His partner's coming up on my side,' the third man announced. 'Looks just like the other one. I guess they're cloning cops now.'

'License and registration, please,' the trooper said in a tone of bored superiority as he reached the driver's door.

'What's the problem, Officer?' the driver asked as he handed over the requested paperwork.

'Just a routine check. Would the three of you mind stepping out of the cab?'

The troopers stood back from the doors, carefully keeping one hand on their holstered pistols. As the driver shut the engine off and slid out from behind the wheel, the two other men stepped down on the passenger side.

'Let's go around to the other side,' the trooper said, indicating that the driver should lead the way.

'Open up the trailer, please,' the trooper demanded as they reached where the second officer stood with the other men.

'Sure,' the driver replied as he unlocked the trailer's side door. 'There's nothing inside 'cept our dollies and some padding. We were just on our way to a pickup.'

The driver swung the door wide open.

'See, just like I told ya.'

'I'll be the judge of that,' the trooper said sternly. 'Step inside please. All of you.'

The three men complied and stepped up into the trailer. They began to sweat, as much from nervousness as the rising temperature inside.

The three men watched as the two troopers climbed up into the trailer.

'Take a look around,' the senior officer said to his partner.

The younger man moved to the front of the trailer and began searching through the pile of padded blankets.

'What're you lookin' for?' the driver asked.

'Drugs,' the trooper answered. 'We got a tip that a local dealer is using moving trucks to bring his drugs in. Where's your pickup?'

'Notre Dame. We're moving some guy's lab to a research park off campus.'

'How's it look?' the trooper asked his partner.

'Clean.'

The trooper nodded.

'Is that it?' the driver asked expectantly.

'Just one more thing.'

In a blur of motion, the trooper drew his weapon.

'Jesus, no!' shouted the driver.

The trooper placed two 9-mm rounds from his suppressed Glock into the skinny man's forehead; the back of the man's skull exploded onto the metal wall of the trailer in a Rorschach of blood, bone, and gray matter. He then adjusted his aim to the right, sweeping to his next target,

49

and fired another double tap between the driver's eyebrows. The younger trooper shot the third mover with equal efficiency.

Both men closed the distance between themselves and the movers. The three young men lay absolutely still as the last seconds of their lives ticked away.

'Clear,' Dmitri Leskov announced. 'Pavel, go get the others.'

'*Da*,' Pavel acknowledged as he jumped down from the trailer.

Pavel was halfway to the unmarked Blazer – blue strobes still flashing – when three men, all dressed in the same tan uniforms that the movers wore, emerged from the rear of the vehicle. The men quickly moved to the back of the Blazer and unloaded a nested set of three orange plastic barrels, three battery-operated caution flashers, a bundle of large gray mats, and a ten-foot-long sausage shaped object emblazoned with the PLG corporate logo at regular intervals along its gray fabric exterior. Pavel grabbed the sausage, retrieved a large canvas gym bag from the Blazer, and then followed the others back to the trailer.

'Hand me the bag,' Dmitri called out from the open door. 'Then feed the Pig to Vanya.'

Pavel tossed the gym bag up to his older brother, then lifted up the end of the sausage. The coarse fabric of the Pig chaffed against his neck and shoulders as Vanya pulled it into the trailer.

'Quickly, Yuri,' Vanya said as he pulled the full length of the Pig into the trailer, 'contain the blood before it covers the whole floor.'

50

Yuri nodded and laid the Pig on the floor to act as a dam around the perimeter of the slowly expanding pool of blood. Vanya then ripped open the package of mats and spread a blanket of thin grey quilted rectangles atop the red-black liquid. Like the Pig, the mats immediately began absorbing the blood.

The fifth man, Josef, had the three orange barrels set with their open bottoms facing up.

'Keys?' Dmitri asked.

'I have them,' Josef replied, patting the key ring in his pocket.

Dmitri and Pavel picked up the skinny mover's body by the arms and legs and carried it over to the first container.

'Steady the barrel, Josef,' Dmitri barked as he and Pavel lifted the body over the open end.

Carefully, they lifted the mover's arms and legs, folding his body at the waist as they lowered it into the barrel. When the body reached the bottom, they folded his arms and legs until the man disappeared into the drum.

They repeated this maneuver twice more as Yuri and Vanya wiped down the trailer walls and floor with the absorbent mats. Drawn by the blood, flies began to swarm annoyingly around them.

Dmitri checked his watch. 'Let's wrap this up,' he announced.

The other men nodded and went about finishing their assigned tasks. Dmitri and Pavel stripped off the police uniforms and stuffed them into one of the barrels.

'Here,' Dmitri said as he tossed his brother new

clothes from the gym bag.

Pavel pulled the snug-fitting work shirt over his broad shoulders and looked down at the embroidered company logo over the left breast.

'I feel like I've been demoted,' Pavel said with a laugh.

Once the trailer was wiped clean of blood and gore, the soiled mats and the sausage were stuffed into the barrels, and Josef snapped the thick plastic lids closed. The men then carefully turned the barrels right side up. The movers' bodies slumped to the bottom, but the lids easily held the weight.

Yuri and Vanya jumped down from the trailer and took the barrels, one by one, from Pavel and Josef.

After Pavel and Josef exited the trailer, Dmitri handed them the three flashing caution lights and the gym bag that contained the two suppressed Glocks. He then leapt down and closed the trailer's side door.

Between the trailer and the Blazer, Dmitri's men arranged the barrels around a wide, deep pothole near the pavement's edge. Snapped in place, the orange caution lights began blinking.

'Let's go,' Dmitri announced, smiling to himself that the barrels might actually do some good.

4

JUNE 23

South Bend, Indiana

Nolan Kilkenny and Ted Sandstrom stood leaning against the wall beside a large window as the movers wheeled another cart of boxes from the nearly empty lab. They heard Kelsey and Paramo engaging in a rapid exchange of words out in the corridor, their voices growing louder as the pair neared the lab's door.

'Problem, Kelsey?' Nolan asked.

'Just a friendly debate,' she replied.

Paramo smiled. 'Kelsey and I were mulling over some of Guth's work on false vacuum theory.'

'False vacuum theory?' Nolan repeated. 'I'm almost afraid to ask.'

'It's one of the more recent theories kicking around about how a universe forms,' Kelsey offered.

Nolan held his hands up as if to push any further explanation away before it could reach him. 'Stop right there! My head still hurts from last night's little after-dinner discussion about M-branes and eleven-dimensional multiverses.'

'Wimp,' Sandstrom said with a laugh. 'Hey, Raphaele, did the movers get those boxes out of our office?'

'Everything went down with the last load,' Paramo replied.

Kelsey eyed the blue plastic cooler near Nolan's feet. 'Anything left to drink?'

'There's one can of Diet Coke with your name on it.'

Kelsey fished the last can from the slush of melted ice and sat down on a lab bench. 'How long before we're done here?'

'Not long. All that's left are those two boxes. It's a short drive to the research park,' Nolan said, running through a mental checklist. 'I figure a couple of hours to unload at the new lab.' Nolan picked up the cooler and dumped the icy dregs into the lab sink, shaking the last few drops out before closing the lid. 'I'm going to take this down to my truck so we can reload it at the gas station. I'll be back in a minute.'

The hallway echoed with his footsteps, the building nearly empty on this early-summer Friday afternoon. Kilkenny took the stairs and exited Nieuwland Science Hall around the corner from the loading dock. A semi filled the single bay, its trailer flush with the elevated concrete dock. The four-wheeled carts were nearly empty; the five-man crew had made quick work of this job.

Kilkenny's truck was parked at the far end of the loading area facing the dock. He fished the key fob out of his khaki shorts and pressed the button that unlocked the lift gate.

As he placed the empty cooler into the back of the SUV, he observed one of the movers pull two canvas bags from the white Blazer parked near the semi. The man then carried the bags back to where the rest of the moving crew waited. Another of the movers crouched down, unzipped one of the bags, and extracted a pistol holster.

'What the hell?' Kilkenny cursed quietly as he watched the distribution of weapons and other equipment among the men.

Using hand signals, the leader of the crew ordered the others into position. One remained on the loading dock while the others went back into Nieuwland Hall.

With his SUV screening him from view, Kilkenny searched the cargo area for a weapon. In the row of bins where he kept his tools, he found a combat knife – a memento from his navy days. He strapped the sheathed blade to his right thigh and carefully closed the lift gate.

As the mover paced along the elevated platform, Kilkenny surveyed the area between the loading dock and the rear of the semi trailer, timing the man's movements. The short span of the platform meant that the trailer blocked the man's view of the parking area for only a few seconds in each circuit.

Realizing that he would have to move quickly, Kilkenny crouched behind his truck, tensed and ready. When the man turned at the far end of the platform and began walking back toward the semi, Kilkenny sprinted across the entire lot using the trailer as a shield. His heart pounded as he slipped under the truck, adrenaline coursing through his body and his senses charged. Loose gravel and chips of broken glass dug at his forearms and shins as he stealthily snaked his way beneath the trailer to the platform.

When Kilkenny reached the space between the double axle at the rear of the trailer, he pulled himself back on his feet and again began timing the man's movements. As the man turned away, Kilkenny shifted closer to the platform, hiding in the space between the right-side tires and the steel-frame bumper.

Soon the man turned facing the driver's side of the semi, walking back toward the open trailer doors.

Kilkenny slipped out from beneath the vehicle and stood next to the rear tires. Carefully, he unfastened the door catch. As the sound of the man's footsteps grew closer, Kilkenny timed it perfectly and thrust the heavy metal door forward. The sudden rush of the door caught the man broadside, striking hard against his shoulder.

'*Blat!*' Vanya cursed as he rolled from the force of the blow.

Kilkenny followed the rotation of the door forward and leapt up on the platform behind it, releasing his grip on the handle and unsheathing his knife to press on with the attack.

Despite the burning pain, Vanya reached for the Glock 9-mm pistol strapped to the left side of his chest. He snapped a glance over his battered shoulder in time to see Kilkenny emerge from behind the steel door.

'*Krasny adin!*' Vanya shouted as he twisted the holstered weapon up and fired from beneath his armpit.

The first round drilled through the muscle of

56

Kilkenny's left thigh, a point-blank shot that struck at almost the same instant it left the Glock. After boring a bloody tunnel, the bullet erupted from Kilkenny's leg and ricocheted off the concrete dock. A second shot flew just inches wide because of the recoil of the first.

Momentum still carrying him forward, Kilkenny grabbed the holster strap and held tight as he drove his combat knife into the man's back. The knife shuddered as its serrated back edge sawed through the cartilage that connected a rib and vertebrae.

Vanya's grasp on his pistol weakened as his heart spasmed, the blade puncturing the muscular walls of the organ. Kilkenny pushed the knife sideways as he extracted it, widening the gash in the man's blood-soaked back. Vanya's legs gave out, and Kilkenny let him fall to the dock.

Kilkenny then rolled the body over onto its back; a blank, open-mouthed stare gaped back at him. Using his knife, he cut two strips of cloth from the man's shirt and hastily wrapped a pressure bandage around his thigh.

Kilkenny found a German-made military-grade radio transmitter clipped to the man's hip, the kind of communications equipment favored by special forces. He flipped the SEND switch into the off position, then removed the earpiece/lip mike component from the man's ear and slipped the gear on himself. His right ear filled with a faint hiss of static, then two sharp clicks crackled harshly in the ear-piece. The clicks repeated a few seconds later.

These guys are operators, Kilkenny thought as he ignored the clicks – a request for the dead man to report in to his commanding officer.

A quick pat search of the man revealed little. The mover carried a silenced 9-mm Glock and two spare clips of ammunition. Kilkenny found no identification of any kind. He pocketed the two ammo clips, chambered a round in the Glock, and carefully moved back into Nieuwland Hall.

One shitbag down, he thought, *four more to go.*

5

JUNE 23

South Bend, Indiana

Krasny adín? Dmitri puzzled over Vanya's urgent warning in his mind.

Yuri, the radioman, sent two more rapid clicks and waited.

No reply.

Yuri looked over at Dmitri, the team leader, and shook his head.

Dmitri knew that things went wrong on missions – it was a fact of life. The Americans had a name for this phenomenon: Murphy's Law. He'd lost radio contact with men before; nine times out of ten it was an equipment failure. But Vanya had broken radio silence and called out

Krasny adín – Red One – alerting them that his position was under attack. Now Vanya was off the air, and his brief warning had stopped Dmitri and the rest of the team just as they got off the freight elevator.

Dmitri carefully moved to a window that overlooked the rear of Nieuwland Hall. Below, he saw the trailer extending from the loading dock and, in the far corner of the paved lot, a black Mercedes truck. The scene appeared just as they had left it moments ago. Other than a few people walking on the campus pathways, he saw nothing to indicate that their mission had been discovered, nothing that would cause Vanya to report that he was under attack.

'I don't see anything,' Dmitri said quietly, wishing he could, 'but Vanya's position is almost beneath us.'

His men were all professionals; each had served under him in the Spetsnaz, the Red Army's elite special warfare unit. He'd handpicked them for this private operations force when paychecks in the Russian military became scarce. Today, they were well-paid and well-equipped mercenaries in the employ of Victor Orlov.

Dmitri scratched at the stubble on his chin. A gritty film of dried sweat covered his muscled frame, the result of moving dozens of heavy boxes containing the equipment, books, and experimental documentation that he had been sent to retrieve.

'You want me to go check on Vanya?' Josef asked.

Dmitri pondered the question, then shook his

head at the swarthy, black-haired Georgian. '*Nyet*. We proceed as planned, but stay alert. It may be nothing more than garbled communications and equipment failure.'

'If not?'

'If not, Josef, then I want you here with the rest of the unit.' Leskov turned toward the two movers watching the hallway. 'How's it look, Pavel?'

'Clear,' Pavel replied confidently. Not so much as a shadow had moved in the empty hallway.

Dmitri smiled, proud of the professionalism his younger brother displayed. Pavel was on point, checking the path ahead as the unit moved forward.

'Move out,' Dmitri ordered.

Pavel strode into the hallway, followed by Yuri and Dmitri, who guided a flat four-wheeled cart. Josef took up position a few steps behind the others, covering the unit's rear. Sandstrom's lab was down at the far end of the corridor.

'This looks like the last of it,' Dmitri announced as they entered the lab, his English flawlessly Middle American.

Dmitri's men spread out, moving toward the last remaining boxes. Paramo was seated in a chair near where Kelsey stood by the windows; Sandstrom sat up on a lab bench, reclining back on his elbows.

As he closed within ten feet of Sandstrom, Dmitri's right hand deftly slipped to the holster nestled in the small of his back and drew his weapon. The muscles in his body coiled tightly as he gripped the Air Taser with both hands and fired.

Propelled by a charge of compressed nitrogen, two needlelike metal probes silently flew toward Sandstrom. In less than a tenth of a second, the twin probes tore through the physicist's cotton shirt and struck his chest. A pulsating electrical current raced from Dmitri's weapon, through the probes, into Sandstrom's body.

Sandstrom shuddered involuntarily and fell back onto the lab bench. His head struck the thick black countertop with a muffled thud.

Across the room Yuri and Pavel's attack mirrored that of their leader. Only the briefest change in expression on the faces of Kelsey and Paramo preceded their sudden incapacitation.

'Josef,' Dmitri called out.

'Corridor is clear,' the Georgian replied.

'The man with the red hair, Kilkenny, he is missing. His truck is still parked by the loading dock. He must be somewhere in the building. Keep an eye out for him.'

As the Taser's pulsating charge attacked Paramo's nervous system, the aging physicist's heartbeat became erratic. The muscle fluttered, struggling to find a steady rhythm until the already weakened organ stopped beating altogether.

'I think I killed the old one,' Pavel announced unemotionally. 'He's not shaking like the others.'

'So much the better for him,' Yuri replied. 'Put those boxes on the cart while I set the explosives.'

Yuri pulled the quilted blanket off the cart, uncovering four pistols in shoulder holsters and a pair of sealed translucent bags, each containing about a quart of fluid. As Pavel loaded the last two boxes, Yuri picked up the two plastic bags and carefully placed them on the lab bench near the sink. He then closed the drain and turned on the water until the sink was about a third full.

'Ready,' Yuri announced.

Dmitri looked at his watch. 'On my mark.' The second hand swept closer to twelve. 'Now.'

Yuri placed the light-colored bag into the water first, followed by the darker bag. Tiny bubbles immediately began to form on the surface of the bags.

'We have five minutes,' Yuri announced as he hastily strapped on his shoulder holster and checked the Glock.

Dmitri nodded. 'Pavel,' he said, handing his brother one of the silenced pistols, 'take the point.'

6

JUNE 23

South Bend, Indiana

Kilkenny carefully worked his way back into Nieuwland Hall and up the building's center staircase. He encountered no one during his ascent to the second floor. On the landing, he cautiously peered through the slit window of wiremesh glass in the fire door. The hallway on the other side was empty, but the window was too narrow to provide a view of Sandstrom's lab farther down the hall.

Slowly Kilkenny pulled open the fire door until a quarter-inch gap appeared. Sandstrom's lab was on the same side of the corridor as the stairwell, so he studied the reflection in the glass doors of a display case on the opposite wall. There he saw one of the movers standing watch beside the lab door.

He had to assume that Kelsey, Sandstrom, and Paramo were in the lab with four armed men. For the sake of the two physicists and the woman his loved, Kilkenny focused on the situation at hand rather than trying to fathom the motive behind it.

The faint hiss of static filled his right ear, as it had for the past several minutes. Unable to raise their man on the loading dock, the Russians had gone off the air completely.

The reflected image in the glass moved as the man in the doorway stepped back into the lab. Another man appeared and moved out into the corridor. He moved cautiously. Visually sweeping the entire length of the corridor, he held a suppressed semi-automatic pistol pointed low in a two-handed grip.

Kilkenny flattened himself against the painted cinderblock wall and slowly closed the fire door. It slid quietly into its frame. As he released the handle, the mortised latch bolts in the head and toe of the door slid home with a metallic click.

Pavel had just raised his hand to motion the rest of the unit forward when he heard the sound of the closing door. He signaled for Dmitri and the others to remain in place while he investigated.

63

'Damn!' Kilkenny cursed under his breath, knowing that the errant sound had exposed his position. He quickly moved against the wall, out of view through the slit window.

A shadow flickered in the thin strip of light beneath the stairwell door, catching Pavel's trained eye. He moved along the wall, approaching the door from the side. With his back against the wall, Pavel inched forward until his shoulder reached the edge of the door.

He adjusted his grip on the Glock and folded his arms close to his chest as he filled his lungs with air. Exhaling with a low, throaty growl, he stepped forward, spun around, and struck the door with a vicious kick. The panic bar slammed into the hollow metal skin of the door, releasing the latch bolts. The door sprang open, and Pavel lunged into the stairwell.

As the Russian leveled his weapon, Kilkenny swung his left arm down in a sharp block that drove Pavel's forearms toward the floor. He then wrapped his hand tightly around the barrel of the Glock. Pavel squeezed the trigger.

Click.

Kilkenny smothered the action of the Glock with his grip. He then brought the muzzle of his own pistol against the side of Pavel's head and fired twice. Blood and bone exploded against the gray metal door.

Pavel shuddered and collapsed to the floor. Kilkenny quickly scanned the hallway for more threats, then retreated down the stairwell.

7

JUNE 23

South Bend, Indiana

Pavel's offensive was over almost as soon as it started. Two muffled shots and then silence. Dmitri moved to the stairwell and found the door held ajar by the body of his dead brother. He quickly shut down the rage he felt, knowing he still had a mission to complete. There would be time to mourn, and to seek revenge.

'Pavel's dead,' Dmitri said quietly as he went back into the lab. 'Yuri, time?'

'Three minutes, forty-five seconds,' the explosives expert replied.

Lying atop the lab bench, Sandstrom groaned and tried to lift his head. Kelsey began to stir as well. It took several minutes to recover fully from a Taser's shock, more time than anyone remaining in the lab possessed. Paramo lay motionless on the vinyl-tile floor, his eyes staring blankly at the ceiling.

'Put the woman on the cart,' Leskov ordered, his mind sifting through his options. 'We may need a hostage.'

Yuri and Josef grabbed Kelsey by the legs and shoulders, quickly loaded her onto the four-wheeled cart. Leskov turned the pistol in his hand and struck Sandstrom in the side of the head; the groggy physicist fell to the floor, unconscious. He would be left for dead.

'Three minutes, Dmitri,' Yuri called out.

Inside the lab sink, the skin of the first bag ruptured and its contents slowly leaked to form a thick layer along the basin.

'I'll take the point,' Leskov announced. 'Yuri, take the cart.'

'And I'll cover our backsides,' Josef said, a mouthful of bad teeth smiling beneath his thick black mustache.

With Kelsey as hostage, the Russians carefully moved into the corridor, wary of who or what might be lying in wait. Leskov held up his hand when he reached the stair-well door, halting his men. He then pointed at Yuri and, with two fingers, motioned for his comrade to join him by the door.

'When I open the door, pull Pavel's body in.'

Yuri nodded. This was not a matter of sentimentality on his leader's part; it was simply the law in the world of special warfare that, dead or alive, no man is ever left behind.

Leskov braced himself against the wall on the hinge side and pushed the door open with a backward sweep of his hand. Crouching, Yuri reached forward and grasped Pavel's leg. He took two steps back, dragging the young soldier's lifeless body through the doorway as a slick red stain spread from the open wound in the side of Pavel's head.

Leskov stepped through the doorway and found the stairwell deserted. 'It's clear.'

'Dmitri, do you see his pistol?' Yuri asked, looking down at Pavel's empty hands.

'*Nyet,* his attacker must have taken it. Put Pavel on the cart. We have to get out of here.'

8

JUNE 23

South Bend, Indiana

After the shoot-out in the stairwell, Kilkenny fell back to regroup. The loading dock was empty when he reached it, save for the body of the man he'd killed earlier.

A bell sounded nearby, indicating that the service elevator had descended to the main floor. Kilkenny searched for a place to position himself.

High ground, he thought when he looked up at the roof of the semi's trailer.

Kilkenny latched one of the rear doors closed, clambered up the thick steel hinges, and pulled himself onto the corrugated roof. Peering just over the edge, he saw the lead man emerge from the doorway. The man swept left to right, weapon held before him, seeking targets. He then checked behind the truck. Satisfied the dock was clear, he motioned for the others to move forward.

A cart rolled through the doorway, guided from behind by one of the Russians. The last man emerged a moment later. Glancing down at the cart, Kilkenny saw the body of the man he had shot in the stairwell and, beneath the body, Kelsey. His heart sank, then Kelsey's arm twitched and her fist clenched.

'Josef, get the truck started,' Leskov commanded, anxious for this mission's end. 'Yuri and I will finish loading.'

Leskov and Yuri holstered their weapons and carried the two remaining boxes into the truck. The starter ground for a moment, then the diesel engine roared to life, belching gritty exhaust into the air. With the greatest respect, Leskov wrapped his brother's body in one of the quilted moving blankets and gently laid it inside the trailer. Yuri repeated the gesture with Vanya, the other casualty of the day.

'Dmitri, what do we do with the woman?' Yuri asked.

'Kill her. Put her body in the back with Pavel and Vanya. We'll get rid of it later.'

Kilkenny listened as the lead man issued orders in Russian. Then the diesel engine growled, and a thick black cloud of exhaust wafted over him. As the truck idled, the trailer's roof vibrated beneath him.

Below, he saw Yuri reaching for his holstered pistol. Kilkenny swung his arms over the edge of the trailer and grasped his weapon with both hands. Aiming down at Yuri, Kilkenny fired two rounds from the elongated Glock that instantaneously penetrated the man's skull. Yuri's head snapped sideways and he collapsed where he stood, his pistol clattering on the concrete dock.

Instinctively, Leskov leapt off the dock, seeking cover. Two more rounds chased after him, chiseling holes in the concrete where he had stood. He had gotten only a brief look at the shooter, but he recognized him immediately. With three of his men dead, Leskov knew that Nolan Kilkenny was more than had been reported to him.

Leskov grabbed the short ladder on the passenger side of the semi and pulled himself up to the window.

'Josef, Kilkenny is on top of the trailer. He's killed Yuri. Cover your side of the truck and meet me at the dock.'

Josef nodded, pulled out his pistol, and checked the mirrors – his side of the truck was clear.

Kilkenny slid over the edge and dropped down, almost landing atop the man he'd just shot. Crouching with the Glock extended at eye level, he scanned the dock for targets. It was clear.

Time to haul ass, Kilkenny thought as he chambered a round, then popped the half-spent clip out of the Glock and slipped in a full one.

Keeping his eyes fixed on the edges of the trailer, Kilkenny grasped the abandoned cart with his left hand and pushed. But one of the turning wheels was jammed in place, stubbornly refusing to rotate into position. Kilkenny furiously kicked the cart twice before the wheel freed up and began rolling smoothly. Once through the doorway, he pulled the double doors closed, then turned down a corridor, hopefully bringing Kelsey toward safety.

As if their timing were choreographed, Leskov and Josef reached the rear of the trailer simultaneously and, with their weapons poised, swept the dock for a target. Kilkenny and the woman were gone – the wide double doors that led into Nieuwland Science Hall were closed. Only Yuri remained, facedown in a growing pool of his own blood.

'Get Yuri,' Leskov ordered. 'I'll cover you.'

Leskov pulled himself onto the dock and took position beside the doors. Josef holstered his pistol, released the catch on the open trailer door, and hoisted himself onto the dock. Quickly, with little consideration for the dead, other than he didn't wish to join them, Josef hefted Yuri's body atop the others and latched the trailer door shut. Josef then slipped the U-shaped bolt of a padlock through the door latch and shut it.

'Done. Let's get away from this fucking place.'

9

JUNE 23

South Bend, Indiana

'Nolan,' Kelsey moaned weakly, her mind still getting reacquainted with her body as she carefully pulled herself into a sitting position.

'I'm here, honey.'

Carefully looking around the corner at the double doors of the loading dock, Nolan saw the semi pulling away. Relieved, he holstered the Glock and sat beside Kelsey.

'How are you feeling?'

'Numb. Kind of tingly, like my whole body went to sleep. They shot us with something.'

'Probably some kind of stun gun.' He picked up her hand, and her trembling stopped – just nerves.

Inside Sandstrom's lab, the second bag ruptured in the sink. Its milky white contents oozed out, then slowly drifted down toward the bottom of the sink. When the contents of the second bag reached the layer formed along the basin by the first, the chemicals ignited in a hypergolic reaction. The initial flash was enough to evaporate the water in the sink. In less than a second from the initial contact, a whitehot fireball erupted inside the lab. The sink, and the bench it was set in, vaporized instantaneously.

A low rumble resonated through the building; lights flickered and dust fell from the ceiling as a shock wave telegraphed the concussive energy of an explosion through the structure around them. A moment later the highdecibel wail of the fire alarm punished their ears.

'Where are Ted and Raphaele?' Kelsey shouted over the din, her recovery almost complete.

'I think they're still upstairs. Come on, we gotta get out of here.'

He carefully helped Kelsey up; then, with one

71

arm around her for support, he quickly walked her toward a side entry. She gained confidence with each step, easily keeping up with his increased pace by the time they reached the lawn in front of Nieuwland Hall.

A pall of smoke billowed out of a series of windows on the second floor where Sandstrom's lab had been.

'Oh my God,' Kelsey cried, sickened by the thought of the two men trapped in the blaze.

A parade of flashing red and blue lights raced down Cavanaugh Road as a convoy of emergency vehicles from the Notre Dame campus police and the South Bend Fire Department converged on the burning science building.

By the time Nolan and Kelsey ran around the building to the loading dock, police officers were starting to secure the area and firefighters were pouring out of their yellow rigs.

'Hey, stay back!' a cop shouted as they approached.

'We were inside when it happened, Officer,' Nolan announced, ignoring the request. 'The fire's in a lab on the second floor. Two people may still be up there; they were unconscious before the blast.'

'Keep your hands where I can see them,' the cop demanded sternly when he spotted the combat knife strapped to Nolan's leg and the shoulder holster tucked under his armpit.

Nolan understood immediately and slowly placed his hands behind his head.

The cop, a fifteen-year veteran of the force, eyed the pair warily. Both were disheveled, and the bloodstained man looked as though he had been to hell and back. The cop reached out and plucked the Glock from Nolan's holster.

'There's another one in my waistband,' Nolan offered, twisting his torso to offer a partial view of his back.

The cop's demeanor eased slightly at this show of good faith. He quickly confiscated the second pistol as well as Nolan's knife.

'Military issue,' the cop commented as he eyed the black-handled blade. 'Looks a little bloody. Anything else?'

'Nothing other than a spare clip in my pocket.'

'You can put 'em down.' The cop checked the safeties on the pistols and signaled for the fire chief.

A stocky man encased in the bulky protective fire gear jogged over from the pumper truck.

'Yeah, watcha want?' the firefighter asked.

'Tell him what you told me,' the cop ordered. 'Then you and I are going to have a chat.'

'The lab's up on the second floor, far end of the corridor. There are two people still inside. They didn't get out before the blast. We haven't seen anyone else in the building all day.'

The chief nodded, then jogged away, calling several members of his crew over to map out a plan of attack.

'Interesting artillery you got here. Now, take a walk with me,' the cop commanded.

They headed over to a police cruiser parked on the grass. The cop tossed the confiscated weapons in his trunk and closed the lid. He then led them over to the paramedic truck.

'What's up?' the paramedic asked.

'Leg wound,' the cop replied. 'Take a look while I have a talk with these nice people.'

The paramedic carefully peeled off Nolan's field dressing. 'Jesus, we got us a gunshot wound. Clean through, all meat. I can clean ya up, but you'll want this looked at in the ER.'

'I just know there's an interesting story about how you acquired that,' the cop said, eyeing the hole in Nolan's thigh. 'Let's start with your names.'

Nolan and Kelsey identified themselves and explained the reason for their presence on campus. The cop jotted down shorthand notes in a pocket pad as the story unfolded. An incredulous look swept over the cop's face when Nolan calmly described killing three men. For Nolan, this was no different from the postmission debriefs from his SEAL days.

'—and when we heard the sirens, we came over to tell you about Sandstrom and Paramo,' Nolan concluded.

'Officer,' Kelsey added, 'these men, whoever they were, have stolen valuable laboratory equipment and over a decade's worth of irreplaceable research.'

'Professor Newton, I'll put the word out on the truck and the Blazer. Maybe we'll get lucky.'

The cop turned and made a beeline for the elevated dock, all the while issuing a barrage of requests into the radio mike clipped to his left shoulder. At the dock, he found the bloodstains and put the call in for Homicide and Forensics.

As the paramedic finished treating Nolan's leg, two teams of firefighters covered with soot rushed out of the building. Each team carried the supine form of one of the injured physicists strapped to a bright red backboard.

The paramedics and newly arrived EMTs met the firefighters halfway and started work on their patients as the backboards hit the gurneys.

'I got a pulse,' one shouted. 'Weak, but there.'

From where they stood, Nolan and Kelsey saw that the burns were serious. Charred flesh, a blend of oozing red and black, covered the entire right side of Ted Sandstrom's body.

'This one's dead,' an EMT working on Paramo announced clinically.

'Oh God,' Kelsey sobbed as she turned and pressed herself into Nolan's chest, his arms holding her. 'That dear, sweet' – her voice cracked with emotion – 'old man.'

10

JUNE 23

South Bend, Indiana

After Nolan and Kelsey received treatment for their injuries, the Notre Dame campus police transported them back to Nieuwland Hall. The blaze that had engulfed Sandstrom's lab was now extinguished, and the exhausted fire crews were slowly stowing their gear. A ribbon of yellow tape surrounded the damaged building, declaring it off-limits while the authorities investigated the incident. Nolan saw a team of forensic technicians photographing the crime scene and gathering evidence around the loading dock.

When the police car reached the cordoned-off area, a man and a woman walked over to meet the vehicle. Over their suits, both wore dark blue windbreakers stenciled with the letters FBI.

'Mr Kilkenny, I'm Special Agent Harris,' the woman announced. 'This is my partner, Special Agent Young. We'd like to have a word with you and Ms Newton.'

'Of course,' Nolan replied.

'Can you tell us exactly what happened?'

Nolan launched into the chronology of events, starting when he and Kelsey had arrived in South Bend the previous evening. The agents waited until the end of his narrative before asking questions for clarification on various points of the attack and details regarding Sandstrom's research on quantum energy cells.

'Bottom line,' Nolan said, 'the men who did this were well trained, possibly former Russian Special Forces.'

'Do you have any idea who might be responsible for this attack?'

'No.'

'Sandstrom and Paramo's research was very cutting-edge stuff,' Kelsey offered, 'and in recent years they didn't publish much of what they were working on.'

'And the device, this quantum energy cell, how

76

many people knew about that?'

Nolan thought for a moment. 'Outside of the boards of MARC and ND-ARC and the regents of their respective universities, I can't think of anyone who knew about the cell or our plans to develop it commercially.'

'Can you provide a list of those who did know about it?'

'Certainly, as soon as we get back to Ann Arbor, I can fax you the contact information. I'd be very surprised if any of those people are involved with this attack.'

'Why do you say that?' Agent Young asked.

'Economics. The people I'm going to name will all be shareholders of the company we're setting up to license quantum energy cell technology. Should things go the way we believe, the shares they purchase as insiders will be worth a fortune. What happened here today is simply not in their best interests.'

'But someone did think this attack *was* worth doing,' Young said.

'Yes,' Nolan agreed, 'but keep in mind that this is more than a violent case of industrial espionage. The person or persons ultimately responsible for this have stolen a technology that could disrupt the industrialized world's economy in a way that hasn't been seen since the Great Depression.'

'Thank you, Mr Kilkenny,' Agent Harris said after a pause. 'If we have any further questions, or information regarding this matter, we'll be in touch.'

'I'd appreciate being kept in the loop. How

77

about security for Sandstrom?'

'The local police have posted officers at the hospital 'round the clock, assuming he survives.'

Young's cell phone chirped in his pocket, and he answered it. After a few single-syllable responses, he scrawled down some hasty notes and finished the call.

'They found three bodies stuffed in some barrels just outside of town, all dressed in the moving company's uniforms. Looks like our gunmen hit 'em on the way in.'

'We have to go,' Harris announced. 'Again, thank you both for your help.'

As the FBI agents left, Nolan and Kelsey began walking over to his SUV.

'Three more innocent people murdered,' Kelsey said slowly, trying to comprehend it all.

Nolan placed his arm around Kelsey's shoulder and pulled her close. He was a former SEAL; violence and death had been a part of his life – a part he'd hoped was behind him.

'Nolan?'

'Yeah, hon?'

'Do you think we're in any danger from these men?'

'No. They got what they came for. We don't know enough about Ted's work to cause them any real concern. The only person who might still be in any danger is Ted. He and Paramo were the ones they were out to kill.'

'This whole situation makes me feel so vulnerable, so helpless. I just wish there were something we could do.'

'Well, there is one more thing I'm going to do.'

Nolan pressed the button of the SUV's key fob and popped the locks. He opened the rear driver-side door and fished out his PalmPilot and a digital phone from his soft-sided briefcase. From the Pilot, he looked up a number and keyed it into the phone.

'Mosley here,' a voice answered.

'Cal, this is Nolan Kilkenny.'

'Kilkenny?' Mosley paused for a moment, recalling the Spyder incident that they had both been involved in a year earlier. 'How've you been, young man? Stayin' out of trouble?'

'Cal, I'd love to say this is just a social call, but it ain't. I've got a problem – something along the lines of the last one we worked on together. I think the CIA might be interested.'

Nolan heard a click on the line.

'I hope you don't mind if I tape this.'

'Not at all.'

'Good, then tell me your story.'

11

JUNE 24

Chicago, Illinois

Dmitri Leskov gazed down at his brother Pavel's body one last time. The open wound, the result of two tightly placed 9-mm rounds, disfigured both the young man's handsome face and

Leskov's memory.

'I'm ready,' Leskov announced.

Out of the corner of the room, Oleg Artuzov appeared, gliding silently across the polished terrazzo floor. The forty-four-year-old mortician plied the same trade in Chicago's ethnic Russian community as he had in Smolensk, before emigrating to the United States. Though profitable in its own right, the Artuzov Funeral Home augmented its bottom line by laundering money and providing discreet 'private services' for the growing community of Russian Mafiya in Chicago.

Artuzov closed the simple casket that bore the body of Pavel Leskov. This was the third and last coffin that he would wheel into the adjacent room for cremation.

Leskov watched through the glass wall that separated the viewing room from the crematory as Artuzov rolled the stainless-steel charge trolley up to the door of the furnace. After docking the trolley, Artuzov moved to a control panel in the far corner of the room. At the press of a button, the automated process began. The furnace door slid upward, revealing a chamber heated to nearly one thousand degrees Celsius. Slowly, Pavel Leskov's coffin moved into the fiery maw. When the coffin's journey was finally complete, the furnace door dropped down and sealed the chamber.

Over the next two hours Pavel Leskov's body would be reduced to a fine gray ash. In that form, the remains would then be mixed in with those of a legitimate client and dispersed over Lake

Michigan. Smuggling three dead men out of the United States and back to Russia, in any form, was far too great a risk.

Leskov stepped outside of the air-conditioned funeral home and walked into a thick wall of humid air. Within seconds, the pressed white collar of his shirt was damp. The day was overcast, which matched his mood.

In front of the funeral home, a corpulent man who was packed like a sausage in an ill-fitting suit leaned against a dark blue Lincoln Town Car. Pyotr Voronin's thinning black hair was slicked back like stringy lines of paint on his fleshy head.

'Did Oleg take care of everything?' Voronin asked.

'*Da,* Pavel and the others will be scattered into your Great Lake Michigan later this week. Thank you for making the arrangements on such short notice.'

'When Victor Orlov asks for a favor, well–' The man shrugged his shoulders. No further explanation was required.

'How are the other arrangements coming?'

'Both trucks were taken to a chop shop and parted out, so neither exists anymore. Your cargo has been placed inside an air freight container with a few nondescript pieces of furniture. The furniture is camouflage; the bill of lading lists the contents as household goods and miscellaneous personal effects. Since there's no contraband, we don't need to lie about what we're shipping. We've insured the entire lot for a few thousand dollars, low enough that no one on either end

81

will be curious about it. It flies out Tuesday and lands in Moscow on Wednesday.'

'Good. And the surveillance?'

'I have a few people, former KGB, working on that. In a few days we should have Sandstrom and his associates well covered. How long do you think Orlov will want us to keep an eye on these people?'

'I have no idea. Just don't drop the surveillance until he tells you to.'

'I'm not that stupid. Orlov will get regular reports until he tells me to stop.'

'I am certain that he will be most appreciative of your efforts on his behalf.'

12

JUNE 26

South Bend, Indiana

'This mass is ended,' Father Blake said from his place on the gilded altar of the basilica. 'Go in peace.'

With that final pronouncement, Sacred Heart Basilica, the ornate centerpiece of the Notre Dame campus, filled with music. The vaulted ceilings and carved recesses shaped each note as it emerged from the organ pipes, transforming 'Amazing Grace' into a triumphant edifice of sound.

A phalanx of priests and altar servers accompanied the polished oak coffin down the main aisle, a somber procession in honor of Raphaele Paramo. Pew by pew, members of Paramo's family and those who held him in regard as a friend, colleague, or mentor filed out into a perfect summer day. High in the carillon, the great seven-ton bell named in honor of Saint Anthony of Padua pealed out its solemn thunder.

'Thank you for such a lovely service, Joe,' Paramo's widow said, clasping Father Blake's hand in both of hers.

'It was my pleasure, Dorothy,' Notre Dame's President replied. 'Raphaele was a good man and a true friend.'

'Yes, he was,' she agreed, knowing both descriptions to be true. 'Excuse me, Joe, but I see someone I have to speak to.'

Dorothy Paramo waded through the milling crowd, leaving her children and grandchildren beside the limousine that was to carry them to the cemetery.

'Professor Newton. Mr Kilkenny,' the diminutive woman called out. 'A word, if I may?'

Kelsey dabbed the corner of her eye with a handkerchief, then smiled bravely at the approaching widow. 'Of course, Mrs Paramo. And please call me Kelsey.'

'I prefer Nolan, ma'am.'

'Very well, but in return you must call me Dorothy,' she replied, a faint smile appearing momentarily on her face. Then the sadness returned. 'The police told me what happened the day my husband was murdered. Nolan, they told me that you risked your life to stop the men responsible for this tragedy.'

'I'm sorry it wasn't enough.'

'It could have been far worse. My only consolation is that the two of you and Ted survived. Did you know that Raphaele and I thought of Ted as a son? Burying a spouse is a sad eventuality, but a child is meant to live on after the parents are gone.'

'Ted will recover from this,' Nolan said reassuringly.

'My prayers are most certainly with him. I was wondering, can you both stop by the house after the reception?'

Kelsey looked at Nolan, who nodded. 'Yes.'

'Good, I have a favor to ask.'

Nolan followed the silver Buick, driven by Dorothy Paramo's eighteen-year-old grandson, into the farm country just outside of South Bend. They stopped at a brick Victorian home with a weathered aluminum mailbox bearing the name PARAMO.

Nolan parked his SUV behind the Buick and followed Dorothy Paramo and her grandson into the house. Once inside, the young man bolted up the stairs, intent on trading his blazer and tie for a pair of loose-fitting jeans and a T-shirt.

'This way,' Dorothy Paramo said, leading her guests through the parlor toward the rear of the house.

She turned the crystal knob and opened the raised-panel door that led to a small room lined from floor to ceiling with books. The only furnishings in the room were a couch, a small desk, and a chair.

'This is where my husband came to think. Please, have a seat.'

Kelsey sat with Nolan on the couch as Paramo's widow sat in Raphaele's chair. A gnarled pipe, unsmoked in almost twenty years, still sat near the corner of the desk.

'Raphaele always said that physicists came in two flavors: thinkers and doers. Einstein was a thinker; Fermi was a doer. In his collaboration with Ted, Raphaele was the thinker and Ted was the doer. My husband was an accomplished thinker and a gifted instructor; teaching physics was his avocation. Raphaele knew his limitations physically and mentally. In both regards he knew he wasn't up to the challenge of tackling Ted's discovery.'

Dorothy Paramo swiveled the chair and leaned forward to open one of the desk drawers. She withdrew a thick clasped envelope from inside the drawer and set it upon her lap.

'Of all my husband's papers, these were the most dear to him. Whenever a particular problem vexed him, he would invariably return to these. They were his inspiration. These are letters – a correspondence he had long ago with the greatest mind he'd ever known. Raphaele never talked about the man; their correspondence was over a year before Raphaele and I met. Once, shortly after we were married, I snuck a peek, thinking they were love letters from an old girlfriend. Except for a few personal notes, I didn't understand a word. Raphaele was quite amused when I told him what I'd done, then he explained how important the letters were to him. He said they were "a brief glimpse into the mind of a genius." I don't know what happened, but their correspondence ended abruptly. This is something that hurt Raphaele deeply.'

Dorothy paused for a moment, collecting her thoughts. She closed her eyes, trying to quell the emotions rising within her.

'A terrible thing has happened. My husband is dead, and our sweet Ted is lucky to be alive. He's going to have a hard time recovering from all this, and I don't want him to give up. Here' – she handed the envelope to Kelsey – 'I want you to take these to Ted. Raphaele wanted him to have them.'

'Shouldn't this come from you?' Kelsey asked.

'No, they were supposed to have come from Raphaele. He was going to give them to Ted after the lab had moved. He said that these letters contain ideas that might help a younger mind solve the riddle of their work. Ted is at the hospital in Ann Arbor now, and I don't know when I'll get up there to see him. The poor man has lost his life-work and his mentor. If these letters are all my husband said they are, I think Ted needs to see them as soon as possible.'

13

JUNE 27

Ann Arbor, Michigan

Nolan and Kelsey followed the blue-and-white directional signs that led them through the first floor of University Hospital. They were there to visit Ted Sandstrom, who had been transported by air ambulance to Ann Arbor after receiving emergency medical treatment in South Bend. Though more than fifty percent of his body was severely burned, Sandstrom's prognosis was good.

Wending their way through the maze of corridors, the two of them finally arrived at the Burn Unit, which was located in a remote corner of the hospital. When they reached the electronically locked double doors of the unit, the head nurse buzzed them through and had them sign the visitors' sheet.

The unit was built in a curved, two-story block that jutted out from the hospital's north face. Twelve single-patient rooms followed the outer curve. Sealed windows in each provided a view of the Huron River. A glass-curtain wall isolated the patient room from the hallway while providing a direct line of sight for the medical staff. Space-Lab monitors hung from the ceiling, displaying the vital signs of each of the patients.

'You have visitors,' the nurse announced pleasantly upon entering Sandstrom's room.

She quickly checked the IV bags and glanced at all the vitals displayed on the small in-room monitor. Satisfied, she moved on.

'Hey, Ted,' Nolan said as they entered.

A knot formed in the pit of his stomach. The sight of Sandstrom's burned flesh didn't shock him; he had seen far worse on SEAL missions around the world. Instead, it triggered memories and feelings he had hoped to leave behind upon his discharge.

'Aren't you going to ask how I'm doing?' Sandstrom wanted to know, a bitter tinge of sarcasm in his raspy voice.

'No, because you'll either lie to spare our feelings or, worse yet, you'll tell us the truth.'

'Nolan,' Kelsey barked, annoyed by his insensitive comment.

Sandstrom feebly raised his hand. 'He's right, Kelsey, I feel as good as I look. At least they're treating me well, and the pain meds keep the edge off. How's Dorothy?'

'She's holding up very well,' Kelsey replied. 'She sends her love.'

Nolan pulled a chair around to the side of the bed for Kelsey and then sat on the chair's flat wooden arm.

'Any word on the guys who did this?' Sandstrom asked.

'Nada,' Nolan answered. 'The police set up roadblocks all over the area but came up empty. The FBI is slowly sifting through what's left of your lab for any physical evidence, but that's going to take a while. I've asked a guy I know at the CIA to take a look at this as well.'

'CIA?'

'Yeah, there's an international angle to this that the folks at Langley are better equipped to handle than the Indiana State Police. The guys who hit your lab looked and sounded an awful lot like Spetsnaz.'

'What's Spetsnaz?'

'Russian army Special Forces. No one in the Russian government is crazy enough to launch a mission like this on U.S. soil, so it's more likely that these guys are mercenaries and somebody with very deep pockets sent 'em here. Enough with this talk, though. How about some good news?'

'Please,' Sandstrom said with a desperate weariness.

'The boards of MARC and ND-ARC had a teleconference this morning regarding the joint venture for your project.'

'I thought you said this was good news?'

'I did,' Nolan replied. 'Despite the setback due to this incident, both boards have decided to pursue the project. This, of course, depends upon your ability to resume your work after you get out of here.'

'So, are you telling me I still have a job?'

'Yep, they still think you're a good bet.'

'As bad as this whole situation is, it's temporary,' Kelsey added. 'You'll recover, the lab will be rebuilt, and your work will proceed.'

'I know, life goes on and all that jazz,' Sandstrom said bitterly, his anger and sadness readily apparent.

'Yes, Ted, it *does*. You and Raphaele made an important discovery, and now you have to follow it wherever it leads. It's what Raphaele would have wanted you to do.'

'How the hell would you know what Raphaele wanted me to do? We were a team. We were going to solve this thing together.'

'Actually, after you moved into the new lab, Raphaele was going to retire.' Kelsey held up her hand to stop the question she saw forming on Sandstrom's lips. 'We had a long talk with Dorothy yesterday after the funeral. She told us that Raphaele felt that he'd done all he could for you, and it was time for him to step aside. Had none of this happened, Raphaele would be telling you this right now and wishing you well. He would also have given you this.'

Kelsey set the thick manila envelope on the edge of Sandstrom's bed. He stared down at it, across the top was his name scrawled in Paramo's hand.

'What's in it?'

'Letters. Dorothy said they were Raphaele's most prized possession. Sometime back in the forties, he corresponded with another physicist. In Raphaele's opinion, the man was one of the greatest minds he'd ever known. He also felt that something in these letters might help you figure out your discovery.'

Sandstrom's eyes never left the envelope as Kelsey spoke. There were only a handful of twentieth-century physicists who Raphaele

Paramo considered truly brilliant, and as best as Sandstrom could recall, Paramo never mentioned having significant communication with any of them.

'Who was Raphaele's pen pal?'

'We don't know,' Nolan replied, just as curious about the letters as Sandstrom was.

'We were tempted to read the letters on the way back from South Bend,' Kelsey admitted, 'but it wouldn't have been right. These letters were meant for you.'

'Well, I want to know. Open the envelope and read me one of them.'

Kelsey smiled as she unclasped the oversize envelope. Inside, she discovered a collection of old brown file folders bound together by string. Each folder bore the date of the letter it contained; the correspondence spanned almost two years.

'I guess we should start at the beginning.'

Kelsey untied the string and opened the first folder. Surprisingly, the paper, which was older than anyone in the room, had barely yellowed – Paramo had kept his treasured letters safe for more than fifty years. The author's penmanship was fluid and precise, like the work of a calligrapher.

'Fifteen September 1946,' Kelsey began. 'Dear Raphaele...'

After a few lines about personal matters, the author shifted direction into the realm of theoretical physics. The tone was conversational, as if Raphaele and the author were sitting in a bar having a discussion over a glass of beer. The man would pose a thesis, then let his imagination run wild, challenging his thesis from several different directions.

More than once Sandstrom had to ask her to stop so he could digest what he'd heard. The beautifully written prose was interspersed with mathematical notations and explanatory doodles. The first four-page letter took nearly an hour to read.

'"–and I look forward to your thoughts on this. Your friend, Johann Wolff."'

'Amazing,' Sandstrom sighed, physically drained by the effort he'd put forward to follow the letter. 'I'd have to study that letter more carefully, but I'd swear that part of what you just read dealt with interaction-free measurement.'

'I was thinking the same thing,' Kelsey agreed.

'I'm sorry to be the dumb guy in the room,' Nolan said, crossing his arms over his chest, 'but what is it about that letter that has you both so stunned?'

'If Kelsey and I understand this letter correctly, Wolff was working on quantum optics.'

'And why is this significant?'

'The significance is not what, but when,' Kelsey said. 'Wolff was thinking about interaction-free measurement in the mid-forties. I've never seen anything on the subject dating that far back. In the early sixties the guy who won the Nobel Prize for inventing holography essentially said such a thing was impossible. No one was even fooling around in this area until the eighties.'

'This is cutting-edge quantum thinking now,' Sandstrom added. 'Fifty years ago, my God. This guy's grasp of the subtle nature of potential and probability is amazing. Las Vegas would hate a guy like this.'

'Shall I read another?' Kelsey asked as she carefully placed the first back in its folder.

'Absolutely,' Sandstrom replied eagerly.

Four hours and five letters later, Sandstrom was ready to get out of bed and go back to work. While Nolan was impressed with the author's ability to describe incredibly complex phenomena lucidly, for Kelsey and Sandstrom the experience was something akin to an epiphany.

'Raphaele was right,' Sandstrom declared, 'this guy's thinking was decades ahead of his time.'

Kelsey nodded her head in agreement. 'I'm just surprised that we've never heard of him.'

'Me, too,' Nolan said as he put the last few folders back in the pile. 'Especially since he was here at Michigan when he wrote these letters.'

'His comments on some of the senior faculty in our physics department sound like they could have been written today. Just change the names,' kidded Kelsey.

'Bureaucracies are eternal,' quipped Nolan.

Still reclining in his hospital bed, Sandstrom stared in wonder at this gift from his mentor. 'It's like Wolff was doing stuff in his head that we're just starting to figure out now using super-computers. Based on what he showed Raphaele, I think Wolff was working toward a theory of everything.'

'A theory of everything?' Nolan asked. 'Sounds like a Monty Python movie.'

'For physicists,' Sandstrom replied, 'a workable theory of everything is the Holy Grail.'

'I'll bite then. What is it?'

'You want to field this one, Kelsey?' Sandstrom asked.

'Sure. The short version goes something like this. Four basic forces are known to be at work in the universe – forces that determine the behavior of everything from the smallest subatomic particle to the universe itself. Current theory predicts that if we were to wind the clock back in time to less than a hundredth of a second after the Big Bang, we should find these four apparently separate forces merging into a single unified force.'

Nolan nodded. 'I'm with you so far. Gravity, which keeps us from falling off the earth and affects all the big stuff in the universe is theoretically related to the forces that hold atoms and all the subatomic bits together.'

'Exactly. A theory of everything, or TOE, describes the linkage between all the forces. If we can ever develop one that can survive experimental testing, we'll have a much clearer understanding of how the universe began, how it works, and where it's going. Now, trying to tie all four forces together in one shot is incredibly difficult. Einstein spent the later years of his life on his unified field theory and came up empty. Taking it one step at a time, we've managed to tie two of the forces – electromagnetism and the weak nuclear force – together. Currently physicists are trying to tie these two forces with the strong nuclear force – the one that holds

94

protons and neutrons together to form atomic nuclei. A theory describing the union of the three nongravitational forces is known in the trade as a GUT, which stands for grand unification theory. The next step after a working GUT is developed is a working TOE.'

'So, based on Wolff's letters, you think he was piecing together a theory of everything?'

'Absolutely,' Sandstrom assured Nolan, 'and he was at least as far along fifty years ago as anyone is today. I'm seeing glimmers of M-brane theory in these letters and hints at strategies for resolving some of the stickier problems that current theorists are wrestling with.'

Nolan nodded. 'Can these letters help you with your research?'

'Who knows? It all depends on how far Wolff progressed with his theoretical work. These letters are just chip shots, snippets; Wolff did his big thinking somewhere else. A guy this bright had to have published somewhere – left some kind of record of his research.' A gleam shone in Sandstrom's eyes, and he looked up at Nolan and Kelsey. 'We have to find Johann Wolff.'

'Ted' – Kelsey's voice carried a touch of concern – 'even if he's still alive, he'd be at least as old as Raphaele was.'

Sandstrom smiled. 'It doesn't matter. A mind like this has to have left some mark behind – some evidence that he was here. Dead or alive, we have to find Johann Wolff.'

14

JUNE 28

Moscow, Russia

Irena Cherny placed the handset back in the cradle of the multiline phone on her desk and sighed. She took a deep breath, attempting to stave off the anger that threatened to disrupt her normally poised demeanor.

'*Yop t'voi yo mat!*' she growled, cursing the man with an expression suggesting an incestuous relationship between the bureaucrat and his mother.

She glanced down at the slip of paper containing the flight and cargo identification numbers for the materials acquired by Dmitri Leskov's team in the United States. Orlov had handed it to her more than two hours ago, requesting that she locate the shipment and arrange for it to be retrieved.

Cherny stood, brushed at a crease in her skirt, and calmly walked to her employer's office. She knocked, and Victor Orlov waved her in.

'Did you talk with the people at Sheremetyevo?' Orlov asked.

'*Da,* Victor Ivanovich, I most certainly did.'

'And?'

'And I have been able to confirm that the

aircraft has indeed arrived and been unloaded.'

'Good, then we can send a truck down to retrieve our shipment.'

'Not yet,' Cherny said.

'Why?'

'As you requested, I called Customs using only the name on the cargo manifest and made no mention of you or the company.'

Orlov nodded.

'After wasting a great deal of my time, they finally connected me with someone who allegedly has enough blood flowing between his ears to generate a spark of intelligence. This individual informed me that the aircraft that arrived from Chicago had no cargo on board that matches our number or description.'

'How can this be? Voronin faxed us all the paperwork. The shipment should have been on that plane.'

'I understand, but according to the people who unloaded the aircraft, it was not on board. Since the manifest that arrived with the aircraft also did not indicate that our property was on board, the man I spoke with suggested that there may have been a clerical error in Chicago.'

Orlov was on his feet, pacing in front of the tall windows that faced the Moskva River.

'Get Voronin on the phone.'

Cherny did a mental calculation of the time difference. 'It's four in the morning there.'

'I don't care if I have to wake that fat slob up. I want to know where my property is.'

Cherny nodded and returned to her desk. In five minutes she connected Orlov with Voronin.

'Victor Ivanovich,' Voronin said groggily, still trying to shake the sleep from his head. 'What can I do for you?'

'You can answer a question, Pyotr Yefimovich. Where is my property?'

'It left Chicago yesterday. It should be in Moscow by now.'

'According to Russian Customs, no cargo containers bearing the numbers that you faxed me were on the plane. Again, I ask, Where is my property?'

Voronin was now fully awake, fear for his life causing an adrenaline-fueled rise in both his heart rate and blood pressure. 'Could the Customs people be fucking around with you?'

'I don't think so, because they didn't try to extort any money from me. They say that there was no cargo on the plane matching the information you sent me.'

'I swear to God, Victor, I wouldn't do this to you.'

Orlov could hear the fear in Voronin's voice, a fear that the man was perfectly justified in feeling. Even halfway around the world, Voronin knew that Victor Orlov could make his life a living hell or, worse, take his life. Orlov did what his business required, and ordering a man's death was no different from cashing a cheque.

'I know, Pyotr. And you know that I don't like excuses. I want results; I want my property. Find it today.'

'*Da,* Victor Ivanovich. I'll call you as soon as I know anything.'

15

JUNE 28

Ann Arbor, Michigan

Nolan walked down East University, or what used to be East University until the dead-end road that defined the eastern edge of the original campus had been closed off and terraformed into a lush pedestrian walkway. To his left was West Engineering, a long three-story Romanesque building topped with a red tile roof and a pair of cupolas.

He smiled as he passed by a series of glass-block windows that punctured the building's thick masonry base. Hidden behind the translucent blocks was the Naval Architecture wave tank and the carpentry shop where his grandfather, Martin Kilkenny, had worked for so many years building large model ships.

Beyond West Engineering, Nolan clambered up the worn granite steps of the Randall Physics Laboratory.

Turning left out of the stairwell, Nolan headed for the office of Kelsey Newton, Associate Professor of Physics.

'Knock, knock,' he said through the partially open doorway.

Kelsey turned away from her computer and

smiled. 'What took you so long? You called almost an hour ago.'

'Same old, same old. Just as I was walking out of my office, I got sandbagged by a couple of calls. I picked up some bagels on the way, and an espresso.'

'Oh, thank you.' Kelsey gratefully accepted the tall, Styrofoam cup.

'How's the search for Wolff?'

Kelsey swallowed a tentative sip of the strong brew. 'I asked a couple of the older professors but struck out. Seems Wolff was gone before any of them arrived for postgraduate work. I also checked the library network. I found quite a few books authored by people named Wolff, on subjects ranging from philosophy to chemistry. I even found a couple of mystery novels, but nothing by a Johann Wolff. There's also no mention of Wolff in the physics journals dating back well before the war.'

'How about departmental records?' Nolan asked as he took a bite of a sesame-seed bagel.

'I was just getting to that. I have no idea how far back the on-line stuff goes.'

Kelsey swiveled her chair back to face her computer. She navigated through the Physics Department Web site, bypassed the public-relations material, and keyed in her ID number and password to log on to the department's restricted server.

'We want Faculty, Wolff, Johann,' she said as she typed in the parameters of her search.

The mouse pointer on her screen changed from an arrow into a cluster of three spinning gears.

Thirty seconds later a new screen of information began to load.

'Johann Wolff, assistant professor of physics,' Kelsey read aloud, '1946 to 1948. Received his doctorate from the Institute for Physics at the Kaiser Wilhelm Gessellschaft in Berlin, 1944. No picture available.'

'He was studying physics in Berlin during the war?' Nolan asked incredulously.

'Apparently so. His doctoral work was in quantum mechanics. He got in on the ground floor.'

'What do you mean?'

'In 1944 the field of quantum physics was about twenty years old. Wolff was studying *the* cutting-edge science of his day.'

'Anything else?'

Kelsey scanned the screen for linking sites but found nothing. 'This is it on-line, so it looks like we're taking a walk over to the archives.'

Kelsey shut down her computer and followed Nolan out of her office. They exited through the west side of Randall onto the Diag, cut through Angell Hall and crossed State Street to the LS&A Building.

They entered the building and descended a side stairway to the basement. After scanning the floor directory, they quickly located the room where faculty, staff, and student records were stored.

'Oh,' said the woman behind the reception counter as they opened the smooth wooden door. She held her hand to her chest reflexively. 'You surprised me. I don't get many visitors during the summer. How can I help you?'

Kelsey quickly glanced at the woman's plastic

ID badge.

'Good morning, Mrs Greene,' Kelsey said politely before introducing Nolan and herself. 'We're looking for some information about an instructor who taught physics here in the late 1940s.'

'That's going back quite a bit, but I'll see what I can do. What's the name?'

'Johann Wolff,' Nolan replied.

'The department's on-line records show that he was here from 'forty-six through 'forty-eight,' Kelsey added.

'Can I see your staff IDs?' Mrs Greene asked.

'Here,' Kelsey replied, pulling it out of her purse.

Nolan unclipped his badge from the collar of his shirt and laid it on the counter. It was similar to the standard faculty picture ID but bore the imprint of MARC as well.

'Always have to check,' Mrs Greene said as she handed the badges back. 'Faculty records, even old ones, are still considered restricted information.'

She keyed the information in to her computer, scribbled down a number on a piece of paper, and disappeared into the stacks of file drawers and shelving units that filled the basement level. Ten minutes later she returned.

'Oh my, it took a little digging to find this one.' she said as she placed a thin file folder on the counter.

The folder's tab contained a bar code strip and the name WOLFF, J. Kelsey turned the folder and opened the cover. Inside she found an ancient university-employee-information sheet listing Wolff's date of birth, citizenship, and other vital data.

'Well, he definitely doesn't live there anymore,' Mrs Greene offered.

'What?' Nolan said, then he skipped down to the home address. 'Oh, you're right.'

'Where is that?' Kelsey asked, trying to get her bearings.

'It was just off campus,' Mrs Greene replied, 'near the business school. It's a parking lot now.'

The remaining pages contained course information, a few letters from the program chairman, and a black-and-white faculty photograph. The last sheet was an official letter terminating Wolff's appointment to the university. The notice was dated January 1949.

'That's odd. The chairman was singing Wolff's praises right up to this,' Kelsey said, still studying the notice. 'Why did they fire him?'

'May I see that?' Mrs Greene asked.

Kelsey handed over Wolff's termination notice.

'They didn't fire him. If they had, this letter would have said so, and given the reasons why. Then, as now, dismissal of a faculty member is a serious matter. This letter is just a piece of paperwork terminating the university's relationship with Wolff – a fancy way of saying he no longer works here.'

'But where did he go?' Nolan asked, knowing the answer wasn't in the file.

'Who knows?' Mrs Greene replied. 'This is all we have on your Professor Wolff. Sorry I can't be of more help.'

'Actually, you can do one more thing for us. Can we get a copy of this file?'

'Sure, but I'll have to charge you for it.'

'Fine,' Nolan replied. 'Put it on my departmental account.'

16

JUNE 28

Dexter, Michigan

'I was beginning to wonder if you two would ever get here,' Martin Kilkenny bellowed in a thick Irish brogue from the swinging bench on the broad covered porch of his farm-house. 'I'll bet it was that no-account grandson of mine making you both miss the fine supper my wife cooked tonight.'

'Nolan and I were up at the hospital visiting Ted Sandstrom, Martin,' Kelsey replied just before kissing him on the cheek.

'A likely excuse.'

'Would either of you like some pie?' Audrey Kilkenny, Nolan's grandmother, chimed through the kitchen window. 'It's raspberry.'

'You bet,' Kelsey replied.

'Let me give you a hand, Grandma,' Nolan offered.

A moment later Nolan followed Audrey back onto the porch carrying a large wooden tray covered with five servings of pie and five cups of tea.

'Ah, that's a good lad,' Audrey said as Nolan served her. 'He'll make a fine husband, Kelsey. These Kilkenny men all do.'

'I'll keep that in mind.'

'So how is Sandstrom doing?' Sean Kilkenny asked, joining them on the porch.

'Good as can be expected.' Nolan replied. 'The docs think he'll recover, but the scarring will be extensive. The plastic surgeon will do her best, but she was pretty frank about the limits of what can be done cosmetically.'

'How about his attitude? Do you think he'll be able to get back to work?'

'He's taking Raphaele Paramo's murder hard,' Nolan answered.

'Raphaele was very much a father figure to Ted,' Kelsey added. 'But I get the sense that when Ted is finally out of the hospital, he'll go right back to the lab. I think he'll continue their work as a way of honoring Paramo's memory.

'For instance, just yesterday he showed signs of being his old self when Nolan and I brought him a bundle of letters that Paramo had wanted him to have. You see, Paramo was planning on retiring once Ted's new lab was up and running, and according to his wife, he felt that these letters might help Ted further his research.'

'Are these letters from Paramo?' Sean asked.

'No, they were written to him by a young physicist who was here at Michigan about fifty years ago,' Kelsey stated. 'I read a few of them to Ted yesterday; they're mind-boggling.'

105

'I can attest to that,' Nolan offered. 'Each letter began with some friendly little chitchat, then this guy would dive into some aspect of theoretical physics that lost me *very* quickly.'

'There are probably fewer than five hundred people worldwide who could follow these letters,' Kelsey explained. 'Each seems to contain some flash of brilliance, some insight into how the universe works.'

'Can the person who wrote these letters help this Sandstrom fellow with his work?' Audrey wondered.

'That's what we're trying to find out,' Kelsey responded. 'The strange thing about these letters is that I've never heard of the author. Our theory is that someone this bright must have left some record of his work somewhere.'

Martin stared down into the brownish liquid in his mug, lost in thought.

'Kelsey and I spent the better part of today just trying to find any mention of this guy on campus,' Nolan offered. 'We came up with next to nothing. The library has no books, articles, or scientific papers with his name on them.'

'That's not too surprising,' Kelsey added, 'considering that he was just an assistant professor and spent only two years here.'

Martin looked over at his wife as Kelsey spoke; his eyes were moist.

'What is it, dear?' Audrey inquired of her husband.

'Johann.'

Audrey clasped her hands to her mouth as if to keep the breath from rushing out of her.

'Dad,' Sean said, worried, 'are you all right?'

'I'm fine, son. Just a bit surprised, that's all.' Martin turned toward Nolan and Kelsey. 'Was the man who wrote these letters, this friend of Raphaele Paramo's, was he a German by the name of Johann Wolff?'

'Yes,' they confirmed in unison.

'How'd you know?' Nolan continued on with his thought.

'I wondered if I'd ever hear that name again,' Martin said absently, aloud. After a moment's silence he glanced at Audrey, who was wiping the tears from her eyes.

'Answer Nolan's question,' Audrey urged as she regained her composure.

'Johann Wolff was a friend. Back in 'forty-six, he arrived here in Ann Arbor with the clothes on his back, a few dollars in his pocket, and a job at the university. The poor fellow was an absolute lost soul, no friends or family – and the anti-German sentiment was still pretty bad. We met, quite by chance, because his office was in Randall and I was in the building next door. He was a wraith of a man when he came through the door of my shop, lost he was and looking for direction. I helped him out, and over time we became friends. A couple of odd ducks we were, with him a highly educated German scientist and me a little-schooled Irish woodworker.'

'Johann was a bright young man,' Audrey added. 'He was handsome in his own way and very sweet. There was also a sadness about him, as there was with a lot of the refugees who came after the war. You see, he lost everyone who was

107

dear to him.'

'Not everyone, Audrey. You're forgetting Elli,' Martin reminded her.

'Who's Elli?' Nolan wanted to know.

'Johann's fiancée. They fell in love just before war broke out. Unfortunately, she and her family didn't get out of Germany and were sent to the death camps.'

'You see, they were Jewish,' Audrey added.

'I think they get the picture, dear. The gobshite Hitler didn't send too many Lutherans to the camps. Anyway, while Johann was working in Berlin, his family was killed in Dresden and Elli disappeared into those camps. He searched for her after the war but was unable to find her. But because he was well educated, he managed to get a teaching job here at Michigan. A little over a year after he arrived, he got a letter from Germany. It turns out that Elli had survived the war and was living in Chicago. They hadn't seen each other in years, but it didn't matter.'

Martin choked back the swelling in his throat.

'In November of 1948 I loaned Johann a few dollars so he could buy an engagement ring for Elli. Nothing fancy, mind you – neither one of us was a Rockefeller – just a simple gold band as a token of his love for her. A local jeweler made it up for him, and he took it to Chicago. The last time I saw Johann was in my shop, when he told me she'd accepted his proposal of marriage. My God, he was happy. He even asked me to be his best man. When we parted company, we'd agreed that he and Elli would stay here with us for the weekend.'

'Grandpa, so what happened to Wolff?'

'I don't know. Nobody does. It's like he fell off the face of the earth. There were rumors, but nothing came of them.'

'What kind of rumors?'

'He was a German scientist, Nolan. Some said the government found out that he'd done some terrible experiments during the war and put him in prison or deported him or had him hanged. Some say that he ran away. Take your choice,' Martin said bitterly. 'It was all a load of malarkey. He wasn't some Nazi bastard. For the first time in his adult life, Johann Wolff had something worth living for. His house was in order; there was no reason for him to run anywhere. Though his body was never found, I still believe that he was murdered. Death is the only thing that could've kept him apart from Elli.'

'So he just disappeared?'

Martin nodded. 'Vanished. As far as I know, Johann Wolff was never seen again.'

17

JUNE 29

Chicago, Illinois

Walter Guk walked into Rollie's Bar just after midnight followed by three of his coworkers from the second shift at O'Hare International Airport. The banter of the broadcasters announcing the

Cubs game blared from a television hanging over the far end of the bar. Three older men nursed a couple of drinks as they watched.

'A round of beers?' the bartender guessed.

'You read our minds,' Guk replied. 'And by the way, is the pool table in back open?'

'Yeah.'

The bartender placed four icy Miller longnecks on the bar. The cargo handlers paid for the round and disappeared into the back. Immediately the bartender pulled a business card from his pocket and dialed the number scrawled on it.

'Yes,' Voronin answered.

'It's Nicolai at Rollie's Bar. Guk just came in.'

'*Spasíba,* Nicolai. A couple of my associates will be there shortly to collect him.'

Leskov entered the bar accompanied by Josef. Both quickly surveyed the room, then moved straight to the bar.

'You Nick?' Leskov asked.

'Yeah,' the bartender replied.

'Where is Guk?'

'In the back, playing pool.'

'How many others?'

'Three men.'

'Give me four beers.'

The bartender eyed Leskov for a second, then thought better of it and pulled four Millers from the cooler.

Leskov nodded, handed two of the bottles to Josef, and then moved toward the short hallway that led past the restrooms into the back of the bar. A burst of shouting erupted from the room,

110

briefly overwhelming the excited voices of the baseball announcers.

'What happened?' Leskov asked.

'The Cubs' first baseman just hit a two-run homer,' one of the men answered without taking his eyes off the replay. 'Game's tied at five.'

As the replay ended, Guk and his coworkers turned to see who had joined them. Leskov smiled warmly as he moved around the table, studying the four uniformed men carefully. A clip-on photo ID badge hung from the left shirt pocket of each man. Josef took up position between the pool table and the hallway.

Leskov took a small sip of beer, then flipped the bottle in his hand and threw it at Guk's forehead. The bottle struck him on the hairline and exploded in a spray of foamy beer and broken glass. Guk's hands covered his face, and he howled in pain.

'What the fuck you doin', man?' one of Guk's coworkers shouted.

'Oh, shit!' another added when Leskov drew a pistol from the small of his back and aimed it in their direction.

'I'm bleeding,' Guk wailed, staring at the reddish smears on his hands.

Josef stood near the hallway aiming a second pistol at the group. Leskov set his remaining beer on the pool table.

'Gentlemen,' Leskov announced calmly, 'this matter concerns only Guk. I suggest you remain where you are and enjoy the rest of the game.'

Guk's coworkers hesitated for a second, then slowly backed away. Leskov stepped over to Guk

111

and struck him in the head with the butt of his pistol. Guk fell facedown on the pool table. Leskov grabbed Guk around the chest and dragged him toward the hallway. Guk hung limply in his arms, unconscious.

Once Leskov and Guk had exited the back room, Josef put his two untouched bottles of beer on the pool table.

'This round is on us,' he said with a laugh.

Guk regained consciousness as the sharp scent of ammonia burned in his nostrils. There was a dull throbbing in the back of his head. He tried to open his eyes but something was holding them closed. He lay flat on his back, wedged between a pair of hard vertical walls.

I'm in a box, he thought, panicking.

Guk tried to sit up, but his arms and legs were bound. A fist struck his abdomen, knocking the wind out of him as he fell back.

'He's awake,' a voice announced.

'Good. Take that thing off his eyes.'

Guk felt fingers probing the material adhered over his eyes, and then a violent tug jerked his head upward as the tape tore the eyebrows and lashes from his face. He blinked repeatedly as tears filled his eyes, as much from fear as from the irritation of salty blood.

Slowly, his vision cleared and he was looking up at a white tiled ceiling. The room was warm and had a clean antiseptic look, like a hospital. Guk heard footsteps. Then a man with a thick fleshy face and stringy black hair leaned his arm against the rim of the box and looked down at Guk.

'Walter, do you know who I am?'

'*Da,* Pyotr Voronin.'

Voronin smiled. 'Very good. Now for a more difficult question. What the fuck happened to the cargo container I sent to Moscow?'

'I don't know what you're talking about! I didn't—'

Voronin smashed his fist into Guk's mouth, splitting the man's lower lip.

'Don't lie to me, Walter. I know how things work at O'Hare – I get a percentage. Yesterday International Airfreight flight number eleven twenty-eight left Chicago for Moscow. I have a receipt confirming that a container of property belonging to an associate of mine was on board that plane. When the plane reached Moscow, the cargo was not on board. How is this possible?'

'I don't—'

Another fist slammed into Guk's face. Blood flowed freely from his lip and nose; one eye was nearly shut from swelling.

'I apologize,' Voronin said as he wiped Guk's blood from his knuckles. 'I must not be making myself clear. If you don't tell me what I want to know, I am going to kill you. It will be slow and most unpleasant. Do you understand me now? Just nod your head yes or no.'

Guk nodded yes.

'Wonderful. Where is my cargo?'

'Moscow,' Guk replied, slurring his words.

'Why you little fuck!' Voronin wound up for another punch.

'No, no!' Guk pleaded. 'It's in Moscow, I swear. It was on the plane.'

113

Voronin pulled his punch, his thick knuckles less than an inch from Guk's damaged face.

'How?'

'I changed the flight manifest to make it look like the container wasn't on board.'

'But it was loaded on the plane?'

'*Da,* it went to Moscow,' Guk replied emphatically.

'Why did you do this?'

'I didn't think anyone would notice. It was just some furniture, a computer, and a stereo. It was insured, so if it got lost, I figured the owner would rather have the money.'

'If you were going to steal my property, why did you send it to Moscow?'

'I didn't know it was yours. God, you must believe me,' Guk pleaded. 'It looked like something no one would miss. I have a cousin in Moscow who is getting married soon. I sent it to him as a wedding present. You know, a housewarming gift.'

'How did your cousin get it if Customs in Moscow says it didn't arrive?'

'He works cargo at Sheremetyevo.'

Voronin saw all the pieces fit together. He'd been a little too clever in packaging Orlov's stolen property, making it so innocuous that this termite Guk stole it without a second thought.

'What is your cousin's name?'

'Konrad. Konrad Guk,' the man blubbered.

Voronin pulled a phone from his coat pocket and selected a number from its memory.

'*Dóbraya útra,*' Voronin said into the phone. 'I have the information Orlov requested. The package arrived in Moscow but was stolen by a cargo worker named Konrad Guk. I have his cousin here who tells me that he's the one who altered the plane's manifest and made Orlov's property disappear. The furniture was to be a wedding gift.'

Voronin paused for several minutes, listening to the other person on the line.

'*Da,*' he replied, 'I'll take care of it.'

Voronin slipped the tiny phone back into his pocket and looked down at Guk.

'Walter, I'm so glad we had this talk, but I must go now. Don't worry, I'm leaving you in very good hands.'

Voronin stepped back. A man appeared on the other side; he smiled and then swung a hinged lid over the top of the box. Guk was again plunged into darkness, and quickly the box reverberated with the sound of a hammer driving a nail.

'Oleg,' Voronin said as Artuzov set the last nail, 'once again, thank you for your assistance.'

'No bother at all, Pyotr Yefimovich. I'm just happy to be of service.'

With that, Artuzov rolled the trolley bearing the wooden box up to the door of the cremating furnace. The wooden box shuddered as Guk thrashed inside, screaming for his life. When the trolley was properly aligned, Artuzov walked over to the console and started the cremation. Slowly, the wooden box glided down the stainless-steel rollers into the furnace. Already the temperature inside the box was over two hundred degrees. The superheated air seared Guk's throat and lungs, each frantic, labored breath more difficult than the last. The thrashing inside the box stopped as Guk lost consciousness.

This isn't the first time Artuzov has incinerated a living person for me, Pyotr Voronin thought with a smile. *No doubt, it won't be the last.*

As Voronin walked out of Artuzov's funeral parlor, he thought about Guk's cousin in Moscow and the visit he would soon receive from Dmitri Leskov.

'Fool,' he said incredulously, 'you stole from the wrong man.'

18

JUNE 30

Sverdlovsk 23, Russia

Lara Avvakum sat back in her chair, her legs propped up on a cushion that lay across the top of an open desk drawer. With a pad of paper on her lap, she stared out her window at the Siberian forest in the distance and the rhythmic swaying of the branches in the wind. The movement was both orderly and complex. In her mind's eye, she could see the ebb and flow of energy within the organic system outside her window, the fluid beauty of nature framed before her like a painting by van Gogh.

Sverdlovsk 23 was the name government planners had given this secret research facility, and

Avvakum had spent the past decade of her life here. It was a remote collection of buildings nestled in the foothills of the Ural Mountains, and its existence was still considered a state secret.

A sharp knock at the door brought her reverie to an abrupt end.

'*Da,*' she said, recovering from her meditation.

The door opened slightly, and the graying head of Boris Zhirov emerged through the crack.

'Lara, you have a visitor,' Zhirov said, his voice carrying equal measures of concern and excitement. 'Georgi just called from the main gate. She'll be here in a minute.'

Visitors were uncommon events at Sverdlovsk 23. One never knew how to take the unexpected arrival of a government official – the only kind of visitor permitted there.

Avvakum stood and adjusted her pale yellow dress. 'What do you think, Boris?' she asked, hoping she was presentable.

'Beautiful, as always,' Zhirov replied. 'Here she comes.'

Zhirov opened the door and stood aside, allowing a tall, well-dressed brunette to enter Avvakum's office. 'Dr Avvakum, I am Oksanna Zoshchenko, deputy director of the Russian Academy of Sciences.'

'I am honored. Please have a seat.'

Zoshchenko nodded, accepting Avvakum's hospitality despite the fact that the long, jarring drive from Yekaterinburg had left her back and buttocks aching. 'Would you like some tea?'

'Perhaps later. Right now, I would like to get to

the purpose of my visit.'

Zoshchenko zipped open her thin leather brief-case and extracted a white file folder embossed with the academy's insignia. The file tab bore Avvakum's name.

'You have worked for the academy since you graduated from Moscow State University, a little over ten years ago?'

'*Da.*'

'Your doctoral work was quite impressive,' Zosh-chenko continued, skimming over the dossier. 'You did your thesis on quantum laser optics, which led to your assignment at this research facility.'

'*Da,*' Avvakum replied, wishing now that she'd studied something less interesting to the acad-emy's military-applications apparatchiks.

'I see that you have requested reassignment on numerous occasions and that each request has been denied.'

Avvakum nodded, her throat constricting. A feeling of dread welled up inside. Her frequent requests had finally been noticed, and this woman had been sent to reprimand her personally.

'Pity,' Zoshchenko said as she closed the file, 'there were a number of more interesting projects that could have used a mind like yours. I offer the academy's apologies for allowing you to rot in this wilderness.'

Avvakum's mouth formed a small O, but she didn't utter a sound. An apology from the academy for wasting so many years of her life was unheard-of. Like the sun rising in the west, this was something that simply did not happen.

118

'You may know that the academy is branching out into new ventures, mostly of a commercial nature. Russia needs truly productive industries if it is to survive. This is the reason we are actively seeking commercial research projects – the academy needs to generate its own revenue, or it will starve.' Zoshchenko stared directly into Avvakum's blue eyes. 'When was the last time you were paid?'

'At the end of last year.'

'Then you personally understand the situation the academy is in. Things cannot continue this way. There is a company, a Russian firm that has requested scientific assistance from the academy. It was involved in a research project with a group of Americans that has since dissolved. This firm would like to continue the research with the intent of developing a marketable product.'

'What kind of product?' she blurted out, curious to know more.

'It has to do with energy production. I'm sorry, but I can't be any more specific than that, except to say that both the firm and the academy believe that you are the most qualified candidate for the project. Under such an arrangement, the firm would pay a fee to the academy and pay your salary directly. It is my understanding that this money would be in hard currency.'

Avvakum's eyes widened at the prospect of not only being paid but being paid in a currency whose value wouldn't evaporate like the ruble.

'The firm would also pay to relocate you to Moscow,' Zoshchenko continued, 'where a private laboratory would be equipped for your work. You will reside in a nice apartment building off Tverskaya Ulitsa, not far from the Bolshoi Theater.'

'How do you know this company can do what it says?' she wondered, afraid it was all too good to be true.

'I can assure you that this firm is reputable and well financed. It has dealings around the world and its founder is a confidant of the President. It has already established an account containing approximately one million American dollars in funding for this project. As an added incentive to you, should any marketable product result from your work, you will be awarded shares of ownership in the company. This is an opportunity to create something worth-while for yourself and your country. In truth, it is far more important than what you are doing here.'

Avvakum felt dizzy. She'd dreamed of escaping this place, of returning to civilization somewhere, but never did she imagine such an opportunity. The world had changed so much in the past ten years. Economics had replaced ideology, and consumer goods were more important than weapons.

'I don't know what to say. Of course I accept.'

Zoshchenko smiled. 'Wonderful. I think you'll find your new position very rewarding. I'll make arrangements for you and your belongings to be transported to Moscow. Make whatever preparations you feel necessary to turn your current work over to your replacement.'

Zoshchenko extended her hand across the desk; Lara Avvakum grasped it heartily.

120

'I can't thank you enough,' Avvakum said, on the verge of tears. 'This is beyond anything I could have dreamed of.'

'Lara,' Zoshchenko said, smiling, 'this is not the same Russia we were born to anymore.'

19

JULY 10

Yekaterinburg, Russia

When she left Moscow a lifetime ago, Avvakum had journeyed east aboard a cramped and ancient car on the Trans-Siberian Railway. For her return trip, a corporate jet waited to whisk her from Sverdlovsk 23 to freedom. As she walked across the tarmac, she saw VIO FinProm's logo, a golden double eagle on a field of royal blue, emblazoned on the jet's triangular tail.

'Welcome aboard, Dr Avvakum,' the uniformed pilot said as she stepped into the luxurious cabin of the needle-nosed aircraft. Inside she saw Zoshchenko talking with a distinguished-looking man. Both rose as she approached.

'Lara, it's good to see you again. I would like to introduce your patron, Victor Ivanovich Orlov.'

Orlov clasped Avvakum's offered hand with both of his; the grip was firm but gentle. 'I've looked forward to meeting you, Lara. Oksanna has told me a lot about you.'

'Thank you,' Avvakum said shyly, not sure how to respond to Orlov's attention.

'What do you think of my new jet?' Orlov crowed proudly.

'I've never seen anything like it.'

'Considering where you've spent the past decade, I'm not surprised. It's the latest design from Dassault. Supersonic. Capable of Mach one point eight. It'll only take about two hours to fly to Moscow from here.'

'Two hours! My last trip by train took days.'

'Welcome to the twenty-first century.'

The pilot sealed the fuselage door and walked into the passenger cabin. 'We're just about ready to leave. If you'll please take your seats.'

'Thank you, Brody,' Orlov replied.

Orlov motioned to a wide leather captain's chair. Avvakum sat and felt herself slowly melting into the supple material as the chair conformed to her shape.

'Don't get so comfortable that you fall asleep on me, *Lara*,' Orlov warned. 'I still want to talk with you.'

Avvakum, Orlov, and Zoshchenko buckled themselves in for takeoff as the jet's three engines began powering up. A subtle change in the frequency of the engines' whine accompanied a gradual forward motion of the aircraft. Were it not for the visual cues passing by the cabin windows, Avvakum might not have been able to tell they were moving.

The sleek white jet taxied out to the end of the runway, where it paused for a minute. In the distance members of the airport ground crew stood outside the hangars watching the jet take off. The engines wound up again, louder than before, and the thirty-four-meter-long, delta-winged javelin hurtled across the runway. The world raced past the windows in a blur of colors as the aircraft's speed increased to the point at which it freed itself from the ground. Minutes later they broke through a layer of low-lying clouds and into a blue sunlit sky.

'It's so beautiful,' Avvakum said as she stared out at the billowy cloud tops.

'Isn't it,' Orlov agreed. 'Shall we get to the business at hand?'

'Of course,' Avvakum agreed, a little embarrassed at her naive display.

'For security purposes, Oksanna has told you little about what you'll be working on for me. I assume that you're curious about the project.'

Avvakum nodded.

'I'll give you a little background information first. My company was involved in a research project with an American corporation. Both sides provided funding and staff, and most of the work was carried out in the United States. This project ran for almost two years, but then there was an explosion in the lab. Following that incident, my American partners dissolved our collaboration claiming a loss of faith in the project.'

'Do you still have people working on this project?'

'*Nyet*. One of the men I sent to the United States was killed in the accident. The other decided to stay there. What I do have is all their research. Are you comfortable with English?'

'I am reasonably proficient.'

'Good, because all the project materials are in English. My researchers were bilingual – theirs were not – so the project documentation was kept in the common language. Since this is going to be your project from now on, you can choose any language you like, as long as it's Russian.'

Avvakum and Zoshchenko laughed along with Orlov's joke.

'Will I be working with anyone?'

'In the beginning, no. Oksanna and I have discussed this, and we believe that it will take you several months to completely familiarize yourself with the work. Once you have an understanding of what you are dealing with, then you can make a recommendation to me regarding your staffing needs. I want you to pick your own people.'

Avvakum smiled. When the time came, she would have the opportunity to select the best people she could find rather than struggling with someone else's castoffs.

'Can you tell me more about the project?' Avvakum asked.

'Oksanna, would you?' Orlov deferred.

'*Da,* Victor Ivanovich.' Zoshchenko took a moment to compose her thoughts. 'You are, of course, familiar with negative energy state theory.'

'Certainly. The early theoretical work in this area brought about the prediction of antimatter, which has since been proved to exist.'

'Well, our researchers were studying the use of fluctuating electrical fields on evacuated chambers to see whether they could develop a better method for producing and containing

124

antimatter. The result of these experiments was a device that outputs roughly two thousand times the amount of energy they put into it.'

'I would like to see that,' Avvakum said skeptically.

'You will,' Orlov promised.

'I understand your skepticism, Lara,' Zoshchenko continued. 'I once shared it. In fact, that's one of the reasons you were selected to continue this line of research. The team that discovered this phenomenon has never been able to explain how it works, which is essential in securing as broad a patent as possible on technological applications. We need to know why this device does what it does.'

'You've brought up another interesting point,' Orlov said. 'Regarding patents. My former partners said they are no longer interested in continuing the project. Both sides parted company with identical copies of the research. While I have no proof as yet, I believe that they may also try to continue working on this project. If so, we are in a race, and the winner will control a technology worth billions of American dollars.'

For a mind that regularly pondered the mysteries of the universe and plumbed the depths of subatomic structures so small that their existence could only he inferred, Avvakum found herself mentally unable to grasp the economic stakes involved in this project. If she succeeded, even a small share in an enterprise so vast could be worth more than the past twenty generations of her family had earned in their entire lifetimes.

Orlov glanced at Zoshchenko, who smiled slyly

back while waiting for Avvakum to recover her senses. A decade in an impoverished scientific backwater had turned Lara Avvakum into the perfect candidate for the job. She had both the ability and, more important, the incentive to succeed.

'Would you like to see where you're going to be working?'

'*Da.*'

Orlov opened his briefcase and pulled out an eight-by-ten photograph of a large, nondescript industrial building. A flag bearing the conglomerate's logo fluttered from a pole mounted on the parapet. Below the flag, a string of large black letters spelled out the name VIO FINPROM.

'I admit, it's not the most elegant building I own, but the renovations are going quite well and security is excellent. It was built back in the time of Stalin; Gipromez used to design metallurgical facilities there. It's on Prospekt Mira, about thirty minutes away from the center of Moscow. Your apartment is just a few Metro stops away, but we've arranged for you to have a car as well – a Saab.'

Avvakum stared at the photograph but saw her new life instead. Here she was, hurtling across European Russia in a supersonic jet. Ahead lay an apartment, a paying job, a new car, and the culture of Moscow.

'Thank you,' she whispered, barely able to speak. She felt as though her life had just been saved.

126

20

JULY 11

Ann Arbor, Michigan

The sun beat down on the cab of Bud Vesper's Caterpillar E120B excavator. Even with the windows open, the temperature inside the cab was a good ten degrees hotter than the ninety-five predicted by the cute weathergirl on the local news.

Yesterday the chairman of the University of Michigan's physics department and several other dignitaries stood on the manicured lawn behind West Engineering and Randall. They wore unblemished white hard hats, and each was armed with an engraved bronze shovel. They broke ground with great ceremony, each turning a spadeful of sod to celebrate the construction of the modern addition that would join together the two old buildings.

Today the steel bucket mounted on the end of the Cat's hydraulic arm bit out thirty times more earth than those ceremonial shovels each time it tore into the ground. After moving several tons of dirt and clay, Vesper called for Darrell Jones, the surveyor on his crew, to check the depth on the cut he was working on.

Jones motioned that they had reached the

specified depth, so Vesper started cutting the next section.

Fifteen minutes into the new cut, Jones walked over with a story pole – an eight-foot metal ruler with markings accurate to a tenth of an inch. Attached to the pole was an electronic target that emitted a loud tone when struck by the oscillating laser on the surveyor's transit. Jones held the pole vertical; the laser line was just shy of the target.

Jones motioned for Vesper to dig a little farther. As the bucket deftly peeled away another few inches of earth, Jones signaled for Vesper to stop as a strange object caught his eye.

Vesper had exposed a sixteen-inch-long piece of something. Jones dug around the edges of the object, which felt soft and rubbery.

'I hope this isn't some damn utility line,' Jones groused.

He gripped the object with both hands and pulled. It easily sprang loose, and Jones quickly realized that it was a human arm.

'Jesus fuckin' Christ!' he yelled.

'Hey, Darrell,' Vesper called out from the excavator.

'Bud!' Jones screamed, still bug-eyed and frantic. 'Bud, somebody's fuckin' arm is in the goddamn hole!'

'Easy, Jones, easy. Say again?'

'There is a fuc-king arm,' Jones replied, enunciating each syllable with deliberate precision, 'in the god-damn hole.'

Vesper looked down into the excavation and saw an arm lying right where Jones had left it.

'I ain't no gravedigger,' Jones complained.

Vesper shook his head in disgust, knowing that this discovery could set his project schedule back worse than a month of heavy rain. He pulled a phone off his hip and called Fred Morrow, the university's project manager for this job.

'Hey, Fred,' he said sarcastically when the other man came on the line, 'guess what I just dug up?'

'Don't tell me you hit the steam tunnel.'

'No, we're well clear of that. Guess again.'

'Bud, I don't have time for this. What the hell did you hit?'

'I didn't hit nothing, Fred. I dug up somebody's fucking arm. I looked at all the as-built drawings for this site, and I don't remember seeing the word *cemetery* anywhere.'

'All right, Bud. Just sit tight. I'll make a few calls and then I'll be right down.'

21

JULY 17

Ann Arbor, Michigan

'Hey, Darrell, you ready to go back to work?'

Darrell Jones walked over to where Bud Vesper sat in the excavator and hesitantly peered down into the pit. 'Did they get all those dead fuckers out of the hole?'

'After knocking my schedule off by a week, they

better have. Fuckin' med school.'

'Med school?'

'Yeah. Up until the late 1800s, the med school had a couple of buildings down here. The Gross Anatomy building stood right about where we were digging.'

'That arm I found looked a lot fresher than the 1800s.'

'It wasn't. The university sent a pathologist down here to collect what we'd found. He told me the reason we didn't find bones was that the parts were too pickled to rot and buried too deep for anything to eat 'em. The guy also said that back then there were rumors about the med school robbing fresh graves to get their cadavers. He assured me that they don't do it like that anymore.'

'I should hope the fuck not!'

'Anyway, they're all gone now and on their way to a decent burial.'

'Glad to hear it,' Jones said as he picked up his story pole and began climbing down into the hole.

By midafternoon Vesper had widened the excavation along the side of West Engineering, but as he dug closer to the old building, he began to encounter construction debris.

'I'd like to beat the crap out of the guy who left all this shit down here,' Vesper said as he pulled out another bucketful of shattered bricks.

Vesper lowered the hydraulic arm back into the hole. When it hit bottom, a loud hollow sound echoed from below. Jones quickly motioned for

130

him to pull out. Vesper parked the bucket off to the side, shut the Cat down, and walked over to the edge of the hole.

'What the hell did I hit now?'

'Beats me, Bud, but it sure sounded funny.'

'Might be a branch off the steam tunnel. What's the invert elevation?'

Jones placed his story pole down in the hole and eyeballed the depth.

'It's about thirteen off the original grade.'

'Too deep for a tunnel. What the...' Vesper thought for a moment as he looked at the masonry, trying to envision the whole structure from the exposed fragment. The rubble they'd cleared appeared to be confined to a circular area ten feet in diameter. 'I gotta check something.'

He climbed out of the hole and walked over to the site trailer that served as his local office. He flipped through a set of drawings he had for the project until he found the campus master site plan. Vesper located the area they were working in, and there, next to a dashed circle, read a note: STACK REMOVED 1948.

'It's a fucking smokestack,' Vesper growled.

Shaking his head in disgust, he picked up the phone and called Murrow.

'Hey, Fred, it's Bud. How's that contingency fund holding up?'

'What is it now?' Murrow sounded as though he could use an aspirin.

'Nothing much, just the foundation of a god-damn smokestack that was yanked out back in 'forty-eight.'

'How bad?'

'The architect wants to put a column right smack on top of the goddamn thing. Looks like there's a cleanout tunnel coming out of one side. Sounds hollow, so it won't bear the weight. The whole thing's gotta come out.'

'Okay, Bud, but take it easy on me. At the rate we're going, the contingency money will be shot before we even get the foundation in.'

'I'll be gentle. See ya, Fred.'

Vesper clipped the phone to his hip and returned to the latest discovery.

'What's the story, Bud?' Jones asked.

'Once upon a time, there was a big old smoke-stack right here.' Vesper pointed at the ring of shattered masonry. He then walked about ten paces west. 'The stack was connected to the boiler house, which sat right about there. When they demolished the stack, they chopped the tree down but left the stump. I talked with Morrow, and he gave the okay to rip it out.'

'Then let's rip.'

Vesper climbed back into the cab of his excavator and carefully began digging out the edges around the stack's foundation. It took almost two hours to expose the base of the demolished smokestack. Vesper widened the trench he'd dug around the stack on the side opposite the presumed access tunnel.

Vesper rammed the bucket into the bricks; a fissure opened in the brittle mortar joints, and two more hits widened the crack that ran top to bottom. Vesper then dug the teeth of the bucket into the upper lip of the cylinder and drove it downward, peeling away the masonry shell.

Broken bricks spilled out of the fractured vessel amid a cloud of dust and ancient ash.

Jones signaled for Vesper to wait while he took a look inside – with their recent luck, he was afraid of what they might find. He switched on his flashlight and pointed it into the tunnel. The dust was still swirling but slowly settling.

'No steam pipes, no wires. So far, so good,' Jones muttered to himself. 'Nothing but broken bricks on the–'

Jones dropped his flashlight and jumped back from the darkened opening, cursing.

Vesper leaned out of the excavator. 'Hey, Jones, what did ya see?'

'Sweet mother of Jesus! I just do not fucking believe this. I'm working in a goddamn grave-yard! I don't need this shit, I really don't!'

Jones was pacing in a circle. Vesper could see panic in the man's eyes. He leapt from the Caterpillar and ran over to the tunnel.

'Darrell, you okay, man?'

'I thought you told me all the dead people were gone! You said we weren't going to find any more! You fuckin' promised me, Bud!'

'I swear, man, I thought we got 'em all.'

'You know how I feel about this shit,' Jones said, slowly recovering his composure while his heart was still trying to pound its way out of his chest.

Vesper nodded, then turned to investigate the latest discovery. He crouched down and peered into the dark tunnel and saw Jones's flashlight lying on a pile of shattered bricks, its beam pointing down. Vesper picked up the flashlight, rotated the bezel for a wide beam, and aimed the light down into the darkened space.

About six feet ahead he saw a body lying prone on the floor of the tunnel. The fully clothed figure of a man looked as if it had been cast aside, like a rag doll, the arms and legs unnaturally askew. Off to one side lay a dust-covered leather briefcase and a rumpled hat.

Somehow, Vesper thought, *I don't think the med school put this guy down here.*

22

JULY 18

Dexter, Michigan

'Kilkenny residence,' Audrey said, answering the phone.

'Ma'am, this is Detective Brian Ptashnik of the Ann Arbor Police Department. Is Martin Kilkenny there?'

'No, he's out running some errands with our grandson. This is his wife, Audrey. Is there something I can help you with, Detective?'

'I'm afraid not, Mrs Kilkenny. We just need to speak with your husband. Could you have him contact me as soon as he returns?'

'Certainly, or if you like, I could call my grandson on his cell phone.'

'I'd appreciate that, ma'am.'

As Nolan and his grandfather walked out of the Dexter Mill with some supplies, the phone clipped to the waist of his jeans purred. He set the large bag of dog food down and answered the call.

'Nolan, is Martin with you?' Audrey asked abruptly.

'Yeah, Grandma, he's right here. Did he forget something?'

'No, dear. I just need to speak with him.'

Realizing that something was wrong, Nolan took the bags from his grandfather's arms and handed him the phone.

'Hello, Audrey.'

'Martin, I just received a call from the Ann Arbor police – a Detective Brian Ptashnik. He needs to speak with you.'

'A detective? I wonder whatever for. Did he say what about?'

'No. He just said that you might be able to help them out with something and that he'd appreciate a call from you.'

'Looks like I'll just have to call him and find out. What's his number?'

'What was that all about, Grandpa?' Nolan asked after Martin ended the call.

Martin momentarily ignored the question as he quickly dialed the number before forgetting it.

'It appears the police in Ann Arbor want to have a word with me. Why don't you finish loading the stuff in your truck while I give this detective a call and see what he wants.'

As Nolan opened the back of his SUV, Martin

135

waited for his call to be answered.

'Major Crimes Unit. Detective Ptashnik speaking.'

'Detective, this is Martin Kilkenny. I'm returning your call. What can I do for you?'

'Well, sir, first off, are you the Martin Kilkenny who worked for the University of Michigan back in 'forty-eight?'

'None other. Why do you ask?'

'Frankly, given the age of this report, I wasn't sure you'd even be alive, much less still residing locally. Something has come up on a very old case and, well, your name was in the file. I can't believe I'm even working on a case that's older than I am.'

'And what case might that be, Detective?'

'In December of 1948 you filed a missing-person report on Johann Wolff. Do you recall that?'

Martin placed a hand on the side of Nolan's SUV to steady himself; he felt the blood rush from his head.

'Are you okay, Grandpa?' Nolan asked when he saw Martin falter.

Martin nodded to Nolan. 'I remember that quite clearly, Detective.'

'Good. Would it be possible for you to meet me down at the Washtenaw County Medical Examiner's Office later today?'

'Certainly. But why?'

'We may have found your friend, sir. I realize that it's been a long time, but I would appreciate your help in identifying the body. Are you sure you're up to this, Mr Kilkenny?'

136

'Johann was my friend. I owe it to him. Would two-thirty be soon enough, Detective?'

'That'll be fine, sir.'

'I'm going to hand you over to my grandson, Nolan Kilkenny. Would you kindly tell him the particulars about where we're going?'

Martin handed the phone to Nolan, opened the passenger door of the black Mercedes, and sat with his head bowed. Nolan jotted down the detective's instructions in his planner and ended the call.

'Grandpa, are you sure you're okay?'

'Johann Wolff is dead, Nolan. My friend is dead. They found his body.' And with that, Martin Kilkenny released the tears that he'd been holding back for more than fifty years.

23

JULY 18

Ypsilanti, Michigan

At two-thirty Nolan and his grandfather met Detective Ptashnik in the lobby of a nondescript municipal building on Ypsilanti's East Side that housed, among other things, the offices of the Washtenaw County Medical Examiner.

'Thank you for coming down so quickly,' Ptashnik said, greeting them as he extended his hand.

'It's not a problem,' Martin assured the detective.

'If you'll both follow me, we'll be meeting with Dr Porter back in the morgue. She's expecting us.'

They followed Ptashnik through a painted steel door marked AUTHORIZED PERSONNEL ONLY and down an antiseptic corridor dimly lit with cool fluorescent lights.

Martin broke the silence. 'I've been meaning to ask you something, Detective.'

'Go right ahead.'

'After all this time, how did you come to the conclusion that this might be my friend Johann?'

'We found some ID with the remains.'

'And where did you find him?'

'In the base of a demolished smokestack not fifty yards from where, according to the report you filed, you last saw him.'

Martin paled slightly, horrified at the thought of Wolff's body lying buried for years just outside his shop in West Engineering.

The short walk ended at the entrance to the medical examiner's office suite.

'Hey, Martha,' Ptashnik shouted in a friendly voice, poking his head into the reception area. 'I've got a pair of visitors that I'm taking back to see Bev.'

'She's expecting you.'

'Thanks.'

Ptashnik led them through a pair of doors clad in stainless-steel protective plates. The room was brightly lit, cold and sterile. The only splash of color amid the whites and muted grays was the strawberry-blond tresses of the woman waiting inside.

'Dr Beverly Porter,' Ptashnik said, 'I'd like to introduce Martin and Nolan Kilkenny.'

'A pleasure, gentlemen, though not under the best of circumstances'

'Dr Porter, the disappearance of my friend has been like an old wound that refuses to completely heal.'

'I hope this will bring you some closure, sir.'

Porter led them into a procedure room where a shrouded figure lay beneath a halo of task lights on a stainless-steel table.

'A word of warning, gentlemen. The body is not in the best of condition'

'Body?' Nolan questioned. 'There's more than just a skeleton left after all this time?'

'The section of tunnel where the body was found acted like a vault, keeping the space inside cool and dry for over fifty years. The environment inside was ideal for preservation. Still, what you are about to see may be a bit of a shock,' Porter explained.

Nolan and Martin both nodded, mentally preparing themselves for an unholy sight. Porter picked up the edge of the cloth and respectfully exposed the head of the corpse. What they saw looked much like an Egyptian mummy – a figure all flesh and bone with the skin shriveled, dark and stiff. Wisps of light brown hair still clung to the head, a subtle reminder that this was once a living person.

Nolan exhaled quietly. In combat, he'd seen more than his share of mangled bodies and gruesome remains – the images in his memory far worse than what he now beheld.

'May I?' Martin asked, indicating that he'd like a closer look.

Porter stepped back to give him room. Martin gazed down at the withered face and compared what he saw with his memories.

'It's Johann,' he said with a mix of sadness and relief.

'Are you sure?' Ptashnik asked.

'Aye, as sure as I can be.'

Martin took out a handkerchief, dabbed at a stray tear, and blew his nose. 'How did he die?'

'He was murdered,' Ptashnik said with absolute certainty. 'His killer nearly decapitated him.'

'Who the hell would want to do a thing like that?' Martin asked angrily. 'Was he robbed?'

'That was our initial thought, but then we found that he still had his briefcase and a wallet with ten bucks in it.'

'If it wasn't for money, then why?'

'Grandpa, what about the rumors?' Nolan asked.

'Rumors?' Ptashnik repeated.

'After Johann disappeared, there was talk about how perhaps the government found out he'd done something during the war and deported him or imprisoned him or simply had him killed. Others said maybe some dark past was catching up with him, and he ran away. It was all a load of hooey; the government cleared him of any wrongdoing before they let him in the country.'

'Detective, you said that Wolff's briefcase was buried with him. Can we see it?' Nolan requested.

'Why?'

'A few weeks ago a physicist I'm working with – a guy named Ted Sandstrom – inherited a collection of letters written by Johann Wolff. Some of the material contained in those letters deals with Wolff's theoretical research. The man who bequeathed these letters, a physicist named Raphaele Paramo, believed that they might help Sandstrom solve a technological problem he's encountered in his own work. After reading the letters, Sandstrom agrees that the answer he's looking for may be somewhere in Wolff's research. Until today, I haven't found any information that could lead me to Wolff or his research. I'm hoping that there might be something in his briefcase that will help.'

'Since you two are the closest thing we have to a next of kin, I don't see any harm,' Ptashnik answered. 'Where are his personal effects, Bev?'

'They're boxed and waiting to go to the state police crime lab. I know this isn't a great time to ask, but who'll be taking care of the arrangements? I'll be finished with Mr Wolff by the weekend.'

'I'll take care of everything,' Martin volunteered. 'The funeral parlor in Dexter will be giving you a call. Thank you for the respect you've shown my friend.'

'You're welcome.'

As the Kilkennys followed Ptashnik out of the procedure room, Porter gently placed the shroud back over Wolff's head.

In the anteroom, Ptashnik located the box Porter had set aside for him on a metal gurney.

141

'Before you touch anything, I'd like you to put these on,' Ptashnik said as he pulled out a pair of white latex gloves from a wall-mounted dispenser. 'I'm going to have the lab people take a look at this to see if they can find any evidence that might identify the killer.'

Nolan and his grandfather complied with the request; Martin's thick callused hands pushed the limits of the glove's claim that one size fits all.

Ptashnik pulled out a pocketknife and slit the tape seal around the cardboard lid. Martin looked down into the open box. Each article of Wolff's clothing was individually sealed in labeled clear-plastic bags. He looked over the tie, the long coat.

'This is what Johann was wearing the last time I saw him,' Martin said. 'He must have been killed that very night.'

The collars of Wolff's shirt, blazer, and overcoat were black with long-dried blood.

'Butchery,' Martin said angrily. 'A horrible way for a man to die.'

Martin laid each of the bagged garments aside gently, as if the spirit of his friend were still somehow connected with his belongings. Brittle mud caked the front of Wolff's coat and pants; the toes of the shoes were scuffed and muddied.

'It was a foul night,' Martin recalled. 'The ground was still soggy from the rains we'd had the day before. Friday afternoon it finally got cold enough to snow. There was a foot on the ground by Saturday morning.'

'Which worked in the killer's favor,' Ptashnik said, absorbing Martin's recollections. 'You reported him missing on Saturday afternoon, but the earliest the police would have started making inquiries would have been on Monday. The snow would've covered any evidence of the crime over the weekend, and then the workmen came back and filled in the hole.'

Martin pulled out Wolff's battered leather briefcase from the bottom of the cardboard box.

'Here it is, Nolan,' Martin announced.

Ptashnik opened the seal on the evidence bag, and Nolan carefully pulled out the briefcase. He then undid the clasp that secured the top flap over the interior compartment. The dark brown leather was cracked and dirty. He lifted the flap and looked inside.

'When I left him, Johann told me that he had some paperwork and a little correspondence to finish up,' Martin said.

Inside, Nolan saw an envelope and six hard-bound notebooks. He fished out the envelope. 'It's another letter to Raphaele Paramo. May I open it?'

Ptashnik nodded his approval.

Nolan carefully ran his gloved thumb under the envelope's seal; the brittle glue released at the lightest touch. He pulled out the folded pages and laid them on the gurney.

'It's like the others,' Nolan said. 'He covers the personal stuff first, then dives into the physics. Take a look at this, Grandpa. He's telling Paramo about his engagement to Elli.'

Martin quickly read the first part of the letter and smiled. 'He was a happy man when he wrote this.'

As Martin read the letter, Nolan pulled a notebook out of the briefcase.

'Johann always kept a notebook with him wherever he went,' Martin recalled. 'He was a very private man, particularly with regard to his work. Some of his colleagues thought he was a bit paranoid, and perhaps he was. After all those years of living with the Gestapo looking over his shoulder, I can understand how he might be guarded about what he was thinking. I'm just wondering, what if he dreamed up something brilliant – like Einstein did. There's a lot of prima donnas running around in a place like Michigan, people who might be a bit put out if a Young Turk like Johann were to show them up.'

'You think one of his colleagues might have killed him out of professional jealousy?' Ptashnik asked.

Martin shrugged his shoulders. 'I don't know. I'm just trying to make sense of something that doesn't make any sense at all. Johann enjoyed what he did; he even tried to explain to me a little about what he was working on, but it flew right over my poor brain. It just seems to me that the only real thing of value Johann had was what he carried around in his head and what he put in his notebooks.'

'It's hard to believe this has been underground for over fifty years,' Nolan said.

The binding cracked loudly as Nolan opened the volume; the pages were still white and showed little deterioration. The first page contained a few carefully drawn sketches and some accompanying text.

144

'What do you make of that?' Martin asked.

'The drawings are mathematical, but I've never seen an algorithm that generates an image that looks like that. One thing's for sure, Wolff could draw.'

'That he could,' Martin agreed. 'He had quite a good fist, like a draftsman.'

Nolan scanned the text – written in the same precise hand that authored the Paramo letters – but found nothing his mind could latch onto.

'This is gibberish,' Nolan said.

'What do you mean, lad?' Martin asked.

'The text. Take a close look at it.'

Curious, Martin and Ptashnik glanced down at the open notebook. The tiny characters Wolff had so precisely drawn on the page were an apparently random mix of letters, numbers, and Greek mathematical symbols. Nolan studied the composition of the page as a whole. Each character was equally spaced, as if laid out on a grid. The page was the result of a deliberate, precise effort.

'Maybe he was dyslexic,' Ptashnik offered wryly.

'I don't think so,' Nolan mused. 'Wolff took his time with these characters; look how carefully each one is drawn.'

'Looks like calligraphy,' Ptashnik noted.

'Actually, I think it's cryptography.'

'Say again?'

'I'm no expert in this field, but I've seen enough encrypted text to think that's what we're looking at here.'

'Why would Wolff do that?' Ptashnik wondered.

'Well, he was a physicist,' Nolan replied. 'What big physics project was going on in the 1940s?'

'The bomb,' Ptashnik quickly offered.

'No,' Martin growled, shaking his head. 'Johann wasn't working on any bombs. He hated the damn things. He once told me that during the war he did everything he could to keep Hitler from getting the bomb. He was quite proud of that.'

'Okay, bad example,' Nolan admitted. 'But you get the idea. Raphaele Paramo once told his wife that Johann Wolff was the most brilliant mind he'd ever met. Coming from a guy who hung out with a lot of very smart people, that's some high praise. What if he was working on something just as important as the bomb?'

'Nolan, Johann wasn't working for anybody on anything. He was an assistant professor teaching first-year physics. Anyway, if his notebooks were so valuable, why are they still here?'

'Good point.' Ptashnik took a look inside the briefcase. 'There's no mud in here, and the letter and the notebooks are all clean. This was a violent killing, and it took place in a muddy pit. The killer had to have been right down in there with his victim. Whatever the motive, I don't think the killer was interested in Wolff's briefcase. You said that the world of physics wasn't all that big. What if it wasn't something he was working on but something he knew? I don't think the Russians had the bomb back in 'forty-eight. Maybe he knew somebody who was helping them.'

'The Russians didn't detonate their first bomb

until September of 1949,' Martin recalled. 'In 1950 Fuchs, the Rosenbergs, and others were arrested for selling atomic secrets to the Russians.'

Ptashnik shook his head and smiled.

'Don't argue with my grandfather, Detective. He's got a memory like an elephant.'

'And the girth to match,' Martin said with a wink.

Nolan carefully turned the next few pages of Wolff's notebook; each was similar to the first.

'The only thing on any of these pages that I recognize are the dates he's put in the upper corners. Here's twenty-two-eight-forty-six.'

'Twenty-two-eight-forty-six?' Ptashnik inquired.

'The twenty-second of August 1946,' Nolan explained. 'He's using European notation: day-month-year.'

Nolan pulled the remaining notebooks out of the briefcase and checked the dates on each.

Martin was curious. 'What are you looking for, Nolan?'

'His last entry.'

The sixth book started with the latest date he'd found. Thumbing through the blank pages in the back, he reached Wolff's last entry about halfway through the volume.

'Ten-twelve-forty-eight.' Nolan read. 'Ten December.'

'That's the last day I saw him,' Martin recalled.

'And likely the day he was murdered,' Ptashnik added.

As Nolan slowly closed the notebook, he noticed some writing on the thick front endpaper. He opened the cover to expose the page and found a series of carefully written mathematical equations. Nolan recognized some of the functions, but others were used in ways that were unfamiliar to him.

'What you got there?' Ptashnik asked.

'I'm not sure, but at least it's in plain text. Maybe this is the algorithm Wolff used to encode his notebooks.'

Martin flipped open the first notebook, then glanced back at the one in his grandson's hands. 'Take a look at this, Nolan. I think this page is the same as that one.'

A quick check revealed that all the notebooks bore the same formula on the front endpaper.

'What are you thinking?' Martin asked, completely confused.

'I'd say there's a pretty good chance that this is Wolff's cipher. Now if we just had the key, we could decode all this. Detective, what are you going to do with the notebooks?'

'The techs will take a look at them for physical evidence, then we'll put 'em in the evidence storage center with anything else we collect. Why?'

'Can I make a suggestion?'

'Shoot.'

'These notebooks are old and potentially valuable. Why don't you take them over to the Preservation Lab at the university library? The people there know how to handle old books.'

'That's probably not a bad idea. We've used their services on cases before. I'll arrange it with our techs.'

'Also, I'd like to get a copy of the letter, to put with the others, he wrote to Paramo. If you like, I can get you copies of what we have.'

'Are they written in code?'

'Plain English. They're a mix of personal stuff and physics. I don't know if they'll be of much help to you, but there's a lot of day-to-day commentary. Maybe there's something in there that you'll find useful.'

'I'd appreciate that,' Ptashnik acknowledged. 'Can I ask a favor in return?'

'Depends on what the favor is.'

'While the books are at the lab,' Nolan explained, 'I'd like to have some work done on them for my project.'

'What kind of work?'

'Nothing destructive, I promise. I just want to scan the pages into the computer for analysis. Raphaele Paramo thought enough of Wolff to suggest that a stack of letters from the guy might help the physicist I'm working with solve a very complex problem. So I want to know what Wolff was working on.'

'All right,' Ptashnik relented. 'Just keep me posted on what you find.'

24

JULY 19

Moscow, Russia

'Dmitri, it's good to see you again,' Zoshchenko said coolly as she walked into Orlov's anteroom. 'My condolences on the loss of your brother.'

'Thank you,' Leskov acknowledged with a nod. 'Pavel knew the risks involved in our work, and he died with honor. He was a good man, difficult to replace.'

'He will see you both now,' Irena Cherny announced as she set the phone in its cradle.

Leskov opened the door for Zoshchenko, then followed her into Orlov's office. The view across Moscow to the Kremlin was breathtaking on this sunlit summer morning.

'Please, have a seat,' Orlov offered, his hand motioning toward the couch and chairs near the window. On the table in the center of the furniture arrangement sat a silver tea service.

'Dmitri, what is the status of our surveillance in America?'

Leskov unbuttoned his blazer before sitting in one of Orlov's prerevolutionary antique chairs. 'The physicist Sandstrom is still receiving treatment for extensive burns at University Hospital in Ann Arbor, Michigan. His condition is stable, but he is in for a long and difficult recovery. Electronic devices have been placed in his room, and his phone has been tapped. The team monitoring him has leased an apartment in a tower across the river from the hospital, high enough that they are receiving very clear transmission from the devices. Sandstrom has two regular visitors – Nolan Kilkenny and Kelsey Newton. Both were present during the raid on Sandstrom's lab. A thorough background check on Kilkenny has revealed that he was once a junior officer in the U.S. Navy SEALs.'

Orlov arched an eyebrow at Leskov's final comment.

'*Da,* Victor Ivanovich. That is why three of my men are dead. Kilkenny's training is equal to Spetsnaz. Per your request, surveillance of both Kilkenny and Newton is also in place.'

'Excellent, Dmitri. Have you learned anything from the surveillance?' Orlov asked.

'*Da.* We have confirmed the assumption that the MARC/ND-ARC combine intends to continue its support of Sandstrom's research. Their support is contingent upon Sandstrom's recovery.'

'It's a little premature to consider any further offensive actions against Sandstrom. Any such move would have to he handled with the greatest care. What is the status of the police investigation into the raid?'

'It's at a complete standstill. Other than the eyewitness reports given by Sandstrom, Kilkenny, and Newton, the police have no leads from which to work.'

'Good. Keep monitoring that situation, but at a safe distance. In all likelihood the whole matter will fade into obscurity due to lack of progress.'

Orlov turned to Zoshchenko, who sat quietly on the couch drinking her tea.

'How are things going at our research facility, Oksanna?'

'There's a lot of material to review, but Lara Avvakum is making excellent progress. She has an almost intuitive grasp of the conceptual aspects of the project. I anticipate that by the end of the month, she will be ready to address the experimental work. She has embraced the project fully and is very enthusiastic.'

'I thought she might be receptive to our offer; ten years in Siberia does that to a person.' Orlov drank his tea, savoring the taste of the imported blend. 'Any other issues we need to discuss?'

'One, sir,' Leskov replied.

'Go on.'

'Our surveillance has uncovered something unusual. On several occasions Newton was heard reading letters to Sandstrom. In analyzing the transcripts of these conversations, I believe these letters were written to Sandstrom's colleague, Raphaele Paramo, several years ago. One transcript shows Sandstrom expressing amazement that the author had a better grasp of quantum physics fifty years ago than anyone today.'

'Do you have the transcripts of those letters with you?' Zoshchenko asked as she moved forward in her seat.

Leskov zipped open a leather binder and handed a folder to Zoshchenko. 'I guessed you

152

might want to take a look. Newton has been reading one or two letters each visit, and the rest of the time is spent discussing what she's read. Both of them seem very excited by the material. I don't know how many letters there are, but we're getting them one at a time.'

'This is very interesting,' Zoshchenko said, thinking aloud as she skimmed over the first letter.

'Could you elaborate, Oksanna?'

'Oh, of course, Victor Ivanovich.' Zoshchenko gathered her thoughts. 'If the first letter I read is any indication of the rest, then I would concur with Sandstrom's assessment that the author is a very gifted individual. He writes about physics like a poet. I freely admit my grasp of the non-deterministic nature of quantum mechanics is weak at best, but even I can see the fog lifting as I read his words. This person's thinking is coherent. It is focused like a laser. I've never read anything quite like this – if I had, I would surely have remembered it. Who is the author?'

'A physicist named Johann Wolff,' Leskov informed them.

'I've never heard of him,' Zoshchenko admitted quizzically.

'Nobody has. Kilkenny and Newton have been looking for some record of this Wolff's work and have apparently found nothing. Sandstrom is convinced that Wolff's research may provide the key that unlocks the mystery behind his discovery.'

'How could a brilliant mind such as this go unnoticed?' Zoshchenko couldn't comprehend it.

'That's where this gets interesting. A few weeks ago Kilkenny and Newton gave up their search for Wolff.'

'Why?' Orlov asked.

'We weren't sure at first, but we eventually learned that Wolff disappeared in December of 1948 and was never heard from again. According to university records, Wolff was a relatively young man – late twenties – when he disappeared. Interest in Wolff was rekindled a few days ago when his body was discovered near the building where he worked at the university.'

Zoshchenko nodded thoughtfully. 'That explains why he never published his work.'

'Wolff was murdered,' Leskov continued. 'Someone practically cut his head off. We intercepted a conference call between Kilkenny, Sandstrom, and Newton yesterday when Kilkenny explained this to his associates.'

'What do we know about this Wolff?' Orlov demanded.

'According to a newspaper article, Wolff was from Dresden and studied physics in Berlin. During the war he worked with a physicist named Heisenberg.'

'Werner Heisenberg?' Zoshchenko mulled over the name. 'He won the Nobel Prize for inventing quantum mechanics and the famous Heisenberg Uncertainty Principle. In the pantheon of great theoretical physicists, Heisenberg is a titan. The main reason the Americans spent so much time and money to build an atomic bomb during the Great Patriotic War was because Heisenberg was working for the Germans. Every physicist in the

154

world believed that if anyone could successfully build such a weapon, it would be Heisenberg.'

'So Wolff was suckled on the tit of the great Heisenberg,' Leskov continued, perturbed at Zoshchenko's minilecture. 'After the war, he went to America and took a job teaching physics at a university. A couple of years later, he was killed.'

'Is that all?'

Leskov looked over his notes regarding Wolff. 'There is one more thing. The reason for the renewed interest is not so much the body, but what was found with it. In that phone intercept, Kilkenny mentioned that Wolff's briefcase contained a letter and six notebooks. There's a problem with the books that Kilkenny didn't elaborate on.'

'If they were buried in the ground with Wolff,' Zoshchenko offered, 'they are probably in very poor condition.'

'Perhaps, but our competitors still believe they are of some value.'

'Then so should we. Good work, Dmitri. Follow up on the notebooks; we'll acquire them if necessary. Oksanna, I would like you to do a little research on Johann Wolff. I believe the Red Army confiscated most of the Third Reich's scientific records. See what you can dig out of the archives. Let's meet on Friday to discuss this matter more fully.'

25

JULY 19

Langley, Virginia

Bart Cooper arrived at the CIA's George Bush Center for Intelligence a little after ten o'clock having avoided the daily rush-hour traffic. Setting his own work hours was one of his perks as a consultant to the Agency, the latest in a long line of titles he'd held in an intelligence career that started when he became an OSS field operative during the Second World War. He'd risen in rank as the Agency grew, and fought on the front lines of America's Cold War. Cooper had survived scandals, various downsizing programs, and micromanaging congressional oversight. And now, he seemed to have survived retirement in his role as adviser to the Director of Central Intelligence. At a robust seventy-seven, he served as counselor emeritus to Jackson Barnett, the current DCI, who valued Cooper for his broad perspective.

After parking in the same spot he'd been assigned back in the sixties, Cooper cleared the main building's security and took the elevator up to the executive level. The place was filled with its usual buzz of activity as information from around the world was gathered, sifted, analyzed, processed, digested, and eventually regurgitated for the elected officials who would decide what it meant. Some things never changed.

'Morning, Bart,' Sally Kirsch, Jackson Barnett's executive secretary, said as Cooper stepped into the office pantry to get himself a cup of coffee.

'Hi, Sally. How are things in the Far East today?'

'No better than yesterday, and Africa is heating up again.'

Cooper sighed at the thought of another military coup in some sub-Saharan country launching yet another round of intertribal genocide. 'There are times when I yearn for the old days, when we would just send a team out and pop these guys.'

'You're kidding, aren't you?'

Cooper just smiled and left with a mug of black coffee.

When he reached his office, he set the mug down on the desk and hung his blazer on the rack. His in-basket contained the files that Barnett wanted him to peruse. Most of them dealt with operational concepts – Cooper's forte – while the remainder were a mixed bag of analysis that somebody, somewhere, wanted a seasoned eye to give the once-over. He wasn't on the front lines anymore, but Cooper was thankful that Barnett valued his insights enough to let him keep his hand in the game. He was the last of the old guard, a cold warrior whose tenure ran back as far as the days of Wild Bill Donovan and Allen Dulles.

He sat down and wiggled the mouse on his

desk, awakening his computer from its electronic slumber. The black screen flickered back to life, rendering the CIA logo against a field of light blue. A small box on the bottom center of the screen waited for him to type in his password. Cooper keyed in the thirteen random characters and pressed ENTER.

'*Ohayo gozamasu,* Cooper-san,' the computer announced in a voice that sounded a lot like Toshiro Mifune. '*Ohayo,* computer-san,' Cooper replied.

Every day, the computer greeted Cooper in the language of one of the countries he'd worked in during his years as a field agent, never voicing the same greeting twice in a month.

Cooper clicked on his calendar and saw that he had a meeting with the Deputy Director in Charge of Operations at 1:30. He then checked his E-mail: a few general-broadcast announcements, a response from Barnett regarding the China-Korea situation, and something generated by the central computer regarding a flagged file.

'I don't recall making a search request,' Cooper mused as he selected the last piece of mail for viewing.

TO: COOPER, BARTHOLOMEW
FROM: CIA CENTER NETWORK
KEYWORD SEARCH FOR FILE OSS-17932
HAS FOUND
1 MATCH FOR KEYWORDS:
WOLFF, JOHANN.

The OSS designator in the file number identified

158

it as something dating back to the Second World War, part of the CIA's inheritance from the Office of Strategic Services. Cooper was the last remaining veteran of the OSS still active with the Agency. While stationed in Germany immediately following the war, Cooper was tasked with weeding out Nazis from the stream of German refugees seeking to emigrate to the United States.

The body of the message contained only a line of blue, underscored text. Cooper selected the hypertext link, and his computer responded by loading an article that the system had culled from the day's electronic edition of the *Ann Arbor News*.

Body that of missing asst. prof.

The remains unearthed Monday from a construction site on the Diag of the University of Michigan have been positively identified as those of Johann Wolff. Wolff was an assistant professor of physics at the university from 1946 until his disappearance on Dec. 10, 1948.

Wolff, originally from Dresden, Germany, received a doctorate in physics at the Kaiser Wilhelm Institute in Berlin and worked with renowned physicist Werner Heisenberg.

Det. Brian Ptashnik, of the Ann Arbor Police, has confirmed that Wolff's death is being investigated as a homicide. No further details regarding the investigation were announced.

The discovery of Wolff's body follows the grisly discovery of the preserved remains of medical cadavers from the 1800s on the same construction site last week. Dozens of handmade grave markers, bearing names like Amelia Earhart, Jimmy Hoffa and Elvis Presley, have sprung up on the Diag as students have transformed the campus lawn into a mock cemetery.

Cooper printed a copy of the article, then closed the window and pulled the single sheet from the printer. After rereading the article for the third time, Cooper scanned the phone list tacked to his wall and dialed the number he was looking for.

'Research, this is Connie,' a whiskey-throated woman answered.

'Morning, Connie. It's Bart.'

'Bart Cooper?' her voice softened with surprise. 'It's been a while. How they treating you upstairs?'

'Same as always, with the great respect due one of my numerous years of service.'

'Sounds like the same old song and dance we get down here,' Connie said with a laugh. 'What can I do for you?'

'I need some research done on an old case.'

'How old?'

'Old, as in before your time.'

'A request like that isn't research; it's archaeology.'

'I know,' he said, laughing. 'But please, I need everything you can find on a Johann Wolff. He was a German physicist, worked on the Nazi A-bomb project during the war.'

'What's the story?'

'They just found his body up in Michigan, fifty years after he disappeared. Looks like murder.'

'A murdered German physicist. How intriguing.'

160

'Might be. See what you can dig up. Full package: German Intelligence, Immigration. The works. You can start with file OSS-one seven nine three two. Also, see if you can get anything from our friends at Lubyanka – they got most of the Gestapo's records out of Berlin.'

'I'll see what I can do. Any rush on this?'

'No, it's just to satisfy my own curiosity. You see, Wolff was one of the German scientists I vetted after the war – I wrote that OSS file I just told you about. Based on what I could find at the time, I cleared him to immigrate into the U.S. Still, I have a few questions about Wolff that I'd like to resolve.'

26

JULY 20

Ann Arbor, Michigan

Kilkenny swiped his ID through the card reader that controlled the electronic lock on the door to the MARC Computer Center. The red light quickly changed to green, accompanied by an audible buzz and the release of the electrified magnets that held the door closed.

Inside, Bill 'Grin' Grinelli rose from behind the cluttered workstation that was the heart of the MARC computer network and smiled. He was a few inches shorter than Nolan and wore a black

T-shirt, a pair of comfortably worn jeans, and his Birkenstock sandals. His shoulder-length brown-gray hair was drawn back in a ponytail, and he sported a pointed goatee that surrounded an infectious smile. Grin was the embodiment of free-spirited mischief, and the tattoo of a mythological Pan seated on a crescent moon scattering pixie dust that adorned his left forearm only enhanced that perception.

'Nolan, what's up, man? Long time, no see. I heard about the excitement in South Bend. I guess trouble just seems to find you.'

'Same old, same old, my friend.'

Grin laughed. 'I hear ya, man. Guys like us don't have to look for trouble; like bees to honey it finds us well enough on its own.'

As MARC's MIS director, Grin kept infor-mation, the lifeblood of the consortium, flowing freely through the building's electronic veins and arteries. The apparent ease with which he handled his job was even more amazing con-sidering the diversity of personal computers and workstations within the consortium.

At the heart of Grin's electronic empire stood a pair of supercomputers that he considered his personal property, a recently acquired Moy Electronics massively parallel machine and MARC's original Cray. The tall, thin Moy machine stood in marked contrast to the squat, cylindrical form of the Cray, prompting Grin to christen them Stan and Ollie. Affixed to the front panel of each machine was a photograph of its comic namesake.

'Miss me down here?' Nolan asked, shaking

Grin's outstretched hand.

'You know it. I had to put Stan in all by my lone-some. Well, me and half a dozen techs from Moy.'

'How's he running?'

'Like a champ.'

'Great, because I've got a problem I'd like him to take a shot at. How are you at cracking encryption?'

'Officially, I never touch the stuff.'

'How about unofficially?'

'You remember that two-hundred-and-fifty-six-bit scheme some genius thought up for the government, supposedly unbreakable?'

'You're the one who cracked it?'

'I must confess. I did have my hand in that little caper. I do so love a challenge.'

'I'm glad to hear you talk that way. Let me show you what I've got.'

Kilkenny pulled a chair around the console, seating himself next to Grin.

'Log in to main campus and jump down to the library's Preservation Lab server.'

'Surf's up,' Grin replied as he clicked on the graphical icons that identified other computer networks connected to MARC. 'And we're in.'

'We're looking for a directory named Wolff Codex.'

'*Kodak,* like the film company?'

'No, *codex,* like Leonardo da Vinci's illustrated notebooks. What I want to show you are high-resolution scans taken from the pages of some very old notebooks that were found with that body down on campus.'

'The murdered professor?'

'That's the one. Johann Wolff taught physics at the university for a couple of years after the Second World War, right up to the day he was murdered. It's the considered opinion of some well-respected physicists, one of whom you know–'

'Kelsey?'

Nolan nodded. '–that the late Professor Wolff may have been one of the most brilliant minds of the twentieth century.'

'Last time I checked the calendar, it was the twenty-first century, big guy.'

'Maybe so, but if Kelsey and Sandstrom are correct, had Wolff not been murdered, the twenty-first century, technologically speaking, might have started thirty years ago.'

Grin let out a long, slow whistle.

'Is there much left of these notebooks?'

'Actually, the books are in surprisingly good shape. The experts tell me that the books were all well-made cloth hardcovers with reasonably high quality paper. The tunnel segment they were buried in protected them like a time capsule. There was very little damage to any of the note-books.'

'I don't remember reading anything about notebooks being found with the body.'

'The police are keeping that quiet because we don't know what's in the notebooks yet. They expect us to keep quiet as well. You'll see why in a minute.'

Grin navigated through the Preservation Lab's file tree, eventually locating the folder icon named

164

Wolff Codex. When Grin selected the icon, a window appeared requesting an access password.

'Well?' Grin said impatiently as he looked to Nolan for assistance.

'I picked something I thought you could remember: MTEV two nine oh two eight.'

Grin turned and smiled. 'The number of feet Mount Everest is above sea level. I'm touched. You remembered my fondness for mountain climbing.'

Grin keyed in the password and was granted access to the file. The Wolff Codex folder split into six subfolders labeled VOL1 through VOL6.

'Click on volume one. I doubt there's anything in the other folders yet.'

As Grin selected it, VOL1 split into dozens of graphic image files. Each file bore the name of the page whose digitally recorded image it contained. VOL1 contained image files PAGE001 through PAGE016.

'Pick page one,' Nolan said.

Grin selected the PAGE001 icon, and his monitor filled with the scanned image of the first page from Wolff's oldest notebook.

'What am I looking at here?'

'This is volume one, page one of the Wolff Codex.'

'What language is this written in?' Grin asked.

'None that I can understand. Zoom in on a block of text.'

Grin selected a section of text from the upper left corner of the page. The enhanced image darkened the characters, amplifying Wolff's bold, confident strokes.

'That look like any code you've ever seen?'

'It's definitely not your basic letter-swap encryption, that's for damn sure. There's no obvious order, but you'd expect that in a serious piece of coding. Is the base language English?'

'Don't know. Wolff was a native German who spoke several European languages as well as English. He'd only been in the States for the last two years of his life.'

'It might be Enigma.'

'Enigma?'

'Yeah, the code used by Germany during the Second World War.'

'I guess it's possible.'

'They didn't happen to find a coding machine with these notebooks, did they? It would look like a typewriter in a wooden box.'

'No, but check out the file called ENDPAPER.'

Grin selected the file. When it appeared, Grin's eyebrows shot up.

'Whoa, that is some serious, heavy-duty math, my friend.'

'Well out of my league,' Nolan admitted. 'I found this algorithm in the front of all six notebooks. My guess is that it's the cipher Wolff used to encrypt the notebooks.'

'Hmm. Didn't happen to see a key for this thing anywhere, did you?'

'No.'

'Too bad. Well, I guess I can try to feed this to Stan and Ollie and see what they come up with. Once I figure out how this algorithm works, I can apply some brute force to cracking it.'

166

27

JULY 21

Moscow, Russia

'Oksanna, have you found out anything more about Wolff?' Orlov asked as he seated himself on the couch, facing Zoshchenko and Leskov.

'Very little, actually, other than to confirm some elements of Wolff's background. He was born and raised in Dresden, the fourth child of an engineer. He attended university in Berlin and, during the war, completed his doctorate under the guidance of Werner Heisenberg. I was unable to locate a copy of his thesis; it was presumably lost during the fall of Berlin. Wolff and several other physicists fled Berlin before the Red Army arrived, hiding in a rural area that was eventually occupied by the Western Allies. As a junior scientist, he was detained only briefly by the Allies and eventually emigrated to America. According to the Gestapo background checks, Wolff was a quiet, introverted young man whose instructors felt showed great promise. Evidently, Heisenberg was so impressed with his young protégé that he used whatever influence he had to protect Wolff from serving in the army. As Dmitri reported on Wednesday, Wolff lived quietly in America until he was killed.'

'Anything else?'

'Just an interesting note. Following the war, several of the German scientists who'd been liberated by the Red Army and became guests of the state were interviewed regarding the German atomic-weapons research. The German effort to build an atomic bomb never really started, because Heisenberg convinced Hitler that even if it were remotely possible to build such a device, research and development would drain billions of deutsche marks away from the war effort, and by the time the first bomb was completed, the war would he over.'

'What does this have to do with Wolff?' Leskov demanded to know. 'He was just Heisenberg's lackey at the time.'

'Heisenberg's recommendations to the Reich were based on what he considered to be irrefutable scientific facts – facts borne out by rigorous manual calculations.' Zoshchenko's tone was snide and superior. 'It was all in the numbers, and those numbers were meticulously ground out by Heisenberg's so-called lackey, Wolff.'

'*Spasiba,* Oksanna,' Orlov chided, politely ending her lecture before she riled Leskov even more.

Zoshchenko bristled but said nothing further. Orlov knew that she and Leskov barely tolerated each other, and did so only because Orlov demanded it. She despised Leskov as a hulking Neanderthal – an unfortunate necessity of Victor Orlov's business. Conversely, Leskov viewed her as an arrogant, self-centered intellectual bitch who could easily be replaced by any of the high-

168

priced whores servicing Moscow executives.

'Dmitri, what do you have to report?' Orlov asked, looking to get the meeting back on track.

'The notebooks found with Johann Wolff have been taken to a laboratory on the campus of the University of Michigan for analysis and preservation. Our electronics team has infiltrated the university's computer network and located information, what they call image files, linked to these notebooks. The files are secured, but they believe they can hack their way in. They have also monitored someone outside the laboratory accessing some of these files, someone named Grin from MARC. We are working to identify this individual.'

'Have you discovered what is in Wolff's notebooks?'

'No, and neither have they.'

'What do you mean?' Zoshchenko was confused. 'If they are interested in these books, then it must be Wolff's research.'

'I have no doubt that that is exactly what it is, but apparently the notebooks are somehow encrypted. Wolff didn't want people to know what he was working on.'

'That's very interesting.' Orlov rubbed his chin as he considered Leskov's report. 'Oksanna, based on Wolff's letters, do you think his work might be of value to our competitors?'

'Absolutely. Wolff's thinking is highly unconventional, and his insights into quantum reality could provide the keys to understanding how Sandstrom's device works.'

'Then we must acquire these notebooks, even if

only to deprive our competitors of them. Dmitri, make the necessary arrangements.'

'*Da,* Victor Ivanovich.'

28

JULY 21

Langley, Virginia

When Bart Cooper entered his office, he found a thick manila envelope resting on his desk. He sat down, undid the clasp tie, and extracted the contents; it was the information he'd requested from Connie. The first few pages laid out a chronology of Johann Wolff's abbreviated life, starting with his birth in Dresden and ending with the discovery of his remains a few days ago.

After the chronology, Cooper found a synopsis of the information about Wolff dredged from a classified report regarding the wartime activities of German scientists issued in September of 1948.

• 10/1947: Workmen clearing rubble in West Berlin uncover a cache of files in the basement of a collapsed building. The building was used by the Reichsforschungsrat – the Reich Science Council.

• The files identified research projects on which prisoners from German concentration camps

170

were used as slave labor and test subjects –
projects that included Wernher von Braun's V-2
ballistic missile program at Peenemunde. Johann
Wolff's name was listed among those responsible
for conducting a horrific series of experiments on
prisoners.

• Investigators were able to confirm, through
witnesses and secondary documentation, most of
the war crimes alleged in the files.

• Since several of the more prominent German
scientists named in the recovered files were
working on classified U.S. military projects, no
action was taken to prosecute them for war
crimes.

• 9/1948: The recovered files and investigative
reports were reviewed by the congressional oversight committee and classified.

'And three months after the files were
suppressed, Johann Wolff was murdered in Ann
Arbor, Michigan,' Cooper said with a sigh.

Cooper recalled hearing rumors about the
recovered files, but only the most senior
intelligence officers were assigned to work with
them. He also remembered the anxiety he felt
over the possibility that a war criminal might
have entered the United States because of something he missed on the background check.

• Review of the still-classified report reveals
that investigators were unable to confirm the
allegation that physicist Johann Wolff partici-
pated in any scientific experimentation on
prisoners. Further, other sources deemed reliable

171

contradict the allegations.

• The evidence found appears to support information provided by Johann Wolff during his interviews with the OSS. Wolff spent the entirety of the war in Berlin, at the Kaiser Wilhelm Gesellschaft, where he was a junior member of the Uranverein – the Uranium Club. The Uranverein was responsible for the German nuclear-research program for both civilian and military applications. This group's work was primarily theoretical, and there is no evidence that Wolff, or any other member of the Uranverein, was involved in human experimentation of any kind.

• Further investigation into the discrepancy regarding Wolff reveals that the Reichsforschungsrat files were intentionally altered by a Nazi scientist named Gerhard Strauss. Strauss essentially traded professional identities with Wolff to cover up his wartime activities. Strauss was killed during the Red Army attack on Berlin.

'My God, he *was* innocent,' Cooper said, his doubts vanishing as he read on.

• As the war in Europe came to an end, Soviet and U.S. forces aggressively sought to acquire German scientists and technology. A few members of the Uranverein were captured by the Soviets, along with a significant amount of research documentation.

• Interrogation of the German scientists revealed the truth about their failure to build an atomic bomb. None of the scientists wanted to construct an atomic bomb for the Führer, but they also truly believed that the job was impossible. When the Uranverein presented their nuclear-research proposal to the Reich, they said that building an atomic bomb was at best impractical and, at worst, impossible. Their conclusion was based on hard numbers that had been painstakingly calculated by hand. These scientists stated that their data had been checked and double-checked by the best mathematician on their staff – Johann Wolff.

• Following the successful detonation of atomic bombs over Hiroshima and Nagasaki, NKVD transcripts indicate that the German scientists were dumbfounded as to the reason for their failure. Using the files captured by the Red Army, the scientists reconstructed the mathematics on which they based their claim that an atomic bomb was theoretically unfeasible.

• After careful review of several years' worth of original calculations, it was the opinion of the German scientists and their Russian counterparts that a number of subtle errors had been introduced into the equations – errors that doomed the German research effort to failure.

Cooper reread the last section and came to an inescapable conclusion. 'They were sabotaged.'

• The review uncovered a deliberate pattern of miscalculation on the part of Johann Wolff. After correcting for Wolff's subtle errors, the Germans realized how close they had come to determining that the atomic bomb was feasible. They also realized that in order for Wolff to have undermined their research efforts so perfectly, he must have known the truth. It was the opinion of the German and Russian scientists that Johann Wolff single-handedly prevented the Germans from building an atomic bomb.

Cooper slumped back in his chair, his face now ashen. He felt a tightness in his chest and, for a moment, wondered if he was having a heart attack. He vividly remembered the day he learned that Wolff, a man he'd cleared to immigrate into the United States, might have been a war criminal. Germany was swarming with rumors then – secret projects, hidden Nazi gold – and it was often hard to separate truth from lies. Rivers of disinformation flowed out of Western and Soviet intelligence services as the Cold War began to set in.

He remembered hearing rumors about a secret cache of files, about records of who did what, and further rumors about how those files were suppressed for reasons of the highest national security. Cooper saw the death camps firsthand and could not fathom how a nation could find any security in harbouring men capable of inflicting such horror.

Then there were those who would not tolerate such an injustice, men and women bent on seeking retribution – the Nokmim. Cooper sympathized with them, exchanged information, and occasionally turned a blind eye when the Nokmim became a court of last resort for war criminals who found refuge under the Cold War umbrella of political necessity. Some of the more radical members of the Nokmim were less interested in due process and reasonable doubt than in vengeance.

'I am responsible for the death of an innocent man,' Cooper admitted, acknowledging something he'd feared since his first contact with the Nokmim regarding Wolff. 'Not just an innocent man, but a hero who prevented Hitler from building an atomic bomb.'

The information he'd had back then was incomplete, but both he and the Nokmim knew that Wolff's name was in the files. At the time, that seemed enough, but now the enormity of that error in judgment bore down upon him.

Clipped to the last page of the report, Cooper found a note from Connie.

FYI. It appears you aren't the only one interested in Johann Wolff. According to the Russians, two search requests were made for information regarding Wolff. That's the reason they responded to my inquiry so quickly; they'd just finished the same search for someone else.

'What the hell?' Cooper's mind raced as he reread the note. He then checked his watch. 'Well, I guess it won't hurt to ask.'

He pulled a tattered address book from the top drawer of his desk and flipped through the pages until he found the entry he was looking for. There was a gray smudge beneath Fydorov's name where the initials *KGB* had been written. In keeping with the new order in Russia, the former Committee for State Security had been rechristened the Federalnaya Sluzhba Bezopasnosti (Federal Security Service), and the initials FSB were now scrawled above the smudge.

Cooper picked up the phone and keyed in the long string of numbers.

'Fydorov,' a voice growled into Cooper's ear.

'*Dóbry viécher,* Igor Sergeevich,' Cooper replied in lightly accented Russian. 'You're working late. It's Bart Cooper.'

There was a pause on the line. 'Bartholomew Georgievich? It's been quite a long time. Are you in Moscow?'

'No, Iggy, I'm calling from the States. How are things with the FSB?'

Fydorov sighed. 'There is a saying in your country that fits perfectly: The more things change, the more they stay the same.'

'Ain't it the truth. I've got a little business I'd like to discuss with you, if you've got a minute.'

'As always, I'll help you any way I can. Go ahead.'

'A few days ago the body of a German physicist was found here in the States. He'd been murdered back in 'forty-eight, and the body had remained hidden until now. This physicist worked on the German bomb project, and I was the intel officer who cleared him to immigrate into the U.S. When his body surfaced, I asked our research department to put together a full package on him, more for my own curiosity than anything else.'

'Did you learn anything interesting?'

'A little, but what stuck out was how quickly we got the information. Your archives turned our request around in a day.'

'A day? What are you bribing them with? I've had requests go weeks before receiving a report.'

'The quick turnaround surprised us, too. The reason your people responded so promptly was that they'd just completed an identical search for someone else, so the information had already been culled.'

'That's quite a coincidence.'

'My old instincts tell me it's more than a coincidence. What I want to know is who was asking for information? As far as I know, the story was strictly local and didn't get picked up by the wire services.'

'And our archives are not exactly as accessible for research as your Library of Congress. What is the name of your dead German physicist?'

'Johann Wolff,' Cooper replied.

'I'll see what I can come up with.'

'I'd appreciate it, Iggy.'

29

JULY 25

Moscow, Russia

It was late when Lara Avvakum decided to make a few notes in the project log before quitting for the night. She reveled in the excitement of this exploration and, for the first time in years, lost track of the hours as she worked.

She clicked on the word-processing icon, and her computer immediately began loading the program. The American-made Gateway that Orlov had provided was by far the most powerful computer she'd ever used, and it was so small compared with the ancient colossus that occupied an entire building at Sverdlovsk 23.

In the corner of the screen, a small window appeared containing an animated representation of Albert Einstein. The figure emptied his coffee cup, tossed it aside with a crash, then waved hello.

'*Zdrávstvuytye,* Albert,' she said.

As always, the words started slowly, but eventually the flow became steady and strong. It all began to come together for Avvakum, how even in a total vacuum there could not be complete emptiness. Mathematically it was one of those odd points that equations reach when they crash into zero or spiral off into infinity, where matter or energy becomes immeasurable and therefore unknowable. As a physicist, she knew that infinities were nonsensical answers that pointed to a flaw in the method of mathematically describing complex phenomena.

Yet, through the work of her unnamed predecessors, Avvakum found herself standing at the threshold of a new awareness, of a dramatic change in her perception of the universe. She was seeing the effects of something beyond the theoretical barriers of infinity, the first cracks in that seemingly impenetrable wall.

It bothered Avvakum that she found no

mention of her predecessors in any of the project documentation. Zoshchenko explained that the names had been expunged as per the terms of dissolution of the original research partnership. As a scientist, Avvakum knew the importance of properly documenting her sources to provide a pedigree for her work. She felt a nagging sense of guilt that she would not be permitted to honor those whose work she was building on.

Two paragraphs into the night's entry, she accidentally keyed in a pair of *ws*. In anticipation of her next stroke, the program offered her a string of underscored, blue text.

www.cse.rid.edu/~sand/

Even though she'd only just begun exploring the Internet after her arrival in Moscow, Avvakum recognized this as the address of a Web page. Curious, she clicked on the text, and a large window appeared as her computer connected to the Internet.

A dedicated line tied Avvakum's computer to a remote network-administration complex inside VIO FinProm's main office. Her request was quickly routed through the FinProm server and out onto the Net.

Seconds later a photograph of a man, possibly in his early forties, with blond hair and a red beard appeared, smiling at her.

'Ted Sandstrom,' she read from the text beside the photo. 'Professor. Ph.D. physics, University of Notre Dame.'

Below the photograph, she read through a long

page that described Sandstrom's background and research interests. Avvakum gasped as she read that Sandstrom's current work was a study of the quantum boundary between matter and energy. The page also listed Sandstrom as being on sabbatical from his teaching duties at Notre Dame for the current term.

I wonder, Professor Sandstrom, if you are the one whom I am following.

30

JULY 26

Ann Arbor, Michigan

'That ought to about do it,' Grin said hopefully as he saved the program file he was working on. 'Now maybe I can get a clearer picture of how Lobo works.'

Shortly after diving into Kilkenny's decryption project, Grin decided that a mathematical algorithm as intricate as Wolff's cipher deserved a name, so he christened it Lobo. The program he had just created was designed to test his assumptions on how Wolff's cipher operated.

Once he finished loading his program into Stan, he switched machines to see how many new pages the Preservation Lab had scanned into their computer. As soon as the window containing the page icons appeared, the individual icons began vanishing. The files were disappearing at a rate of one every three seconds. No doubt, someone was moving the files off the server. But who, and why?

Grin moved to the Wolff directory – which held the six separate subdirectories for each of the notebooks – and selected everything to be downloaded to his machine.

FILE ACCESS DENIED

He stared at the monitor in disbelief. 'What the hell is going on!'

Grin grabbed the phone. 'Please, somebody, still be there,' he pleaded as the line rang.

He got a fast busy signal and slammed the handset in the cradle. Seven more files were now gone.

Suddenly, the window displaying his link to the Preservation Lab server closed – the connection cut.

'Red alert! Red alert! All hands to battle stations!' a voice clip of Patrick Stewart from *Star Trek* shouted out from Grin's workstation. Whoever was erasing files down on campus was now attacking Grin's machines.

Grin swiveled to view the large monitor just as the screen went blank and a new window appeared. In the upper-left corner was a white square that held a black spider graphic.

'All right, Spyder, sic 'em,' Grin commanded, as if the computer were listening to him.

Nested deep within the MARC network was a Spyder, a black chunk of artificial intelligence that a year earlier had nearly cost Nolan and Kelsey their lives. The device was the offspring of a similar piece of computer hardware designed by Moy Electronics to defend computer networks against hacker attacks. The Spyder carried all the tools of its parent, the Gatekeeper, and several offensive weapons designed by the CIA for use in gathering intelligence. Following the Spyder incident, Nolan and Grin worked out a deal with the CIA that allowed them to retain the device and work with Moy on improvements.

Grin watched as a graphical depiction of the affected computers appeared on his screen. From MARC, the trail led back to the Preservation Lab server on campus, through the university's central server, and then out into the world.

'You may be good,' Grin said with grudging admiration, 'but your ass is mine.'

System by system, Spyder followed the hacker's electronic trail, identifying each step along the way. The hacker had covered his tracks well, snaking his way through dozens of Internet servers to create a labyrinthine trail that was nearly impossible to follow.

Grin reset the window view from a schematic line drawing of the hacker's route to one superimposed over a map of the earth. The hacker blazed an impressive path across the globe, even managing to penetrate a Web server at a research station in Antarctica. Ten minutes later the trail reached Moscow.

'Say cheese, you asshole,' Grin said, knowing he'd nailed the malevolent intruder.

The map of the world faded and was replaced

by the image of a black IBM server tower. Just as the window containing the machine's schematics and serial numbers started to appear, the window went blank.

'What the fuck do you mean the connection has been lost?' Grin screamed as the Spyder reported its status.

Grin instructed the Spyder to show him a network diagnostic. A graphic depiction of the MARC network appeared, followed by one of the university's network. The Spyder showed him every machine it could touch. Both networks appeared fine, except for the hole in the picture where Grin knew the Preservation Lab server should be. The server was physically in the basement of the Harlan Hatcher Graduate Library on main campus but, from Grin's point of view, it was gone.

31

JULY 26

Ann Arbor, Michigan

Leskov looked down at the broken remains of the beige network server, its thin metal shell stripped open to reveal the delicate circuitry. Five minutes into their assault of the Preservation Lab, he'd received a panicky report from Orlov's electronics group in Moscow about some difficulty they were experiencing with the MARC network. Apparently, their attempt to penetrate that network had met with an effective resistance and retaliation. Leskov answered their request to break the connection by destroying the lab's network server.

'Moscow confirms that contact with the MARC network has been terminated,' the young man in charge of communications reported.

'Obviously, Misha,' Leskov said, laughing. Although his solution to the possible security breach might be considered crude, it was decidedly effective. 'Hand me the magnet.'

Misha, a lanky twenty-five-year-old with ice-blue eyes, slipped the backpack off his shoulders and extracted the electromagnet.

Leskov kicked several pieces of broken plastic away from the exposed metal supports to reveal the server's stack of hard drives. He flipped the switch on the powerful magnet and began slowly waving it over the stack. A strong electromagnetic field bathed each of the sealed drives, obliterating the organized patterns of information stored on the thin disks within. In seconds, the drive stack was wiped clean.

From the rear of the lab, Josef, the thickset Georgian who'd been part of the team that struck Sandstrom's lab a month earlier, walked quickly toward Leskov.

'I have the notebooks,' Josef said as he zipped his backpack closed and slipped it over his shoulder. 'The technician was very helpful.'

Leskov glanced back at the small room that Josef had just left and saw a pair of legs lying on

184

the floor. The technician was either unconscious or dead. Leskov checked his watch – in a few minutes he would know for certain.

'Time, everyone.'

Josef and two other men, Kiril and Grigori, moved out into the hallway where Evgenii, the point man, stood watch.

'Burn it.'

Misha nodded, held out a plastic squeeze bottle, and squirted a clear golden fluid throughout the room. When he reached the door, he capped the bottle and slid it into his pack.

'Ready,' Misha announced.

Everyone backed away from the door as Misha, using a handheld spark igniter, set a nearby puddle of the fluid aflame.

32

JULY 26

Ann Arbor, Michigan

As he reread the message that the Preservation Lab server was off-line, Grin remembered that Nolan was in town with Kelsey at the Art Fair. Two of the annual fair's three venues bordered the university's main campus and were a short walk from the lab. Grin punched in the number of Kilkenny's phone.

'Kilkenny here.'

'Yo, Nolan. It's Grin. Something bad is happening down at the lab where they're keeping those notebooks.'

'What do you mean?'

'I was just loggin' on to download the latest pages and I waltzed right into someone swiping the Wolff directory. I tried to grab what was left, but they locked me out. When I called the Preservation Lab to find out what was happening, the phone line went nuts. Then somebody tried to take a run at my machines.'

'Everything okay?'

'Yeah. The Spyder slammed the door, then went after 'em, but that's why I think you need to check on the lab. I was just about to nail the hacker when the lab's server went off-line. I got a funny feeling about this. I think somebody's trying to ace us out of those notebooks. Are you anywhere near the Grad Library?'

'Kelsey and I are down near West Engineering. We'll head over and take a look.'

Nolan ended the call and located Kelsey at a nearby booth haggling with an artisan over an inlaid wooden box.

'We'll have to come back,' Nolan announced as he put his arm around Kelsey's shoulders, guiding her away from the booth.

'What's going on? Who was that on the phone?' The words raced out of Kelsey's mouth.

'Grin. We need to check on the Preservation Lab, right now. It looks like somebody's after Wolff's notebooks.'

They moved as quickly as they could through the crowd and passed through the West

Engineering arch into the Diag. To their right was the fenced-off pit where Johann Wolff's body had been discovered. They broke into a run, weaving their way through the crowd toward the Diag. Ahead stood the Harlan Hatcher Graduate Library.

Kelsey followed Nolan up the granite staircase to the portico of the library. A welcome rush of cool air greeted them as they passed through the bronze-and-glass doors into the building's ornate vestibule.

Moving quickly, they reached the far end and turned the corner into a side hall where the elevators and the basement stairs were located. They noticed one of the old elevators preparing to descend and slipped through its closing doors.

A moment later they exited the elevator car into the basement lobby, followed by a librarian carrying a small stack of books. The footsteps of several people quickly climbing up the wide stair-case echoed off the marble treads and smooth plaster walls.

'It's around the corner,' Nolan directed as he ran toward the Preservation Lab.

Nolan saw that the hallway was empty, which wasn't unusual during summer months and almost expected for a building surrounded by the madness of the Art Fair. Then he noticed the temperature rising around them.

He signaled for Kelsey to hang back and carefully approached the lab. As Nolan reached out to place his palm against the door, the frosted-glass sidelight erupted from its frame, expelled by a shock wave of superheated gas. The shattered pane narrowly missed Nolan as it hurtled down the corridor, its imbedded wire mesh barely keeping the hundreds of pebble-sized fragments together. A second explosion thundered from the lab as containers of volatile chemicals exploded in the heat.

'Let's get the hell out of here!' Nolan shouted.

Kelsey was halfway down the corridor before the words were out of Nolan's mouth, and he was just a few steps behind her.

33

JULY 26

Ann Arbor, Michigan

Quickly making their way to the main floor, Nolan and Kelsey rounded the corner into the vestibule and raced out through the front doors. As they reached the top of the steps, Kelsey looked down into the crowd on the Diag. Below, in the mass of people who now stood bewildered as the library burned, she noticed a group of men forcefully working their way through the crowd. In the middle of the group, one of the men quickly glanced back at the burning building.

'Nolan, over there!' Kelsey shouted, her voice full of surprise and anger. 'That's one of the movers.'

Nolan immediately shifted his gaze to where

Kelsey pointed. The taut, muscular men stood out from the crowd like a team of athletes walking among the fans. They carried themselves differently than normal people, their posture and movement the result of skillful training.

'I got 'em, Kelsey. Looks like a six-man unit in a close formation. You're right about the tall blond one in the middle. The big guy in front of him was there, too. Come on.'

As they stepped down into the crowd, Nolan keyed through his phone's memory and selected a number. 'Major Crimes Unit, Detective Ptashnik.'

'Nolan Kilkenny here. The Preservation Lab where Johann Wolff's notebooks are being stored is on fire. Anyone who was inside is probably dead. I'm on the Diag headed toward the intersection of State and North University. About fifty yards in front of me is a group of six men who I believe are responsible for the fire. All are probable ex-Russian Special Forces. Two of them are wanted for murder, theft, and arson in Indiana. You need to get some cops down here ASAP.'

'Shit. You sure about this, Kilkenny?'

'Absolutely.'

'All right, I'll put the word out and get a car' – Ptashnik paused – 'fuck, the streets are blocked off for Art Fair. I'll get the foot patrols moving to your location. What's your number?'

Nolan carefully recited his phone number.

'I'll call you as soon as I get something moving on this end. Where are the suspects at now?'

'They're crossing State, looks like they're heading into Nickels Arcade.'

'Keep an eye on 'em. I'll call back in a minute.'

189

34

JULY 26

Ann Arbor, Michigan

Leskov heard the sound of approaching sirens and instantly knew that firefighters were en route to the burning building. He scanned the crowded plaza; people were starting to edge away from the library as clouds of thick black smoke roiled upward. Bright orange-yellow flames danced at the base of the smoky column. The accelerant had completely engulfed the lab in seconds. The firefighters didn't know it, but soon there would be nothing left for them to salvage.

'Misha, where is rendezvous?'

'The driver reports very heavy traffic, as expected, Dmitri. An accident is causing problems at the primary pickup site. He suggests we meet at the backup location:

'Approved,' Leskov said. 'Evgenii, take us to the backup site.'

'*Da,* Dmitri,' the point man replied.

The Russians waded through the audience gathered around a quartet of Peruvian musicians. Leskov smiled; the crowded streets were the ideal place for him and his men to disappear.

Evgenii led the way across State Street toward Nickels Arcade, a two-story glass-roofed gateway of small shops that bisected the long block of continuous storefronts.

The phone purred in Nolan's hand.

'Kilkenny,' he answered.

'It's Ptashnik. I've got you on a speakerphone so we can relay information to the cops on the street. Where are you?'

'We just crossed State and are moving toward Nickels Arcade.'

'Understood. I want you to stay out of sight – do not let these guys see you following them. They'll bolt or worse. There's a pair of uniformed officers on Washington moving toward Maynard. What do these guys took like?'

Nolan described each of the men as best he could. As he spoke, someone in the background on the other end of the line parroted what he'd said.

'Got it. Our patrol has spotted your Russians just exiting the arcade.'

'That's them,' Nolan confirmed.

From where they stood, Nolan and Kelsey saw the six men leave the arcade onto Maynard Street. An earful of static told Nolan their signal was fading as he and Kelsey moved deeper into the arcade.

'I'm losing you,' Nolan hollered, hoping the detective could still hear him. 'Call me in a minute.'

The connection was gone.

'What's going on?' Fear resonated in Kelsey's voice.

'Two cops on Maynard have spotted the

191

Russians. I just hope to God they hang back until they can get these guys in the clear, or we are going to have a genuine, grade-A clusterfuck. Look at all these people – nothing but shields and hostages.'

'Oh my God.' Kelsey's fear grew stronger.

'The tactical situation here is completely skewed in their favor,' Nolan continued. 'What we need is a handful of two-man teams on the ground, roving in the crowd, and a sniper team up above if we're to have any chance of taking some of those men alive without killing a lot of bystanders.'

'Dmitri,' Josef said in a low voice. 'Police.'

Leskov looked to the left. About twenty feet back, two uniformed police officers carefully waded through the crowd, moving in their direction. The younger of the pair tilted her head slightly as she spoke into a microphone clipped to her shoulder.

'Continue moving,' Leskov quietly ordered. 'It's probably nothing.'

Evgenii led the team right, veering away from the approaching officers. A concrete parking structure spanned over the midsection of the street, casting a dark, cool shadow where they walked. The crowd thickened in the sheltered space, seeking some relief from the sun.

'Excuse me,' the senior cop announced in a stern, serious voice.

Pivoting on his left leg, Kiril quickly spun around and drove the ball of his right foot into the side of the cop's head. The momentum of the vicious spin kick flung the man headlong through a plate-glass window and into a large bookstore. The officer lay in a torn, bloody heap atop an overturned floor display of anthropology texts.

'Officer down!' the younger cop shouted into her radio as she drew her weapon.

In a swift, fluid motion, Josef drew a 9-mm Glock from the holster concealed against the small of his back, aimed, and fired three rounds through the woman's chest. She fell back, collapsing on the pavement.

A woman screamed, and the crowd on Maynard Street panicked, spreading out away from the scene like a rippling aftershock.

'Move!' Evgenii shouted as he pushed a couple into a booth of hand-tooled leather goods.

The metal frame supporting the light fabric roof over the booth buckled as the couple grabbed for anything to halt their fall. They toppled through the fabric wall into the next booth, setting a domino effect in motion that brought the seven consecutive booths down to the ground. Ceramics, jewelry, and blown-glass art crashed onto the pavement and was trampled by the fleeing throng.

Josef holstered his weapon as the team moved toward Liberty Street. Leskov's team pressed farther into the crowd, hoping to lose themselves amid the chaos.

'Shit, gunfire!' Nolan growled as he broke into a run toward Maynard Street, leaving Kelsey in his wake.

He took defensive cover behind the pillars at

the end of the arcade, scanned the situation, and moved out into the street. Kelsey emerged onto Maynard just as Nolan reached the officer who'd been shot. The crush of people emptying out onto the adjacent streets turned the area into complete chaos. Several bystanders were trampled, including artisans who were crawling out from beneath the wreckage of their booths.

'She's dead,' Nolan pronounced angrily. 'What a fucking waste.'

He rose, looked around, then spotted the other officer through the shattered plate-glass window. Kelsey followed, and they traipsed over the debris from the ruined booths and stepped into the bookstore. Carefully, they lowered the fallen cop onto the carpeted floor.

'How is he?' Kelsey asked as Nolan checked for a pulse.

'Unconscious, and cut to hell.'

Nolan pulled the microphone off the cop's shoulder and keyed the switch. 'This is Kilkenny. There are two officers down on Maynard between Liberty and William. One's dead and the other needs a medic, stat. Over.'

'Help's on the way, Kilkenny,' Ptashnik promised, his voice filled with concern. 'Where are the fucks who did this?'

'They're somewhere on Liberty, probably heading west, away from the fair. They've done what they came to do, so they're looking to exfiltrate. Kelsey Newton is going to stay here with your people until the ambulance arrives.'

'Where are you going?' Ptashnik asked.

'I'm going to try and get my hands on these

guys for you.'

'Don't you even think about it, Kilkenny!' Ptashnik shouted.

'You're going to have to trust me on this one.' Then he cut the transmission.

Nolan turned to echo the same thought to Kelsey, but before he could say a word, she handed him the wounded officer's weapon. After checking the safety on the SIG-Sauer P226 and clipping the police radio to his waist, Nolan turned and disappeared down the street.

35

JULY 26

Ann Arbor, Michigan

Kilkenny cautiously approached the intersection, edging alongside a brick building that housed a copy center in its basement level. He slowly peered around the corner and saw that the Russians were moving west down the center of Liberty Street, between the parallel rows of booths that temporarily occupied the metered parking spaces.

He moved onto the sidewalk, using the booths as a screen between himself and the Russians. At the end of the block, he passed a seven-foot-tall bomb, painted like Old Glory, that stood beside the entrance of a military-surplus store. The

Russians cleared the last booths and stepped onto the sidewalk opposite Kilkenny – about half a block ahead of him. He easily picked them out in the thinning stream of people.

'Ptashnik, this is Kilkenny. Over.'

'I read you, Kilkenny.' Ptashnik sounded pissed-off. 'What's happening?'

'The Tangos are still on foot moving west on Liberty. They crossed Division and are nearing Fifth.'

'Oh my God! He's got a gun!' a woman screamed when she saw Kilkenny crossing Liberty with his weapon drawn.

Leskov and two of his men turned at the scream and saw Kilkenny. The Russians immediately broke into a run toward Main Street.

'Shit! They spotted me,' Kilkenny cursed into the handset. 'Tangos are heading toward Main.'

The radio chattered with commands and responses as the police drew their forces in. Officers on foot and in cars moved to cordon off the two-block stretch of Main Street where the cop killers were headed.

The Russian in the rear position turned and aimed his weapon. Kilkenny dove behind a parked minivan as the man fired; two rounds shattered the vehicle's windshield. The sounds of gunfire cleared the sidewalk for two blocks as people ran for cover. Ahead, the Russians pressed forward into the thick crowd on Main Street.

'They're on Main, heading north from Liberty,' Kilkenny reported.

He sprinted down the street, slowing when he

reached the edge of the Art Fair's downtown venue. Thousands of people had replaced the normal gridlock of cars.

The atmosphere was still festive as the panic of Liberty Street had not infected this area yet. The aroma of spiced lamb and onion accompanied the bouzouki music wafting from a Greek restaurant's temporary sidewalk café. Up the block a nine-foot-tall inflatable Mongol warrior greeted passersby, encouraging all to dine at BD's Mongolian Barbeque.

'Ptashnik, Main Street is packed, and the Tangos are right in the middle of it. Where are those other cops?'

'On the way,' Ptashnik promised.

The police radio crackled as officers reported their positions, converging on the scene. Kilkenny pressed the two-way against his ear to better hear over the din around him. Frustrated, he pushed his way onto the sidewalk and began hurdling over the chain partitions that defined the outdoor seating areas of the Main Street restaurants.

'Sir!' a hostess shouted angrily. 'You can't do–'

'Dmitri, on the sidewalk,' Josef said.

'I see him. It's Kilkenny, the one who killed Pavel and the others. Josef, you're with me. The rest of you follow Evgenii to the pickup. We'll be right behind you.'

Leskov and Josef broke ranks, moving to intercept. Each readied his weapon as they approached their prey. The four other Russians hurried their pace, moving onto the last city block closed by the fair.

Kilkenny pushed his way through the long line of people waiting to be seated at the Mongol warrior's restaurant, and finally reached the intersection of Main and Washington. From behind a wooden barricade, he surveyed the milling crowd, searching for the Russians. He spotted them as they passed into the next block, then realized that two were missing. Nearby, a patrol car quietly approached the intersection.

'Turn around and keep your hands where I can see 'em!' a cop shouted as the doors on the police cruiser flung open.

Kilkenny froze, then put both hands in the air.

As one of the officers approached, Nolan saw two of the men who attacked Sandstrom's lab muscle their way through the restaurant's queue. The Russians spotted Kilkenny and raised their weapons.

'Gun!' Kilkenny shouted as he dove for the curb.

The cops hit the pavement just as two shots roared past Kilkenny. Both flew wide of the mark, ricocheting off the pavement.

A woman screamed, pulling her children away from the restaurant's giant mascot. Her youngest, a three-year-old boy, stumbled, and she lost her grip on his tiny hand. Hearing gunfire, the young man inside the inflatable suit dove over the child. The next shots ripped through the costume's thick nylon skin, sending an explosion of pressurized air and fabric upward.

'Time to go,' Leskov announced as the window of opportunity for revenge closed.

Both men rushed with the crowd up Main Street toward Huron. On the other side of the barricade that marked the northern edge of the fair, Leskov saw the rest of his team climbing into the dark green Suburban that had brought them there.

Kilkenny stood up and began scanning the crowd for the Russians. He caught sight of the two men who'd just shot at him halfway up the block.

'Freeze!' the cop shouted.

'Ptashnik!' Kilkenny said angrily into the microphone, 'tell the two cops at Main and Washington to lay off me right now. Your cop killers are getting away!'

Kilkenny watched the Russians move farther away while he impatiently waited for a reply.

'Rookie, lower your weapon!' the cop's partner shouted as he jogged over from the patrol car. 'This is the guy who was tracking these fucks for us. We're here to back him up.'

'Then let's move it,' Kilkenny ordered, leading the way down the sidewalk.

The crackling sound of automatic-weapons fire filled the air.

'Oh my God!' someone shouted, terror-stricken.

When he reached the toppled barricades at Huron Street, Kilkenny saw a plume of pale yellow steam rising from the grille of a police cruiser. Dozens of holes pockmarked the dark

199

blue sedan. On the pavement, two more officers lay clinging to life. Farther up Main Street, a green Suburban with tinted windows sped north toward the highway.

36

JULY 26

Ann Arbor, Michigan

It was well past nine and evening was ebbing into night by the time Nolan and Kelsey's question-and-answer session with Detective Ptashnik was finally through. After the debriefing, an Ann Arbor police patrol car ferried them down to the southeast corner of the Diag. They picked up a carryout of General Tso's chicken from their favorite Chinese restaurant, then walked over to Kelsey's old sorority house, where Nolan's SUV was parked.

'Do you mind driving?' Nolan asked, offering Kelsey his keys. 'There's a call I need to make.'

Nolan set the bag of food cartons on the floor behind the passenger's seat and pulled the Palm-Pilot from his briefcase. As they drove toward Dexter, he searched through the handheld computer for Cal Mosley's number, which he keyed into his phone.

'This is Mosley.'

'Cal, it's Nolan Kilkenny.'

'What can I do for you?' Mosley asked.

'The Russians struck again today, this time in Ann Arbor. Four people dead. Cal, these were the same guys who hit Sandstrom's lab in South Bend.' Nolan then launched into a brief report of the latest attack.

'So they were after these old notebooks?' Mosley asked.

'Yes. Definitely. After Wolff's body was found, the police made no public mention of the notebooks. Only a handful of people even know about their existence and their potential importance to our project – and I trust all of 'em. My best guess is that these guys are still watching Sandstrom and probably have his hospital room bugged.'

'They got their intel from somewhere,' Mosley agreed. 'Get the hospital to move him and ask the FBI to sweep his old room for any surveillance equipment. In the meantime, I'm going to run this latest information past some people here and see what I can come up with. Thanks for the update.'

'Cal, I need all the help you can give me. This project I'm working on has the potential to become a multibillion-dollar-a-year industry. If whoever's behind these attacks succeeds in taking control of Sandstrom's quantum technology, they'll have the power to pull the economic equivalent of a coup d'état on the rest of the industrialized world.'

37

JULY 27

Moscow, Russia

The numbers from the Far East exchanges looked flat, the third straight day without any sign of the occasional exuberance or volatility that made watching the markets interesting in the first place. A day without winners or losers, without victory or defeat – so far. The day was still young, and the Western markets had yet to open.

Orlov shuffled around a few positions, much like placing bets on a roulette table – only on a global scale. His bets were spread over the three Cs: companies, commodities, and currencies. The billions under his control allowed Orlov to cover a wide field of opportunities; since the beginning of the year, his portfolio had already increased sixty-five percent.

The phone on his desk rang softly.

'*Da*, Irena,' he answered.

'You have a call from Dmitri Leskov.'

Orlov glanced at his watch; it was just after midnight in the eastern United States. 'Put him through.' There was a click, and then a dull hum that often accompanied overseas phone calls. 'Dmitri, what news do you have?' Orlov asked.

'The materials are en route to you now. The courier should deliver them to you by the end of the day.'

'Excellent.'

Cherny quietly walked into the office and laid several laser-printed pages on his desk. It was a copy of a news article she'd retrieved from a wire-service Web site on the Internet. Orlov's left eyebrow arched slightly as the headline caught his eye.

FOUR KILLED, DOZENS INJURED IN ART FAIR ATTACK

'Did you encounter any problems that I should know about?'

'Nothing we weren't prepared for. Did Irena locate the information I wanted you to see?'

'I have it right here.'

Orlov skimmed the article, noting that three of the slain had been police officers. The search for the men responsible would undoubtedly be thorough, making it dangerous for Leskov's team to travel.

'Dmitri, there are many difficulties surrounding this assignment. I think you and your men should remain where you are for a while, just to make sure the situation resolves itself. I'm certain our associates there can find a comfortable place to house all of you.'

'They already have, Victor Ivanovich.'

38

JULY 28

Moscow, Russia

'Oksanna,' Orlov said with a smile, the syllables of her name rolling almost musically off his tongue.

Zoshchenko passed through the tall French doors of his office, moving with poise and grace. The well-cut lines of her jacket and skirt accentuated her trim figure.

Orlov stood in front of his desk, enjoying every step of her approach. When she reached him, he clasped both her hands in his, leaned forward, and kissed her gently.

'Will Dmitri be joining us today?' she asked.

'*Nyet*,' he replied, looking amorously into her eyes.

Orlov reached over his desk to activate his speakerphone.

'Irena?' he called out. 'While I am meeting with Dr Zoshchenko, please see that we are not disturbed.'

'*Da*, Victor Ivanovich.'

Orlov switched the speakerphone off, then motioned for Zoshchenko to accompany him into the adjacent room. Once inside, she turned and embraced him, pressing her body tightly against his, fueling their arousal.

She pulled back far enough that her hands could find space between them to begin the unfastening. Orlov carefully worked the buttons of her jacket and slid the garment off her shoulders.

Orlov stepped out of his Italian loafers, then bent down and caressed each of her calves as he removed her pumps. He lingered there, gazing up at her as his hands roamed up beneath her skirt to slowly draw down her tights.

His silk tie fell to the floor, quickly followed by his shirt and trousers, then her blouse and skirt. They kissed each patch of bare skin as it was revealed.

Orlov appraised her nude form with delight. She guided him to the ornate bed that dominated this private chamber. The headboard bore the carved image of a Romanov double eagle – Orlov had once told her that the last czar had commissioned this bed. Now, they shared it.

When their sexual relationship had begun to evolve, she found Orlov's technique to be like that of most men she'd been involved with – crude and clumsy. Slowly, patiently she trained him and as a reward for his efforts brought him to dizzying heights of ecstasy. Orlov eventually developed a sense of improvisation, and their passion play now took occasional ventures into the exotic.

An hour later they both lay exhausted, their bodies entwined in the rumpled and sweat-soaked linen sheets

'Victor,' Zoshchenko whispered as she ran her hand through the graying hair on his chest, 'I had a chance to take a look at the notebooks you acquired.'

'And?'

'And I don't know what to make of them.'

'What do you mean?' he said, a bit irritated. 'Dmitri and his men went through a lot of trouble to get those notebooks.'

Zoshchenko propped herself up on her elbow to face him. 'No, you misunderstand me. Acquiring the notebooks was definitely worthwhile. Wolff's drawings give a hint at what he was thinking, but without the narrative and his calculations, they're just a collection of very interesting pictures. I've put a former KGB cryptographer to work on them, but he doesn't hold out much hope.'

'Why? Isn't he a very good code breaker? If not, get someone who can break the damn code.'

'Actually, he's one of the best the KGB ever employed. I know because I'm the one who found him for them. He's never seen anything quite like the mathematics of Wolff's cipher – he's not even sure where to start.'

Orlov's hand caressed the curve along the small of Zoshchenko's back as he considered the notebooks. 'Will this have any effect on Avvakum's work?'

'There's no way of knowing until the notebooks are decrypted. According to your surveillance, Sandstrom believes Wolff may have had a working theory that can explain the quantum effect he discovered. If this is true, such information would go a long way in bolstering our claim on all technology derived from this discovery. Such knowledge would be almost as valuable as the device itself.'

Zoshchenko lifted her head off Orlov's chest and rolled to prop up her upper body on her elbows so she could face him. 'I believe then that we must maintain electronic surveillance on Sandstrom and his associates indefinitely.'

'The longer we keep watching them, the riskier it becomes,' Orlov reminded her.

'I understand, but we don't know how much of the notebooks they have stored in their computers. Our hackers were met with heavy resistance when they tried to access the MARC network. Someone shut them out completely and then began tracking them. If Dmitri hadn't destroyed the lab server when he did, our hackers might well have been identified. Regardless, we have to assume that they are working to decrypt whatever portion of Wolff's notebooks they have. Should they succeed, that might put their effort ahead of ours.'

'And if their patent claim has priority, we lose.'

'Precisely, Victor.'

39

JULY 28

Moscow, Russia

It was nearly midnight, but within the windowless lab the distinction between night and day wasn't readily apparent. Lara Avvakum's fascination with her work caused time to slip past more quickly than it ever had before. Her workdays grew long; spans of eighteen, even twenty, hours weren't uncommon as the feverish passion of discovery consumed her.

She stared blankly at the screen, unable to get Ted Sandstrom out of her mind. The possibility that he might be the one who started this project whetted her desire to learn more about him.

But surely, Avvakum reasoned, *Victor Orlov's prohibition against contact with my predecessors on this project doesn't extend to knowing something about them. After all, is it not wise to know all you can about the competition?*

A moment later she accessed the Web search engine on her computer and keyed in a deliberately broad search for Ted Sandstrom. Within seconds there were seven responses to her query.

Avvakum selected an article from *USA Today* and waited while her computer connected with the newspaper's Web site and downloaded the article. The peripheral elements of the Web page loaded first, then the story and accompanying photographs. In bold text, the headline appeared.

ND PROF KILLED, ANOTHER INJURED IN LAB BLAST

Avvakum scrolled down to the article and read about an attack on the professors' lab that left Raphaele Paramo dead and Ted Sandstrom severely burned. Five unidentified men posing as a moving crew were responsible for the blaze and the theft of Sandstrom's lab equipment and research. The article cited FBI sources in claiming that industrial espionage was the apparent motive for the attack.

Two other individuals, Nolan Kilkenny and physicist Kelsey Newton, were treated for minor injuries and released from the hospital. The article went on to describe how Sandstrom had recently signed with two consortia to develop commercial applications related to an undisclosed discovery.

Am I working for thieves and murderers? Avvakum thought fearfully as it all became painfully clear. *No one just walks away from all this research; it was stolen, and the minds that created it trampled.*

Avvakum pored over the other articles, searching for further information pertaining to the incident. She soon learned that once Sandstrom's condition had stabilized, he had been transferred to the University of Michigan Hospital. The investigation lab was currently at a standstill because of a lack of evidence.

The more she read, the more the name Nolan Kilkenny kept cropping up. As a project director for the Michigan Applied Research Consortium, Kilkenny was noted as being involved with the commercial application of Sandstrom's work – an effort she'd been hired by Orlov to pursue.

Avvakum continued to investigate and found herself at the MARC home page. She navigated through the site until she found a staff listing for Nolan Kilkenny, complete with his E-mail address. She clicked on the address and began typing her message.

Is this file the work of Ted Sandstrom?

Avvakum then browsed through a directory of files and selected one that dealt specifically with the quantum energy device and attached it to her message.

She looked at the one-line message she'd written. If her suspicions were wrong, then she was about to violate the trust of her employer – a man who'd saved her from a life of scientific exile in Siberia. But what if her suspicions were right? If Orlov truly was responsible for the attack on Sandstrom, then by developing this research, she became Orlov's accomplice.

Avvakum carefully weighed the options before her, balancing her need to know the truth against the fearful hope that ignorance could somehow protect her.

She sighed, then clicked the SEND button.

40

JULY 28

Langley, Virginia

Mosley's knuckles rapped against the partially open door of Cooper's seventh-floor office.

'Bart, do you have a minute? There's something I'd like to discuss with you.'

'Ah, sure, Cal,' Cooper replied, surprised by the visit. 'C'mon in.'

Mosley sat in one of the upholstered chairs opposite Cooper's desk. 'I'm working on an industrial-espionage case, something involving a radical new technology.'

Cooper leaned back in his chair, getting comfortable. 'Tell me about it.'

Mosley quickly ran through the information Kilkenny had provided regarding the quantum power cell, the attack in South Bend, and his lines of inquiry.

'So what you're telling me is that you've got squat as far as any solid leads.'

'The trail was getting pretty cold, until a couple of days ago. Two of the same men who hit South Bend led another team to Ann Arbor, where they struck a rare-books lab.'

'How does that fit in with your technology case?'

'They were after a set of notebooks, and it's these notebooks, or rather their author, that led me to you. The man who wrote them was a German physicist named Johann Wolff. When I called down to Research for some information about this guy, they told me you'd recently made a similar request. That led me to wonder what your interest is and if there's any overlap with what I'm working on.'

'There might be,' Cooper replied. 'Have you gotten the report from Research?'

'No, I spoke with them just before I came here. So far, these attacks have left eight people dead and one hospitalized with severe burns. I'd appreciate any help you can give me on this.'

Cooper leaned his head back and composed his thoughts.

'As you probably know, I've been with the Agency for a long time. In fact, I've been in the intelligence business since the Second World War, when I worked for Bill Donovan in the OSS.' Cooper pointed to a black-and-white photo of him with the legendary spymaster on the wall. 'When the war in Europe began to wind down, the OSS launched an active campaign to capture as many German scientists as we could find – especially the ones working on rocketry, jets, and atomic research. Wolff was part of the group that was working on the German bomb project. I interviewed him and cleared him for entry into the U.S. When his body was found, the computer system matched his name with the keywords on his old 055 file and, since I'm still here, notified me.'

212

'If it's just an ancient case, why'd you request a full background check?'

'Professional curiosity. When I checked out Wolff, I didn't find anything that tied him to the nastier stuff the Third Reich was into. He looked like a bright young guy who spent the war doing math exactly the kind of highly educated professional that the government wanted us to import. After his body was found, it made me wonder if I'd missed something. I requested a full check because there's a lot more information available now than back in 'forty-six.'

'Did you find any skeletons?'

'Just a rumor that turned out to be false. I did learn one new thing about Wolff; he was a lot smarter than he let on.'

'How so?'

'Did you ever hear the story about how Einstein and a group of top physicists wrote a letter to Roosevelt explaining why the U.S. needed to build the bomb?'

'Yeah.'

'Well, in Germany, Wolff's boss, a guy named Werner Heisenberg, did the opposite with Hitler. Heisenberg and his team ran the numbers and determined that even if it were possible, it would cost too much and take too long to build an atomic bomb.'

Cooper then explained how the Soviets and their captured scientists reconstructed the German nuclear research and discovered that Wolff had sabotaged the calculations, thus preventing the Nazis from pursuing development of atomic weapons.

'So you're telling me that Wolff kept the Nazis from building an A-bomb?'

'That's what his colleagues thought after they put all the pieces together. He was the best mathematician on Heisenberg's staff, and they trusted his skills implicitly. If he said two plus two equaled five, they believed him. That's pretty much it as far as background for Wolff. Now, you said that the teams that hit the two labs were apparently Russian?'

'Yeah, that was the impression they left. Why?'

'When our people asked the FSB in Moscow to check their archives for information about Wolff, we learned that I wasn't the only one asking about him. I called a guy I know over there and asked him to see if he could find out who put in the other request.'

'Did you get an answer?'

'Yeah. The other interested party is a woman named Oksanna Zoshchenko. She's a high-level apparatchik in the Russian Academy of Sciences. My contact is digging up some information on her. Whatever I get, I'll pass along.'

'Thanks.' Mosley scribbled a few more notes on a legal pad. 'So, just days after Wolff's body is discovered, both you and this Zoshchenko put in a request for information about him.'

'The timing's a bit much for mere coincidence, wouldn't you say?'

'That and the guys hitting these labs have the look of Russian Special Forces.'

'Odd thing, though. If the Russian government is behind this, then why let us peek into their archives about Wolff and why tell us about

Zoshchenko? That part doesn't fit.'

'No, but none of this has played out like a typical government-run intelligence operation. Somebody doesn't just want to acquire this technology, they want to own it completely.'

41

JULY 28

Dexter, Michigan

Martin and Audrey Kilkenny were seated on the porch of their farmhouse when Nolan's SUV rode up the long gravel drive. He parked near Martin's old Ford pickup, then walked around to the passenger side and opened the door. Tears welled up in Audrey's eyes as a woman handed Nolan a cane, then reached for his offered arm and carefully stepped out of the vehicle.

Nolan towered over the thin wisp of a woman who stood beside him. A halo of snow-colored hair framed an oval face. At the sight of Audrey and Martin Kilkenny, her dark eyes grew moist with emotion.

'Elli, it's so good to see you again,' Audrey said as she carefully stepped down from the porch.

Elli Vital nodded, unable to express her feelings. The memories of this place, of the long weekends she'd spent here with Johann Wolff, all came back.

The last time she had walked up this drive, the father of the young man whose arm she leaned upon was just a boy. It was December of 1948 and Johann had failed to meet her at the train station. Instead of a weekend spent in celebration of her engagement, Elli and Martin searched in vain for her missing fiancé. She returned to Chicago heartbroken, fearing that Johann's disappearance was like that of everyone else she'd embraced as family – permanent.

So when Martin Kilkenny called her, the day that Elli had long dreaded finally came. Now she was here, reunited with old friends to honor the memory of her beloved Johann.

Elli released Nolan's arm and walked the last few steps toward Martin and Audrey on her own. She trembled as more than fifty years of emotions resonated deeply within her.

'You always said someday we would know the truth.'

Martin wrapped his arms around Elli in a display of love and support, as he had at the end of that terrible weekend when the man she loved was taken from her.

'I had faith in Johann. I knew there was only one thing that could keep him from you.'

Elli pulled back and turned to embrace Audrey. They'd kept in touch over the years, exchanged letters and holiday cards, but the unknown always lingered like an un-welcome guest. Johann Wolff was the link that tied her to the Kilkennys, and his unresolved absence was a gulf that could never be completely bridged.

'I've missed you so,' Audrey said tearfully.

'And I've missed you.'

'That was a wonderful meal, Audrey,' Elli declared.

Martin inched his chair away from the table. 'That it was. And now that we're fed, there's some business we need to discuss. Kelsey, I have a wee bit of a favor to ask you. As you may have noticed, Elli here is getting around these days with the help of a walking stick. You see, she had her hip replaced a few months back and she's still recovering from it.'

'Martin, you don't have to tell them my entire life story,' Elli interrupted, a hint of her native German still present after half a century. 'The point I hope Martin was eventually going to arrive at is that I need a place to stay. Because of my hip, I can't climb stairs, so staying here is out of the question. Audrey mentioned that you have a nice one-story condo with a guest room. Would it be too much of an imposition?'

'Not at all,' Kelsey replied.

'I told you she was a fine girl,' Audrey said proudly. 'We have high hopes for her and Nolan.'

Kelsey beamed as Nolan reddened.

'The only advice I have to offer on that matter,' Elli said with the confidence of age, but her voice a curious mix of regret and hope, 'is that you must seize this time, for you never know what tomorrow will bring.'

Martin perked up. 'Now that we have that problem solved, Nolan, do you happen to have a copy of that letter that was found with Johann?'

'Not on me, but if you let me use your com-

217

puter, I can probably print one out.'

'You know where it is.'

Nolan exited the kitchen and walked into a small adjacent room. He switched on the computer and logged in to the MARC network and saw that he had new mail: a message with an attached file from avv@vio.com.ru. The subject of the message was SANDSTROM.

Nolan clicked on the message. It asked a single question: *Is this file the work of Ted Sandstrom?*

He selected the attached file.

'What the hell?'

The file contained several pages of technical information concerning an energy device that sounded suspiciously like Sandstrom's.

'If this *is* real, then it could have only come from the people who stole it. But why send me a piece of it?'

Nolan quickly decided he needed to verify the authenticity of the correspondence, so he forwarded copies of the message and the attached file to Sandstrom and to Grin, hoping MARC's computer guru might be able to identify who sent the E-mail. He then forwarded it to Mosley, just to cover all his bases, and printed out a copy for himself.

'Nolan, did you find the letter?' Martin called from the kitchen.

'Working on it,' he replied automatically, his mind still occupied by the E-mail.

'Here it is,' Nolan announced when he returned to the kitchen.

'Would you do the honor of reading the first page to Elli.' Martin's voice cracked with emotion.

Nolan sat down and began to read.

10 December 1948

Dear Raphaele,
Yesterday, I summoned up the courage to abandon myself to my dreams. I moved beyond the comfort of my existence and made a leap of faith. My actions were not based on any rational, cognitive process, but on those elements of hope, wonder and discovery that make life itself worth living.

I have discovered beauty and truth, and in the immortal words of Keats, that is all I need to know. Truly, it is all I want to know.

I have given myself fully to the woman I love, and she now holds the key to my heart, my mind, and my soul. Elli has accepted me and offered herself fully in return. The emptiness is now filled.

42

JULY 29

Dexter, Michigan

Nolan reached out from his bed and fumbled for the cordless phone. The digital clock on the nightstand read 6:30 A.M.

'Yeah,' he answered, still groggy.

'Good morning, sweetie,' Kelsey said in a singsong voice.

'Oh, hi, Kelsey,' he replied with a yawn. 'You're up early.'

'I couldn't sleep. I need to talk to you about something.'

'Now that I'm awake, go ahead.'

'Do you think your grandfather is up?'

'Now? Yeah, probably.'

'Could you put a three-way call together? I need to talk with you both?

'Let me see. Hang on.'

Nolan put her on hold, then dialed his grandfather's number on his second line.

'Is everybody there?' Nolan asked when the connections were made.

'Yes,' Kelsey answered.

'I'm here,' Martin replied. 'So, Kelsey, what's so important that you had to interrupt my grandson's beauty sleep? God knows he needs all he can get.'

'Martin, when Nolan and I first started looking for Wolff, I seem to recall you telling us that you loaned him some money for an engagement ring.'

'Aye, I remember. I sent him down to my friend Urban; he did a real nice job for him, too. His son's running the place now. You two should stop by there when you're ready.'

'When we're ready?' Nolan asked. 'You sound pretty sure of yourself, Grandpa.'

'You're halfway down the aisle right now. It's only a matter of time. Is there anything else, Kelsey?'

'Yes, do you know if Johann had the ring inscribed?'

220

'I believe he did. In fact, I'm sure of it because I remember Urban telling me it was the strangest thing he'd ever etched into a piece of jewelry.'

'What do you mean?' Nolan asked.

'I mean he put down whatever it was Johann asked him to, but he had no idea what it meant. He said it didn't look very romantic, but he figured it must have been something between Johann and Elli. As long as his customer was happy, who was he to judge?'

'Thanks, Martin. That's all I needed.'

'You're entirely welcome, Kelsey. And don't forget to bring Eli over by noon. We're meeting with some folks from the university to discuss the memorial service.'

'I'll have her there. Nolan, could you stay on after your grandfather hangs up?'

'You bet.' Nolan paused until he heard the click of his grandfather's line disconnecting. 'What's this all about?'

'I was just reading Wolff's last letter.'

'I hope you had a box of tissues handy.'

'So I'm a romantic, sue me. But the letter got me thinking. It says here that Elli "now holds the key to my heart, my mind, and my soul." What if he meant that literally?'

'How could he give her the key to his heart, mind, and soul?'

'Nolan, Wolff was a physicist who loved his work. He lived at a time when physics had just turned the world upside down in a way that hadn't happened since Galileo and Copernicus. Quantum physics was still a very young field, and he studied under the man who practically

221

invented it. Physics wasn't a job for Wolff, it was a passion. Everything he was – his heart, mind, and soul – was bound up in that. The most valuable possession he had to offer Elli, as a token of his love for her, wasn't a ring but his lifework.'

'You think Elli has the key to Wolff's cipher?' Nolan asked as Kelsey's logic became crystal-clear. 'The ring. My God, you're brilliant.'

'After what Martin said about the unusual inscription, I'm sure of it. Now I just have to wait until Elli gets up, so I can ask her about it.'

'Well, I'm up now, so call me as soon as you know. Grin still has a good chunk of the first notebook on disk. If we get the key, I think we can decrypt it.'

'I'll let you know.'

A second after Kelsey hung up, Nolan heard another, distinct click on the line. He thought about the sound as the dial tone buzzed in his ear. Nolan rolled onto his side, reached over, and depressed the cradle switch; the dial tone disappeared. He then lifted his finger up – the line clicked, then clicked again. Nolan hit Kelsey's number on his speed dial and got a steady busy signal.

'Shit!' Nolan cursed as he slammed the phone into its cradle and rolled out of bed.

He dressed hurriedly in a T-shirt and shorts, then unlocked the safe in his walk-in closet and retrieved a teak storage box that contained the pistol he'd used during his days as a Navy SEAL – a Heckler & Koch USP Mk 23. He strapped on a shoulder holster, then quickly checked over his weapon. Satisfied, he slipped a magazine containing ten .45-caliber ACP rounds into the USP, chambered a round, then sated and holstered the weapon. He then stowed three more clips in his pocket.

Three minutes after Kelsey's call, Nolan fired the ignition of his SUV and put it in gear.

'I hope I'm just being paranoid about this,' Nolan muttered, a cloud of dust in his wake as he sped down the driveway.

43

JULY 29

Moscow, Russia

The speakerphone on Orlov's desk buzzed quietly.

'*Da,* Irena,' he answered.

'I have Dmitri Leskov on line one. He says that it's urgent.'

'Put him through.'

Orlov heard the line click.

'Dmitri, what do you have to report?'

'The two people working with Sandstrom, Kilkenny and Newton, may have identified where Wolff hid the key to his notebooks.'

'Do they have it?'

'Not yet. We intercepted a telephone conversation between Newton and Kilkenny. Newton believes that Wolff had the key to his cipher engraved on a ring that was given to his fiancée. This woman is currently staying at Newton's home in Ann Arbor. Newton has not spoken with the woman about it yet – it's still quite early in the morning here.'

Orlov glanced at his watch and subtracted the eight-hour time difference. 'What do you think of Newton's theory?'

'It makes sense. No one creates a cipher without putting the key for it someplace safe. What is Zoshchenko's opinion of the notebooks? Are they important to the project?'

'She believes so. She has a very high opinion of this physicist Wolff.'

'Then I think we have an opportunity here, if we act quickly.'

'What are you proposing, Dmitri?'

'From our current position, I can deploy my team at Newton's residence in fifteen minutes. I've already had Newton's phone line disrupted.'

'Do you know if the ring is actually there?'

'No. If Wolff's fiancée is sentimental, I suspect she would have the ring with her. If not, she knows where it is. In either case, we'll deal with it.'

'Very well, Dmitri. Proceed.'

44

JULY 29

Ann Arbor, Michigan

Elli woke up while Kelsey was in the shower, and she made herself at home in the kitchen. By the time Kelsey emerged from her bedroom in a pair of khaki shorts and a coral Polo shirt, Elli had split open a grapefruit and turned on the television.

'Good morning,' Kelsey said as she wrapped a towel around her long mane of wet blond hair. 'Did you sleep well?'

'As well as I can with this hip of mine. Thank God for ibuprofen.'

Kelsey smiled. 'Elli, there's something I want to ask you.'

'Go right ahead, dear.'

'Do you still have the ring that Johann gave you?'

'Oh my, yes. Of course I do. I keep it with me always.'

'Did Johann have something inscribed on it?'

'Yes, he did.'

'May I see it?'

'Certainly. But why?'

'Six notebooks were found with Johann's body. They appear to be his research, but we don't know for certain, because he wrote them in a very sophisticated code. I was rereading Johann's last letter to Raphaele Paramo this morning and I noticed something. He wrote that he gave you the key to his mind, and I wondered if perhaps he meant it literally.'

With her right hand, Elli carefully slipped the plain gold band from her ring finger and offered it to Kelsey. The metal showed the signs of a lifetime of wear.

Kelsey held it in the palm of her hand. She then picked up the ring with her fingers and brought it close to her eyes, tilting it to see the curved plane of the interior. She saw the jeweler's mark and a number indicating that the ring was fourteen-karat gold. She turned the ring slowly counterclockwise, rolling it with the tips of her fingers. Then she saw it. Delicately inscribed, in characters so small that at first she thought it was a decorative design, was the numerical key to Johann Wolff's cipher.

'It was our secret,' Elli said when she knew that Kelsey had found the inscription. 'Johann was a brilliant man – my father said he was the most gifted student he ever had. Johann knew that his work had value, that someday it would provide a comfortable life for us and our children. He wrote his work in code so he could keep it to himself until he was ready to publish. He was near to a breakthrough when he asked me to marry him, when he gave me the key to his mind and his heart.'

Kelsey looked up from the ring, knowing that she was the first person Elli had ever told this story to.

'After he disappeared, this was all I had left to remember him by. I've owned other rings over the years, but I've always loved this ring most of all. Why don't you try it on?'

'I couldn't,' Kelsey stammered, surprised by the request.

'Please, for me. I suspect that young man of yours will be giving you one quite soon. I hope it means as much to you as this one has to me.'

Kelsey relented and slipped the gold band around her finger.

'There, now your hand doesn't look quite so naked. It looks good. Kelsey, bitter experience has taught me to embrace every moment of life as if it were the last. I can see you and Nolan are very much in love, just as Johann and I were. Grab hold of this time and don't let it escape you.'

Before Kelsey could find any words to respond, the front door of her condo burst open and four men rushed in. The first two moved straight for the kitchen with pistols drawn and aimed at her and Elli. The other two split off to search the rest of the condo. When they returned seconds later, one of them went to the front door and made a motion with his hand.

'Good morning, Professor Newton,' Leskov said as he walked into the condo, his voice hard and flat. 'It's a pleasure to see you again.'

'You know this man?' Elli asked.

'Yes,' Kelsey replied, her eyes locked on the approaching Russian. 'He's a thief and a murderer.'

Leskov backhanded Kelsey across the cheek;

the towel fell from her head. She fought off the stinging pain and turned back to face him, her eyes burning angrily.

'Get the hell out of my house!' Kelsey commanded through clenched teeth.

'All in good time,' Leskov replied, sneering.

Leskov pulled a chair away from the table, turned it around, and straddled it, resting his elbows on the back. On the table he saw the copy of Wolff's final letter.

'Ah, one we don't have yet.' Leskov folded the page and slid it into his shirt pocket. 'Thank you. I have just one matter to discuss with your guest, then my men and I will leave.'

'What do you want?' Elli said defiantly.

Leskov turned his head slowly in her direction, a bit surprised by her lack of fear.

'Madam, I would like the ring that was given to you by Johann Wolff.'

'What a coincidence,' Elli replied without a hint of humor in her voice, 'Kelsey was asking me about that just as you and your men stormed through her front door. I no longer have the ring.'

Kelsey sat still, hoping her face wouldn't give away the truth.

'Where is the ring?' Leskov demanded.

'I am not going to tell you that.'

'Madam, I had hoped that you would be more cooperative. If necessary, I can make this situation very unpleasant for you.'

Elli's mocking laughter shocked everyone in the room.

'*You* are going to make things unpleasant for *me?* I was beaten, degraded, raped repeatedly, starved, and left for dead by the Nazis. What do you think you can do to me that hasn't already been done?'

'Perhaps you're right, there may be nothing I can do to you.' Leskov reached out and grabbed Kelsey's wrist. 'But perhaps watching this young lady suffer might change your mind.'

'If you harm Kelsey in any way, I swear I will kill myself at the first opportunity. I am not afraid of death and I am not afraid of suffering. This is a waste of your time and ours. Go back to wherever you came from and leave us alone.'

Leskov grudgingly admired the woman's nerve. Their eyes locked, and he saw nothing but steel. She meant every word.

The stare down ended when Leskov's earpiece crackled to life.

'Kilkenny has turned into the cul-de-sac,' the man reported. 'Black Mercedes truck. He's seen our vehicle.'

'Everyone, we're moving out,' Leskov announced.

'Good riddance,' Elli said.

'You misunderstand me; you two are going with us. We are not finished with this conversation. Kiril, Misha, bring the women.'

Two of Leskov's men roughly grabbed Elli and Kelsey, pulling them out of their chairs and marching them out the front door.

45

JULY 29

Ann Arbor, Michigan

Kilkenny sped to the far end of the development where Kelsey's condo overlooked a wooded ravine. As he approached her unit, he saw a full-sized dark green Ford van with smoked windows backed up in her driveway – the driver was the large black-haired man he'd seen at Sandstrom's lab and the Grad Library.

'Damn it!' he shouted as he braked and turned hard to the left.

The screech of rubber dragging over asphalt echoed loudly off the walls and windows of the surrounding condos. Kilkenny brought the SUV to a stop in the center of the narrow drive, nearly perpendicular to the road. As he rolled out of the driver-side door onto the road, a fusillade erupted from Kelsey's front door. Bullets tore into the exposed side of the SUV, puncturing metal and shattering the windows into pebble-sized chunks of glass. An explosion shook the vehicle as one of the bullets struck the compressed gas cylinder of the air bag in the passenger-side door.

Kilkenny crouched behind the front tire with his weapon drawn, glass fragments raining down on him and bullets ricocheting off the road beneath the SUV. The ML 320 lurched away from him as the tires on the passenger side ruptured and the vehicle fell onto its rims.

'Nolan!' he heard Kelsey scream.

Glancing up over the hood, Kilkenny saw a pair of men firing submachine guns while two others forcefully moved Kelsey and Elli into the van. Orchestrating the attack and kidnapping was the tall blond Russian. As Nolan took quick aim at their leader and fired, a short burst riddled the hood. Kilkenny fell back, hot metal fragments biting into his face and arms.

Leskov felt a burning sensation across his forehead, followed by an intense rush of pain. Instinctively, he clasped his hands over the wound just as blood began to ooze from the groove dug in the skin by Kilkenny's bullet.

'Grigori, Evgenii, kill him!' Leskov shouted as he staggered toward the van, his hands and face now soaked with blood.

Without a word, the two shooters began leapfrogging toward the bullet-riddled SUV – one firing while the other moved ten feet forward, then reversing roles until they covered the distance.

Hop and pop, Kilkenny thought as he listened to the regular, short bursts of approaching gunfire. *Question is, Which side of my truck are you two gonna try and nail me from?*

Crouching down, Kilkenny moved along the side of his truck until he was able to grab hold of the rear door handle, and opened the door.

Evgenii caught the opening of the rear door as Grigori ran past his position and reached the shredded rear wheel. Using hand signals, he informed his partner that Kilkenny had moved into the backseat. Grigori nodded, and shifted his crouch to better position himself to fire into the shattered rear window.

Evgenii then ran toward the front of the SUV, firing until he came to a stop, crouched against the front wheel. Beneath him, a widening puddle of sickly sweet smelling antifreeze spread slowly over the asphalt.

Both men nodded that they were ready. Evgenii held his fingers up and mouthed a three count.

Kilkenny waited for the pause in the gunfire. Staying low, he moved around the rear corner of the vehicle, then rose up with his pistol aimed through the shattered rear window.

The two Russians came into Kilkenny's view simultaneously. Both were focused on the rear seat when he fired a two-shot burst into Evgenii's forehead. He then swept right and drilled another pair through Grigori's temple. Both men collapsed on the ground without firing a shot at him.

'Fuck!' Josef cursed.

The Ukrainian put the van into gear and punched the accelerator – the large V-s roared loudly as he drove straight at Kilkenny.

'What the fuck is happening?' Leskov shouted,

wiping the blood from his eyes.

'Grigori and Evgenii are dead,' Josef reported. 'We have to get out of here now.'

Leskov saw two of his men lying in the street and Kilkenny turning to fire on the van.

'Kiril, shoot him!' Leskov shouted.

Leaning out the passenger window, Kiril aimed his submachine gun and opened fire, pinning Kilkenny down behind his damaged truck as Josef drove over the shallow curb and across the lawns of Kelsey's neighbors.

'Shit!' Kilkenny cursed, unable to find a clear shot at anything.

As the van rounded the corner, he saw only the shadowy forms of the people inside through the vehicle's smoked glass. Kilkenny didn't dare shoot for fear of hitting Kelsey or Elli.

46

JULY 29

Ann Arbor, Michigan

Nolan winced as the EMT extracted another metal fragment from his bloodstained cheek.

'Good thing none of these hit you in the eye,' the EMT said.

'Just get 'em out and patch me up,' Nolan replied, sitting impatiently on the ambulance's chrome bumper.

A second ambulance pulled away from the crime scene, this one ferrying the bodies of the two Russians he had slain. Outside the perimeter the police had established, Sean Kilkenny leaned against his Explorer, waiting for his son.

Once the bodies were removed and the forensic techs finished photographing Nolan's ML 320 in situ, the driver of a flatbed wrecker ran a steel cable around the SUV's undercarriage and slowly began pulling the damaged vehicle up the ramp. The winch howled under the load, and the shredded tires alternated between flopping and dragging across the wrecker's diamond-plate steel bed. Once the SUV was secured, the driver handed Ptashnik a receipt and drove off. Nolan watched until his truck disappeared from view.

'I'll bet your insurance company is going to love this,' Ptashnik said.

Nolan glowered back in stony silence.

'You're right. Bad joke. Here,' Ptashnik handed him the receipt. 'We're impounding your truck so we can collect evidence. The yard will call when we're done with it.'

'Are you done with me yet?'

'Pretty much. I'll be in touch if we need anything else.'

'Can I have my pistol back?'

'No, we have to hang on to that until we run this mess past the DA. Don't worry about it, though. This was clearly self-defense, and you were attempting to prevent a kidnapping. There's no way she's gonna press charges against you for killing those two guys. Once the paperwork

234

clears, I'll release your weapon.'

'Thanks. I see you got somebody from the phone company checking Kelsey's line for a tap. Anybody working on my phone?'

'The sheriff is out there right now with a line crew. Your phone should be clear in about an hour.'

'Good.'

'I'm finished,' the EMT announced as he taped a dressing over the gouge on Nolan's right shoulder 'Keep your wounds clean and have a doc look at 'em in a couple of days.'

Nolan nodded, then stood up. 'I'm outta here. Call me if you hear anything about Kelsey and Elli.'

'I will,' Ptashnik promised.

Nolan walked over to where his father had waited for nearly two hours.

'You okay, son?' Sean asked.

'I'm fine, Dad. Did you call Kelsey's folks?'

Sean nodded gravely. 'I hate being the bearer of bad news. These Russians, do you think they'll—'

'Kill Kelsey or Elli? God, I hope not, but their pattern to date suggests otherwise. They're after the engagement ring Wolff gave to Eli.'

'Why?'

'Kelsey believes Wolff had the key to his cipher engraved on it. She told me this morning, and that's how these fuckers found out! They tapped our phones, Dad.'

'Nolan, it's not your fault.'

'I should have had the lines checked. We *knew* we had a leak when they took the notebooks. These people have been one step ahead of us all

235

the way. We've got to find out who's running this op if we're going to have any chance of stopping 'em.' Nolan took a deep breath and let it out slowly, trying to calm himself. 'Do you have your phone on you, Dad? I don't trust mine right now.'

Sean reached into his Explorer and pulled a small digital phone from the center console.

'Here you go.'

'Thanks,' Nolan replied as he began dialing a number.

'Grin,' the voice answered, as if it could be no one else.

'Morning, Grin. It's Nolan. Did you get that E-mail I sent you last night?'

'Yeah, and got two things for you. First, Ted Sandstrom called a little while ago sounding very excited. He said he replied to your E-mail, but he hadn't heard back from you yet.'

'What's his message?'

'He said the file you sent him was one of his.'

'Good. What else you got for me?'

'The *ru* in the sender's E-mail address told me right off that the host server is in Russia. I tracked it back as far as a company in Moscow called VIO FinProm. I tried to tickle the sender's name out of their E-mail server – to find out who a-v-v is – but the server was having none of it. I went in with a light touch, but they got pretty decent security. If you want, I can be a little less subtle.'

'Let's hold off on that for the moment,' Nolan replied. 'What I would like you to do is dig up whatever you can on this VIO FinProm.'

236

Nolan then told Grin about Kelsey's theory and the kidnapping.

'I'm sorry to hear that, my friend.'

'Yeah, this thing has really gone into the shitter.'

'I'll get on this FinProm thing right away. If there is *anything* that I can do...'

Nolan smiled, knowing the offer amounted to carte-blanche access not only to Grin's formidable hacking skills but to those of his inner circle of like-minded associates.

'When the time comes, I'll let you know. Also, could you page Cal Mosley for me? Have him call me on my dad's phone.'

'Consider it done.'

'Thanks, Grin.'

Nolan ended the call. A few minutes later Mosley returned the page.

'What's happening, Nolan?' Mosley asked.

'Cal, in the words of my late mother, this whole mess is going to hell in a handbasket.'

Nolan then brought Mosley up to speed on everything that had happened that morning.

'Was Kelsey able to confirm her theory about the ring?'

'I don't know. She was going to call me back once she had a chance to talk to Elli about it. She never made that second call.'

'This thing is moving a little faster than I anticipated. Do you know if Elli had the ring with her?'

'No, but I would have to assume that she would have kept it for sentimental reasons. I have no idea whether she brought it here or left it at home.'

'Do you have an address?'

'Not on me, though I can call you back with it once I get home.'

'Fine. Once I have that, I'll give the FBI a call and have them coordinate with the local cops to secure her house and give it the once-over. If Elli doesn't have the ring with her, that's likely to be their next stop. I'll also see if we can't do a bank search for any safety-deposit boxes where she might have some jewelry stashed.'

'Cal, did you get that E-mail I forwarded to you?'

'Yes. I passed it on to our technical staff; they're working on it.'

'Do you remember Grin, from the last time we worked together?'

'Ponytail. Goatee. Yes, I remember him.'

'I gave him that same message. We still don't know who a-v-v is, but the E-mail was sent from a Russian company called VIO FinProm. That mean anything to you?'

'Yes, it does. Let me pull some stuff together. I'll see you tomorrow.'

'You'll *see* me tomorrow?'

'I don't like the way this thing is moving, and you're where the action is. I'm bringing an associate of mine, too. A guy by the name of Bart Cooper. We'll be on the first flight in the morning.'

'I'll be waiting for you.'

47

JULY 29

Dexter, Michigan

'What are you going to do now?' Sean asked as he pulled his Explorer up to the barn.

'I'm not sure,' Nolan replied pensively.

The ride back from Kelsey's condo had been quiet as Nolan struggled to find some course of action.

'Dad, you had some jewelry made for Mom, right?'

'Yes, some rings, a few necklaces, and a charm bracelet.'

'Do you know what kind of records a jeweler keeps?'

'Very detailed ones, especially for custom work. Every piece I bought came with an appraisal that described it fully for insurance purposes.'

'Including the inscriptions?'

'Yes,' Sean replied. 'You think there might still be a record of the ring Wolff bought for Elli?'

'That's what I'm going to find out,' Nolan said as he began walking toward the garage inside the barn.

'Not like that, you're not,' Sean said firmly. 'Take a quick shower while I pull the Viper around. Do you want me to call Urban's and let

239

them know you're coming?'

'No, I don't. After this morning, I'm a little worried about announcing my plans publicly.'

'May I help you?' an attractive, stylishly dressed woman said, greeting Nolan from behind one of the jewelry shop's countertop display cases.

'Yes,' Nolan replied, introducing himself. 'Is the owner in? My grandfather is an old friend of the family, and I'd like to have a word with him.'

'Yes, he is. I'll see if he can come up front.'

Nolan saw that behind the main display area, the shop split into two levels, each a half flight of stairs up or down from where he stood. The woman descended to the lower level and disappeared behind a gray metal door. A moment later she reappeared, followed by a blond man wearing a light blue smock.

'Mr Kilkenny, a pleasure to meet you. When your grandfather was in a few weeks ago for your grandmother's birthday present, he mentioned that you might be in the market for an engagement ring soon. What can I do for you?'

'No rings today, unfortunately. What I'm looking for is a little information. Do you still have your father's records?'

'Of course. I still see a few of his pieces from time to time for cleanings and repairs, that sort of thing. Why do you ask?'

'Well, I'm looking for the details about a ring your father made back in the fall of 1948. I'm trying to find out what was inscribed on the ring.'

'If my dad didn't pitch it, then it should still be down in the files. What's the customer's name?'

240

'Johann Wolff.'

'Wait here a minute, and I'll see what I can do.'

The jeweler disappeared into the shop's lower level, leaving Kilkenny alone in the glittering display area.

'Excuse me,' the saleswoman said, 'but while you're waiting, would you like to take a look at our ring selection? We've just completed a new series of rings that are simply stunning.'

'Why not?'

Nolan looked down at the felt-covered tray of beautifully crafted rings, each a unique work of art. Simple gold bands gave way to more complex geometries; stones ran the gamut from traditional diamonds to more playful displays of brilliant gems.

'I think I found what you're looking for,' the jeweler announced as he climbed up from the lower level.

He laid an old brown file folder on the glass display case, next to the tray of rings Nolan had browsed. He opened the file to a yellowed page of handwritten notes.

'The customer was Johann Wolff, a referral of your grandfather's. In December of 1948, Mr Wolff purchased a fourteen-karat yellow gold engagement ring. The ring was an original design. The style of the ring was a heavy band, high polish. The ring was inscribed as follows...'

The jeweler flipped through the next few pages until he reached a sheet of graph paper that contained a long string of numbers.

'Not terribly romantic, as far as inscriptions go, is it?'

'No, but it's exactly what I'm looking for,' Nolan replied. 'Can I get a copy of this?'

'Sure.'

'Another thing. After I leave, put that file in your safe.'

'Why?'

'The people who shot up the street in front of your store on Wednesday are also looking for this. If anyone else comes in here asking about this ring, tell them you gave the file to me.'

As he walked out of the store, Nolan pulled out his phone and pressed the speed dial for Grin.

'Yo, this is Grin.'

'Hey, Grin, it's Nolan. Do you have any of the image files from Wolff's notebooks handy?'

'I got a couple of Zip disks in my backpack.'

'Great, bring them with you. I'm downtown right now. Meet me out at my place in half an hour. I'll fill you in on the rest when you get there.'

48

JULY 29

Dexter, Michigan

Grin arrived right after Nolan and parked his yellow VW bus next to the red Viper. With any luck, he planned to have the thirty-five-year-old vehicle restored to her original glory by the end of summer.

'I'm here,' Grin said as he stepped out of the van in cutoff jeans, a tie-dyed tank top, and a pair of yellow-andblack-checkered high-top canvas sneakers. 'What's up?'

'I found Wolff's key,' Nolan said. 'Let's head upstairs and crack Lobo.'

Nolan led the way up to his loft. Grin set his backpack on the kitchen table and began pulling out disks and printouts.

'Let me fill you in on what I got so far; Grin said. 'For starters, do you know anything about quantum computing?'

'Just what little I've read in the journals.'

'Well, you know how in a digital computer, like the one sitting on your desk over there, information is stored in a series of ones and zeros – bits?'

'Yeah. I remember that much from my high-school intro to computer class,' Nolan replied.

'I'll bet you do. In a quantum computer, the quantum bits, or qubits, exist in multiple states simultaneously. I won't get into all the wave/particle duality and superposition stuff, but bottom line, a qubit can represent a whole lot more information than the plain old digital bits you and I are used to playing around with.'

'I read about a couple of research projects where they assembled a rudimentary quantum computer.'

'One team of people from IBM, MIT, Berkeley, and Oxford put together a hydrogen-chlorine processor and used it to sort an unordered list. 'We can do the same thing using conventional programming algorithms, but a quantum computer can sort a list of one million names about five hundred times faster. On more complex problems, the quantum advantage grows larger exponentially.'

'Don't tell me Wolff built a quantum computer to encrypt his notebooks.'

'No, they didn't have the technology required to tackle that kind of problem back then. Heck, the big-brain folks working on quantum computing today are just scratching the surface. Like conventional computers, though, quantum computing comes in two distinct parts.'

'Hardware and software,' Nolan offered.

'Give that man a cigar. About six years ago a guy at AT&T labs named Shor wrote a quantum algorithm for factoring integers. On paper, this piece of code looks like it'll smoke anything written for digital machines. Shor scared the hell out of all those folks who write data-encryption software because an algorithm like his could eat those codes using big-bit prime-number keys for lunch.'

'Lucky for them nobody has a machine to run it on.'

'Not yet they don't, but in about twenty years quantum-programming techniques are going to turn the computer world upside down. You think that Y two K stuff was bad? Internet security will evaporate the second machines capable of running quantum programming go on-line.' Grin paused to catch his breath. 'Getting back to Wolff, this cipher of his reminded me of some of the research papers I've seen on quantum computing, so I pulled a few of them off the Net to see if my hunch was right.'

'What's your conclusion?'

'Johann Wolff developed a new form of mathematics and, as a by-product, wrote his quantum encryption algorithm. And if you think elliptical curve schemes were hard to crack, you ain't seen nothing yet. Do you want to know the really wild thing about this?'

'Yeah.'

'Algorithms, whether they're quantum or conventional, are essentially a list of instructions that tell you how to do something. You and I are spoiled. We're used to writing up our programs, plugging them into a computer, and letting the machine do all the grunt work.'

'That's why people made computers.'

'That's right, but Wolff didn't have a computer back when he did this. There were only a handful of crude digital machines in the entire world in 1948, and quantum computing is something the long-term research types didn't start looking at seriously until the early nineties. From today's point of view, Wolff's algorithm is an astonishing piece of programming. The fact that he wrote it over fifty years ago is almost unbelievable. The thing that really blows my mind is that not only did he write this little mathematical symphony, he played the thing in his head and used it to encrypt his notebooks. Wolff's cipher is a truly incredible piece of work,' Grin said respectfully. 'I tried graphing portions of Lobo, and it's working with something on the order of eleven dimensions. The mind this guy must have had – the focus! We're talking Einstein and the Rain

Man all rolled into one.'

'I get the picture. But can we decode his note-books?'

'Yeah, but you and I have some serious work ahead of us. You see, we got his key and his quantum algorithm, but no quantum computer to run it on. We're going to have to reconstruct this algorithm using conventional programming techniques:

'Well, let's get at it. Cracking Wolff's code is our ticket to getting Kelsey and Elli back unharmed.'

'Say no more. I'm staying right here until we get plain text coming out of this thing. I'll need caffeine and some coding music. Whaddya got?'

'How about Diet Coke and the Ramones?'

'It's a start.'

Grin cracked his knuckles and began spreading out a schematic flowchart of the programs they would have to write. Nolan handed him an ice-cold can as a pounding bass and a grungy three-chord guitar riff roared out of the recessed wall speakers, flooding the loft with hard-driving sound.

49

JULY 29

Moscow, Russia

'Working late, I see,' Orlov said as he entered Avvakum's office.

From behind, he saw her convulse as if suddenly struck by an electric shock. Startled, she quickly turned around to face the unexpected visitor. The sight of Victor Orlov standing in her doorway did little to ease her discomfort.

'I didn't expect you, sir,' Avvakum said as she quickly stood.

She absently brushed a few strands of hair out of her face.

'I don't doubt that. Please, sit down.'

Avvakum complied automatically, still trying to compose herself. Orlov unbuttoned his blazer and sat down on one of her guest chairs.

'What can I do for you?' she asked, her voice aquiver.

'You are already doing what I hired you to do, Lara. According to Oksanna Zoshchenko, you are making excellent progress. This pleases me.'

'Thank you.'

'Unfortunately, I'm not here to discuss your work. It seems that we have a security problem.'

'Oh?'

Orlov's eyes narrowed, and Avvakum felt his gaze boring into her; his manner changed perceptibly.

'*Da*. I have many talented people, such as you, in my employ. A group of these people care for all the computers in use by my various businesses.' Orlov pointed at the machine on her desk. 'The network your computer is attached to is monitored by these people. They see everything that moves across that network, including the E-mail message you sent yesterday to a man named Nolan Kilkenny.'

Avvakum's heart seemed to stop for a moment, pausing until a surge of adrenaline sent the muscle galloping in her chest.

'Since you contacted him, I assume you know who Kilkenny is and what he represents.'

'He works with Sandstrom, the man who made this discovery.'

'You fucking whore! Is this the gratitude you show me for rescuing you from that rathole in Sverdlovsk? These men are my competition, my enemies! The message you sent might have compromised everything I'm trying to accomplish here. This is a race between them and me – winner take all! I intend to win. I will win.'

'At any cost?' Avvakum asked bravely. 'Is murder and theft an acceptable part of this competition? You've killed one man and stolen the lifework of another. How can you justify that?'

Orlov stood and struck her across the face with the back of his hand; the blow nearly knocked her to the floor. Her cheek went numb, and she tasted blood in her mouth as her lip split and began to swell.

'Dr Avvakum,' Orlov replied icily as he wiped her saliva from his hand, *'this* is how the game is played.'

'If this is how you run your business, then I want no part of it.'

'I've already made that decision. You have violated my trust. Zoshchenko is already looking for your replacement – someone better suited to work in the private sector. I expect you to stay on until your replacement is found and brought up to speed on the project.'

'No, I can't continue working for you any longer.'

Orlov struck her again, splitting her lip further. Avvakum turned back to face him, her bloodied lip ballooning out grotesquely.

'I'm not giving you a choice. You are going to remain *right here,*' Orlov growled, pointing at her desk, 'in this building, until your replacement is found. All your access to the outside world is gone. You will be under armed guard twenty-four hours a day.'

'You're insane. Do you actually think I am going to continue to work for you? You can imprison my body but not my mind.'

'You will continue to have access to project materials on your computer, but that access has been reduced to read-only.' Orlov leaned down so that his face was just inches from hers. 'What you do while you are here is your concern, but any attempt to damage project materials will be dealt with harshly.'

'Are you going to kill me, too?' Avvakum said defiantly.

'If that had been my intent, we wouldn't be having this conversation.' Orlov stood up and buttoned his blazer. 'The quality of your work during the remainder of your time here will greatly affect the nature of your eventual severance from my employ. Work or die, Dr Avvakum. The choice is yours.'

Orlov walked out of her office. As he turned and disappeared down the corridor, a large muscular man in an ill-fitting tan suit filled her doorway. His stony face lacked any sign of intelligence or even humanity.

50

JULY 29

Pine River, Michigan

Leskov completed his inspection of the grounds surrounding the remote hunting cabin where he and his men now took refuge. The cabin, which belonged to a business associate of Victor Orlov's, sat near the southern edge of a six-thousand-acre parcel of marshy forestland. The northern border of the property abutted the Ogemaw State Forest; along the southern border lay Saginaw Bay. The nearest homes along the shoreline to either side were miles away.

The isolated location and marshy terrain made the property ideal for holding hostages. The approaches to the cabin by either the narrow dirt road or the bay were easily defended, and an airdrop of any kind was too hazardous to be considered by anyone attempting a rescue.

As he approached the cabin, Leskov saw the dark muscular form of Josef on watch outside.

'Josef, how are our guests?'

'We have made them comfortable. They aren't giving us any trouble. I was pleased to see the kitchen was stocked for our arrival.'

'I'm sure our hosts wish to remain in good standing with Orlov. How are communications?'

'Everything is fine. The satellite phone is working well. We should get word from our eavesdroppers if they pick up anything on the police frequencies. I've also confirmed that two new men will make their way across the Canadian border tonight.'

'Good. Now we settle in and wait.'

'Are we going to interrogate the old woman?'

'Not yet. At this point I think it would be counter-productive. She's tough, and we don't have a lot of leverage with her.'

'Do you think it was wise to take these women hostage?'

'Taking hostages was the only reasonable choice open to us. If Kilkenny has the ring, he will trade it for the women.'

'I still don't like it. In the old days, we went in, we killed, and we got out. If we had to snatch some Afghani chieftain, we did the job and dropped him off for interrogation. We never trained for baby-sitting jobs.'

'It was simpler in the old days, my friend,' Leskov agreed. 'But remember, our paychecks were a lot smaller back then.'

'And rarer, too,' Josef said with a brusque laugh.

'Has the video clip been sent off to Moscow?'

'*Da.* Misha took care of that fifteen minutes ago. Moscow acknowledged receipt, and they are satisfied.'

'Good. Now Orlov can start his negotiations.'

51

JULY 30

Dexter, Michigan

Cal Mosley brought the rented Taurus to a stop beside Grin's faded microbus. As he and Bart Cooper stepped out of the car, two overly friendly yellow Labradors ran up to greet them. They heard a loud whistle from the front porch of the farmhouse.

'Buckley, Babs! Get over here!'

The two dogs bolted toward the porch, coming to rest at the feet of Martin Kilkenny.

'Thanks,' Mosley said, then introduced himself and Cooper as they approached the porch. 'We're looking for Nolan. He's expecting us.'

'Indeed he is. Go in the side door of the barn,

there. Take the stairs up to the loft – that's where you'll find him.'

Mosley led Cooper into the massive renovated barn and up the spiral staircase to the loft. Nolan and Grin sat amid a field of debris from their all-night assault on Wolff's encryption algorithm. Neither took notice of the other men's arrival.

'Good morning, gentlemen,' Mosley called out. 'I believe we had an appointment.'

'Morning, Cal,' Nolan said as he rose stiffly from the floor. 'I assume this is Bart Cooper.'

'A pleasure,' Cooper said as he shook Nolan's hand.

Nolan then completed the introductions. 'Can I get you guys something to drink? I've got a pot of coffee going or some juice.'

'Coffee would be fine. Black,' Cooper replied.

'Same,' Mosley added.

'I could use a reload myself,' Grin said as he slowly ambled into the kitchen. He filled his mug and the two that Nolan had set on the counter.

'Judging from those dark circles under your eyes,' Cooper commented, 'I'd say you two have been at it awhile. What are you working on?'

'We're decrypting Wolff's notebooks.'

'You've cracked the code?' Mosley asked, surprised.

'It's a lot easier when you have the key,' Grin replied.

Nolan then explained how he acquired a copy of the ring inscription from the jewelry store.

'How are you coming with the decoding?' Mosley asked eagerly.

'We're making slow progress. Grin, give the

man a demo.'

'Sure thing, boss.'

Grin walked over to Kilkenny's computer.

'Gather 'round,' Grin said, 'but fair warning, this is not the prettiest piece of programming ever written. It's downright crude compared with Wolff's method, but it does get the job done.'

With Mosley and Cooper watching over his shoulder, Grin enlarged the decryption program window to fill the entire twenty-one-inch monitor on Nolan's desk. The screen displayed two blank windows placed side by side.

'I'm going to pick page six out of Wolff's first notebook. We've already decoded the first five.'

The top window filled with a wide column of apparently random symbols and characters. After the encrypted text was loaded, the program highlighted the first row of text and the cursor changed from an arrow into a tumbling hour-glass.

'Wolff deliberately used a column format in recording information in his notebooks because it helped keep the information ordered in his mind. You see, he was using matrices, but in a multidimensional way like nothing I've ever seen. I am still floored that this guy could do in his head what Nolan's top-notch computer is struggling with.'

The decrypted version of the first few characters began appearing in the window on the right side of the screen. The characters came in bunches, with the time between each character's appearance being randomly shorter or longer.

'Why is it so jumpy?' Cooper asked.

'It's just the way our program was written,' Nolan replied with a yawn. 'The method Wolff devised to encode his notebooks is an offshoot of the mathematics that he invented for his research. How a piece of data is processed by this algorithm is governed by probability.'

'What? You lost me, Nolan,' Mosley said.

'Don't feel bad. Grin and I went round and round on this one until the fatigue set in and we suddenly caught a glimpse of how this thing really works. Most codes rely on some form of one-for-one substitution – A becomes Q, or Z or fourteen – whatever the method, the readable text gets transformed from one thing into another. It's a very black-and-white kind of process.'

'I'm following you so far,' Mosley said.

'Quantum reality is shades of gray. A can become Q, Z, and fourteen all at the same time. Effectively, each character has an infinite number of simultaneous possibilities. It then falls to probability to discover the answer you're looking for.'

'Thankfully, Wolff devised only a simple quantum algorithm – something he could do in his head,' Grin added. 'We were able to cobble together a very crude conventional program to simulate Wolff's method – a lot like rescoring a Mozart symphony for a washtub bass and a kazoo. If we had a working quantum computer, it would've been done with a whole notebook by now.'

'Why don't you get one?' Cooper asked.

'A quantum computer?' Nolan replied. 'They haven't been invented yet.'

Grin rapped a knuckle against Nolan's computer. 'For the time being, this is as good as it gets.'

Mosley and Cooper watched the first few strings of deciphered text emerge in the window on the monitor's right side. Then he noticed the small stack of printed pages on the desk. 'This the part you already finished?'

'Yeah, have a look,' Nolan offered.

Cooper put on a pair of reading glasses and picked up the loose pages. 'It's in German, which makes sense. It was Wolff's native tongue. Unfortunately, that's about all I recognize. Science was never one of my strong suits.'

'I don't think anyone in this room can truly appreciate Wolff's work,' Nolan remarked. 'We're all going to need someone to spoon-feed us on this stuff.'

'Well, this is definitely beyond me,' Cooper agreed, setting the pages back on the desk.

'Enough about the notebooks,' Nolan said. 'What's the latest on our kidnappers? Do we know who we're dealing with yet?'

'To answer your first question, we don't have a fix on the hostages. I've been in contact with the FBI, and we don't believe they've been taken out of the country. I also think we've confirmed that Elli does not have the ring with her.'

'Why do you say that?' Nolan asked.

'The FBI has Elli's house under watch, and they spotted a couple of guys snooping around. They ran the plates and found that a high-level boss in the Russian Mafiya owns the car. That tells me Orlov is still looking for the ring. Given that, I'm sure Kelsey and Elli are fine – they have to be, or Orlov doesn't have anything to bargain with.'

'Who's Orlov?' Nolan asked.

'The man who's responsible for this whole mess. Let's have a seat, and Bart and I will walk you through what we've come up with.'

Nolan cleared an empty pizza box from his dining table, and the four men took their places around it. Cooper pulled a file from his briefcase and set it on the table.

'First of all,' Mosley began, 'our people confirmed Grin's trace of that E-mail you forwarded to me. It originated from an Internet server owned by a corporation named VIO FinProm. This corporation is based in Moscow and serves as a holding company for a widely diversified collection of financial and industrial businesses. FinProm is short for *finanzava promuchistva,* which is Russian for "financial-industrial".'

'And the VIO?' Nolan asked.

'Those are the initials of the owner of this business empire,' Cooper replied as he laid a photograph on the table. 'Victor Ivanovich Orlov.'

Cooper then placed another photograph next to the one of Orlov, this one of an attractive brunette in her mid-forties.

'The woman is Oksanna Zoshchenko, an assistant director of the Russian Academy of Sciences. Shortly after the body of Johann Wolff was found, Zoshchenko and I both, independently, requested a search for information about Wolff from the old KGB archives at Lubyanka. I found this coincidence odd, until Cal told me

257

about his investigation. A further check on Zoshchenko revealed two very interesting facts. First, she was in Ann Arbor this spring as a guest of the university. Apparently, one of the regents brought her to a MARC board meeting, the one where Ted Sandstrom made a presentation.'

'So that's how they found out about Sandstrom,' Nolan said.

'She even signed a nondisclosure agreement, not that she kept that promise. The second thing I learned about Zoshchenko is that she's supplementing her income by providing consultation services to Orlov. This kind of arrangement would be considered a clear conflict of interest here, but it doesn't appear to be a problem in Moscow.'

Cooper then laid a third photograph on the table. It was an enlarged headshot of a man with blond hair. 'This guy is Dmitri Leskov. Currently, he's Orlov's fixer; he handles the dirty jobs, the wet work. Leskov's a former captain in the Spetsnaz – Soviet Special Forces.'

'A real bad-ass, I take it?' Grin asked.

'That's putting it mildly. Leskov is a highly trained and very capable mercenary. You don't want to underestimate him. My contact in Moscow and I ran some checks on border crossings, and we found arrivals and departures that put Leskov and four other Russian nationals in the U.S. at the time of the attack on Sandstrom's lab.'

'Nolan, you ever see this guy before?' Mosley asked.

'Yeah,' Nolan seethed with anger. 'He led all

three attacks.'

'Of the four other individuals who entered the U.S. with Leskov on that first trip,' Cooper continued, 'only one made the trip home.'

'I took out the other three,' Nolan offered matter-of-factly, his voice displaying neither pride nor remorse.

'I gathered as much from the police report,' Cooper said. 'None of those bodies have been found, and I don't expect they ever will be. Interesting thing about one of the men you dispatched' – Cooper thumbed through the other photographs until he found what he was looking for – 'this one is Pavel Leskov, Dmitri's younger brother.'

'That's bound to piss off his big brother, Nolan,' Grin said, looking at the dead man's photo.

'Leskov's reputation says he's a coolheaded professional. Whether something like this is going to affect how he deals with Kelsey or you is unknown. I just thought I'd let you know in case Leskov has an agenda outside Orlov's game plan. The rest of these' – Cooper laid out a series of grainy pictures – 'came in with Leskov last week. This is the crew that hit the library and snatched Kelsey and Elli. All are Spetsnaz veterans who either served with or were trained by Leskov. It's a handpicked crew.'

'Two of these guys are in the morgue, right now,' Nolan added. 'What about the man who's holding Leskov's leash?'

'Victor Orlov gets as much press in Russia, both good and bad, as someone like Bill Gates does here. His wealth gives him access to the highest levels of the Russian elite. For every friend, he has a bitter enemy. When communism fell, this guy was a nobody. Now he's one of the richest men in the world, and the road that got him there is littered with dead bodies.'

'I take it you are not speaking metaphorically?' Kilkenny asked.

'No, I am not. Orlov's not a sociopath; to him, murder is just another business tool. If putting a bullet in a rival's head gets him what he wants, that rival ends up dead. Moscow has received a lot of bad press about car bombings and the assassinations of Russian businessmen – most of what you heard is attributable, in some way or another, to Orlov.'

'Do you think he'll kill his hostages?' Nolan asked, respecting Cooper's experience with such people.

'Truthfully, Nolan, if he feels that killing them is in his best interests, then that's what he'll do. This whole situation is like a chess match for Orlov, and at this point in the game, I don't see what value killing Kelsey and Elli will bring him. Orlov wants the key to Wolff's code, and the women are his best means of getting it.'

'Changing the subject,' Mosley interjected, 'we think we've ID'd the author of that mysterious E-mail that came out of VIO FinProm.'

'My contact,' Cooper continued, 'says a-v-v is a woman named Tara Avvakum, a physicist with the Russian Academy of Sciences. She's currently on loan to VIO FinProm for an industrial research project. Orlov and Zoshchenko pulled

Avvakum out of a Siberian research facility and set her up in one of Orlov's buildings in Moscow.'

'If she works for Orlov, why'd she send the E-mail?'

Avvakum's relationship with Orlov is barely three weeks old. Prior to that, she was so far out of the loop that I doubt she'd ever even heard of him. Zoshchenko is the connection between Avvakum and Orlov; her position in the Russian Academy of Sciences allowed her to locate a bright young underpaid physicist to continue Sandstrom's work to the point where Orlov could file patents and become father of a new industry.'

'So Avvakum's just a means to an end,' Kilkenny concluded.

'That's our take on it. She's just a specialist hired to do a job. I think she wrote to you because Orlov didn't tell her where her project research came from. Orlov surely had the files he stole from Sandstrom sanitized, but something must have been missed that allowed Avvakum to identify Sandstrom and you. I think she's the one person on Orlov's team that we can trust.'

'Why?' Kilkenny asked.

'She took the job not knowing what kind of man she was working for. According to my contact, I think she now knows. Avvakum appears to be under house arrest in that building where she works. Orlov paid her a visit yesterday and left a big ugly man to keep her company. My guy over there tried to send her an E-mail; it was returned as undeliverable.'

'Makes sense,' Nolan said. 'She's become a security risk, so they cut her off.'

261

Grin shook his head. 'If Avvakum's a threat, why didn't Orlov just have her killed?'

'Simple, Grin,' Nolan answered. 'Orlov still needs her. She's a skill player. If he kills her, he's got downtime until he can get a replacement. Better to put Avvakum on a short leash and keep her working until he finds a new physicist for the job.'

'Then she gets whacked,' Mosley added.

A small window appeared in the corner of Nolan's monitor, and a voice announced the arrival of a new E-mail message. Nolan got up and walked over to his desk. He didn't recognize the sender's E-mail address, which was a string of random letters and numbers. The subject of the message read: *Trade two for one, Kilkenny?*

Nolan selected the message.

We have Kelsey Newton and Elli Vital. We will return them unharmed in exchange for the key to Johann Wolff's notebook code. Attached is a video clip of our guests. You will be contacted on the morning of July 31 with instructions for the exchange.

'It's a message from Orlov,' Nolan announced.

Cooper, Mosley, and Grin gathered around the computer.

'May I?' Grin asked as he reached over Kilkenny's shoulder and typed a quick command that displayed all the message's header information. 'They covered their tracks really well; this could have come from anywhere.'

'Pretty straightforward demand,' Cooper said. 'Let's have a look at the video clip.'

Nolan downloaded the attached file. A moment later Kelsey and Elli appeared on the screen. They were seated at an old wooden table in a rustic, wood-paneled room. Both sat rigidly, with their forearms resting on the table. For the first few seconds, neither moved.

'Hi, Nolan. Elli and I are all right. The people who took us want the engagement ring Johann Wolff gave to Elli.'

The clip ended with the final frame frozen on the screen.

'Short and sweet,' Cooper said. 'Just enough to let us know that they have them.'

'Actually,' Nolan said, the tone of his voice revealing his curiosity, 'I think it might have told us something else.'

'You spot something, Nolan?' Mosley asked.

'Maybe.'

Using his mouse, Nolan enlarged the still image to the screen's full size. The resolution went from crisp to grainy with the enlargement.

'There it is,' he exclaimed.

'What?' Cooper asked.

'Elli's ring.'

Everyone looked at the older woman's hands but saw no ring.

'Elli's not wearing a ring,' Grin said.

'No, she's not, but Kelsey is. Kelsey doesn't wear rings. I think the only one she owns is from high school, and she hasn't worn that since she was eighteen. Look at the ring, it's a thick gold band. That's a match for the jeweler's description of Wolff's ring. It's gotta be it.'

'Gentlemen,' Mosley said sternly, 'that piece of

information does not leave this room. For those two ladies, it's a matter of life and death.'

Everyone nodded.

'We need to respond to this,' Nolan urged.

'I'm already working on it,' Grin announced. 'I can put together a Trojan horse program that we can imbed in our response. Once they open our message, our Trojan horse will load and contact us over the Net. From there, we can use the Spyder to track 'em down.'

'That's not what I had in mind, Grin. They'll be expecting something like that. Orlov's feeling secure right now, thinking he's in control of the situation. We need to shake things up a bit. I say we call him.'

'Call Orlov?' Grin said. 'Nolan, are you nuts?'

Mosley nodded as he thought through Nolan's suggestion. 'Actually, it's not a bad idea. We'll catch Orlov off guard and can push for terms of our own.'

'We are going to give him *everything* he wants – the cipher key, our decoding program, everything – in exchange for Kelsey and Elli.' A devious smile curled across Nolan's face.

Mosley caught the glint in Kilkenny's eye. 'Nolan, after our little trip to London last year, I know you're not the type who just rolls over. What are you working on?'

'A plan, Cal, a plan.' Nolan turned to Cooper. 'Do you think that Orlov has any highly placed enemies in the Russian government – people who might enjoy watching him take a fall?'

'The sense I get from my contact in Moscow is that if Orlov ever made a serious mistake, the

264

wolves would be all over him.'

'Good, because I think I need to pay a visit to Orlov at his office in Moscow.'

Grin shook his head in disbelief. 'You're talking crazy, man.'

'If we're going to win this fight with Orlov, we can't just cut a deal with him. We have to take him out completely. To do that, I have to go there – I'm going to be our Trojan horse.'

Over the next hour Nolan proceeded to outline his plan of attack, refining elements as he brainstormed with Mosley, Cooper, and Grin.

'We're in agreement then?' Nolan asked.

The three other men nodded.

'Done.' Nolan then handed Cooper the cordless phone. 'Bart, it's time to make some calls.'

Cooper flipped through his legal pad until he found the sheet with the list of phone numbers, and dialed the first one.

'Electronic surveillance. Gardner speaking.'

'Gardner, this is Bart Cooper.' He then recited his Agency identification number. 'I need a flashback trace on this number for all incoming calls, starting from the second I hang up. I have the owner of the line right here, so I don't need a warrant.'

Cooper could hear Gardner entering his ID number into a computer, running a check on Cooper's authority to make a flashback request. Cooper smiled; there were few spooks in Langley who carried more clout than he did.

'It's all set, Mr Cooper. The NRO will be monitoring your line as soon as you hang up.'

265

'Thanks, Gardner.'

Cooper ended the call and then keyed a long string of numbers into the phone.

Nolan pulled Mosley aside so as not to disturb Cooper. 'Cal, what exactly is a flashback trace?'

'It's like a regular phone trace, but a whole lot faster. It can also run down mobile phones and triangulate their location using cell towers or satellites. With it, we can pinpoint a call anywhere in the world, and since we don't know where the hostages are, that's exactly what we need.'

Cooper stood in the center of the room with the phone still pressed against his ear.

'Orlov *rezidence*,' a brusque voice answered on the other end of the line.

'*Dóbry viécher. Vy gavárite paanglíyski?*' Cooper said.

'*Da*, I speak English,' the man replied, his accent thick but understandable.

'Good. My name is Bart Cooper, and I wish to speak with Victor Orlov.'

'Mr Orlov does not want to be disturbed. This is a private line. How did you get this number?'

'That's not important, but what I have to tell Orlov is. I don't care if you have to pull him off his mistress, you just get him on the phone now. If he asks, tell him that I have the key to Wolff's notebooks.

The man mulled all this over. 'Hold on, I'll see if he can take your call.'

'You do that. I'll wait.'

A moment passed, with Kilkenny and the others wondering what was happening on the other end of the line.

266

'Mr Cooper,' a man's voice answered with only a hint of a Russian accent. 'I am Victor Orlov. Do I know you?'

'No, you don't, but I'm very well connected. I'm here with Nolan Kilkenny. We received your message regarding the hostages.'

'What are you talking about?'

'Cut the crap, Orlov. This little game is over, and you've won. I'm calling to cut a deal so we can put an end to this. We have the key to Wolff's codes. Kilkenny has successfully decrypted a couple of pages from the notebooks, so we know the key works. If you want it, now's the time to talk.'

'Very well, Mr Cooper, but I like to know who I'm dealing with. Who are you?'

'Let's just say that I'm someone with powerful enough friends that I can get your home phone number, and that's all you need to know about me. My primary interest in this is getting those two women back safe and sound. If you deal straight with me, we won't have any problems.'

'Very well,' Orlov replied, intrigued by Cooper. 'What do you propose?'

'First, the video clip you sent is worthless. We need a live phone contact to verify that the hostages are still unharmed.'

'That can be arranged.'

'Good, because that's a deal breaker. I'll expect the call within ten minutes after we hang up. Here's the number.' Cooper read the numbers off his list. 'Now, I assume that the hostages are still nearby. Don't worry, I'm not going to ask you where they are. You wouldn't tell me anyway.'

'That is correct.'

'As a measure of security for both sides, I propose we break up the exchange. The hostages are to be released at a very public location of your choosing. When you give the word, your people will simply drop them off and drive away. The women will call to tell us they've been released.'

'How do I get the cipher key?'

'That part is a little trickier. Nolan Kilkenny and I will travel to Moscow, where we will meet with you at your office on Prospekt Mira.'

'You seem to know a lot about me, Mr Cooper,' Orlov said warily.

'Like I said earlier, I'm very well connected. We'll fly out of the States later this afternoon, which puts us in Moscow tomorrow afternoon. Let's say the three of us meet at your office around six o'clock. When we arrive at your office, you will tell your people to let the women go. When the women are free, we will turn over Wolff's key and Kilkenny's decoding program.'

'These terms are unusually generous, Cooper. Why?'

'Write it off to goodwill. All we care about are the hostages. Kilkenny's got copies of maybe a dozen pages from Wolff's notebooks, so the key doesn't really do his people a lot of good. Like I said earlier, you won. Let's settle up and call it a day.'

'Agreed. I look forward to meeting you tomorrow, Mr Cooper.'

'Likewise.'

Cooper set the phone back in its cradle. 'I haven't had to do something like that in a while.'

'An impressive performance,' Kilkenny said.

'Now we just have to wait for the call.'

A moment later the phone rang. Kilkenny quickly snatched it off the table.

'This is Nolan Kilkenny,' he answered.

'Nolan, it's Kelsey.'

'How are you and Elli?' he said loud enough for the others to hear.

'We're fine. They haven't hurt us.'

'We found Wolff's key, so they're just going to hold you both until we can make a trade. It'll all be over tomorrow, I promise.'

'I love you, Nolan.'

'I love you, too, sweetheart.'

The line went dead.

'They cut her off,' Kilkenny said as he switched off the phone. 'She sounded okay, just scared. She said they're both fine.'

'They should stay that way until tomorrow,' Cooper said reassuringly. 'Now, I have to make my next call.'

Cooper took the phone from Kilkenny and punched in a number.

'Gardner, it's Cooper. Did you get a trace on that last call?'

'Yes, sir. It originated in Arenac County, Michigan, near a town called Standish. I've got an address and precise coordinates.'

'Read them off to me.'

Cooper took notes as Gardner read off the trace results.

'Gardner, this is a hostage situation with national-security implications. Get in touch with the folks in Research. I want a full package on

269

this property, everything you can get your hands on. And I need it yesterday. I got an E-mail address for you.'

'I'm ready,' Gardner replied, his adrenaline up.

Cooper read off Kilkenny's address carefully. 'Got that?'

'I got it, sir. I'll have something for you in thirty minutes.'

'Good. Next thing, I need some discreet surveillance of this property. See if you can't get a little time on one of the satellites to pull some images. Send them to the same address.'

'Sir, has Kilkenny been cleared for satellite imagery?'

'Yes, he has, on my authority. If you like, I can have DCI Barnett call you to confirm it.'

'I can accept your word on it, sir,' Gardner said meekly.

'Good.' Cooper hung up and set the portable phone on the desk.

'I got the GPS mapping program up,' Grin announced. 'I just need the coordinates.'

Cooper read off the precise longitude and latitude figures that Gardner had given him; Grin typed in the coordinates and pressed ENTER. The global positioning satellite program rendered a globe on the screen that began to spin and grow large, as if the viewers were flying toward Earth from space. North America filled the screen, then the mitten shape of Michigan's Lower Peninsula came into view. Finally, the program zoomed in on the northern shore of Saginaw Bay, where the Rifle River flowed out into the bay.

'I canoed that river as a Boy Scout,' Kilkenny

said, looking over Grin's shoulder. 'Once, we followed the river all the way out to the bay. It's mostly wetlands and trees in this area, with a few cabins along the shore. A lot of duck hunting up there. I think my friends will be able to handle this.'

52

JULY 30

Moscow, Russia

The phone rang, breaking the silence that filled the room where Orlov was waiting. He answered it quickly, fully aware it was Dmitri Leskov on the other end.

'The call to Kilkenny is done.'

'Any problems?'

'*Nyet*. We kept it short, not enough time for a phone trace. Newton said nothing other than what we told her to say.'

'Good. Put Josef in charge of the hostages. With Kilkenny and Cooper coming to Moscow, I want you here handling security. Your tickets are waiting for you at Tri-City Airport. Flight arrangements have been made that should get you here a few hours ahead of our visitors.'

As he wrote down the flight information, a surge of anger flushed Leskov's skin. Kilkenny's hands touched nearly everything that had gone wrong with this operation, including the death of his brother Pavel. He toyed with the idea of letting his men rape Kilkenny's woman just for spite, but such an action didn't fit in with Victor Orlov's plans.

'I'm on my way, sir. Any change to our plans for the hostages?'

'None.'

'Do you expect any trouble from Kilkenny or from this Cooper?'

'No, but I want you here to make certain that things go smoothly. Once I have the ciphers, you can settle things with Kilkenny.'

'I understand, Victor Ivanovich,' Leskov replied. '*Spasiba.*'

53

JULY 30

Ann Arbor, Michigan

Kilkenny stood outside the airport hangar and watched the small, military passenger jet taxi off the runway. The pilot deftly brought the aircraft to a stop over the painted markings on the tarmac just a few feet from where he stood. The twin-jet engines mounted on the tail slowly wound down, their high pitch dropping in both tone and volume.

The door of the aircraft shuddered, then slid

open. The copilot lowered the built-in stairs and stepped aside to let his passengers disembark. First off was a muscular man of about fifty with dark ebony skin and a close-cropped Afro flecked with gray. He stood a few inches shorter than Kilkenny; the collar of his battle-dress uniform bore the stars of a newly frocked rear admiral. Over his right breast was the gold pistol and trident emblem of Navy SEALs.

Kilkenny greeted Rear Admiral Jack Dawson with a crisp salute.

'Good to see you, Nolan,' Dawson said as he returned Kilkenny's salute. 'Sorry it's not under better circumstances.'

'Thanks for coming, Jack.'

'Just following orders. After the folks at Langley gave the Secretary of Defense the situation report, he agreed it would be best if we dealt with these Spetsnaz mercenaries.'

Dawson and Kilkenny first met back when the admiral was still a captain, then in charge of the SEALs training facility in Coronado, California, and Kilkenny was a BUD/S trainee. A few months after Kilkenny was assigned to SEAL Team Four in Little Creek, Virginia, Dawson assumed command of the team. The respect and loyalty the two men had for each other led them to become close friends.

'The stars look good on you,' Kilkenny said, commenting on Dawson's recent promotion to flag rank and his new assignment as commander of Navy Special Warfare Group Two.

'The upgrade has some benefits, but it's added another layer of bureaucracy between me and my men. At least I'm in a position to do some good for 'em.

'The maps and intel are waiting for you back at my place, along with a CIA guy named Cal Mosley. He's coordinating things on this end. My dad will lead you back there,' Nolan said, pointing to his father's truck.

The nine men who followed Dawson off the jet formed a human chain that ran from the plane's cargo hold into Sean Kilkenny's Explorer and a pair of rented Ford Expeditions that were parked beside the hangar. They quickly off-loaded the duffels containing their gear and stowed them in the SUVs for the next leg of their journey. Master Chief Max Gates, a balding, barrel-chested NCO with forearms that would make Popeye proud, led the obscene cadence that accompanied their labor. Gates had been Kilkenny's right hand during his tour with the SEALs.

Kilkenny recognized most of the men. In his past life, he and Gates had led Gilgallon, Hepburn, Darvas, Rodriguez, and Detmer on missions around the world, and each was like a brother to him. Edwards, the young lieutenant who'd replaced him, Kilkenny knew only by reputation. The two remaining men, Ahsan and Gorski, had worked with Kilkenny's squad on several occasions – they were the sniper team.

After the squad stowed their gear, the Lieutenant led them over to Dawson and Kilkenny.

'Squad One is ready to move out, sir,' the young man said with a crisp salute.

'Well done, Lieutenant,' Dawson replied as he returned the salute. 'At ease, men.'

274

The SEALs relaxed, broke ranks, and encircled Kilkenny and Dawson.

'Lieutenant Jeremy Edwards,' Dawson said, 'I'd like to introduce your predecessor, Nolan Kilkenny.'

'A pleasure to meet you, sir. Chief Gates and the men speak highly of you.'

'They're a good crew,' Kilkenny replied as he shook Edwards's hand. 'You're a ring-knocker, I see. I'm an Annapolis grad, too. Good luck, Lieutenant.'

'Thanks.'

'Men,' Dawson boomed out so all could hear, 'a little background on this op. One of the hostages we're going after is a very close personal friend of Kilkenny's. Now he may no longer be in uniform, but he's still one of us. That makes this personal.'

'Hoo-yah!' the squad shouted back.

'Nolan,' Gates said in a thick Oklahoma drawl, 'you have my word, we'll get Kelsey back for you.'

Kilkenny grasped Gates's hand firmly. 'I know you will, Max. I know you will.'

'All right, everybody!' Dawson shouted, excited at the opportunity to operate at the squad level. 'Let's move out.'

Dawson rode with Sean Kilkenny in the Explorer. Behind them, Edwards and Gates piloted the Expeditions. Kilkenny watched as the small convoy rolled onto State Street.

As they disappeared from view, Cooper walked over from his rented Taurus.

'Bet you wish you were going with them.'

'You'd win that bet,' Kilkenny admitted. 'But this is the way it has to be. Hell, I've been off the team for almost two years. That's an eternity in terms of training. If I went along, I'd just be baggage. The lead belongs to Edwards now, and my old NCO tells me he's good at it. They'll get the job done, and that's exactly what Kelsey and Elli need right now, not me riding in with guns blazing, playing the hero.'

'Well, we've got our own job ahead of us,' Cooper said, 'and it's time for us to catch our flight to Moscow.'

54

JULY 30

Northwest Flight 0030

Shortly after the flight lifted off from Detroit Metropolitan Airport, Kilkenny fell into a deep and much-needed sleep. Seated beside him in business class, Cooper made a series of phone calls, then nursed a Bloody Mary.

The clatter of the beverage cart awoke Kilkenny. He yawned, checked his watch, and looked out the oval window. The sky was clear and dark; the Atlantic spread out calmly beneath them, shimmering under the light of a gibbous moon.

'How are you feeling?' Cooper asked as he

traded his empty glass for a full one.

'Like I could use another day in the sack. How about you?'

'I'll sleep on the flight back.'

'Would you like something to drink?' the flight attendant asked.

'An orange juice,' Kilkenny replied, his mouth thick, as if it were packed with wet cotton.

After Kilkenny received his drink and a couple of packages of peanuts, the flight attendant moved on.

'Bart, I've been meaning to ask you something.'

'Go ahead.'

'You mentioned that after Wolff's body was found, you ran a background check on him. Why?'

'Professional curiosity, mainly. Wolff worked for the Germans during the Second World War. After the war he wanted to emigrate to the States. I was with the OSS back then – I'm the guy who checked Wolff out and certified he wasn't a Nazi. When the story about his body being found hit the papers, the computers at Langley picked it up and matched it with the report I wrote back in 'forty-six and sent me a notice. Wolff's murder looked enough like an execution for me to wonder if I'd missed something when I vetted him, so I took another look.'

'Did you find anything?'

Cooper stared down at the ice in his glass.

'Yeah, I found out he was an okay guy.'

'When Cal found out you were both looking into Wolff's background, why didn't you just turn over what you'd found? He had an active investigation, and no offense intended, you're a few years past field-duty age.'

'That's a polite way of putting it, and you're right, I have a quasi-retired status with the Agency. I hung on because I thought I could give Cal a hand. I know a few well-connected people in Russia, and that's where his investigation seemed to be pointing. I thought I might be of some use.'

Kilkenny nodded, taking in what Cooper had said.

'Bart, I don't mean to sound like I'm suspicious of your motives, because my gut and Cal Mosley both say I can trust you. So, given that you're on my side, all the reasons you cited still don't add up to why you personally are doing this. You're over seventy years old; you've done your bit for flag and country. It just seems to me that you have a deepseated passion for this case, something that's stronger than I would expect, given that you first heard about any of this just two days ago.'

Cooper remained still for a moment, not responding to Kilkenny, just staring blankly ahead at the projection screen.

'At my age, there's this inner need to know that you've done some good with your life. If you have, then you're content. If you haven't, you try and make up for it somehow. After the war there was a lot of intel work to do. There were war criminals to track down, evidence to collect. In the OSS, we were concerned with scientific information. We wanted to find everything the Reich had been working on – rockets, jet propulsion, atomic energy – before the Soviets did. We probably got a sixty-forty split with regard to people, records, and equipment. Some of the scientists we recovered were, without a doubt, Nazis. A few should have been tried as war criminals for the things they were involved in, but they weren't for reasons of national security. Instead, they got a free pass to America, where we put them to work on our weapons.'

'Moral expediency.'

'More like *immoral* expediency. I interviewed a few of these scientists, and they were proud of what they'd done. If people had died, that was acceptable in the advancement of their work. Watching these evil men go off to a pampered life in the States after what we found in the death camps made me sick. As both a human being and a Jew, I found the hypocrisy intolerable. While I was stationed in Germany during the occupation, I became involved with a group of European Jews seeking justice against their former persecutors. They were known as the Nokmim – the Avengers – and they took it upon themselves to root out every war criminal they could find. On several occasions I provided them with evidence that justified action against specific individuals; some were German scientists and engineers who'd been captured by the Western Allies.'

'Was Johann Wolff one of these German scientists?' Kilkenny asked, sensing where this story was leading.

'Yes. In 1947 some documents were found that implicated Johann Wolff in war crimes. The evidence was thin, but enough for the Nokmim to put a death sentence on Wolff's head. By this time, Wolff was already in the U.S.'

'So they sent an assassin here to kill him?'

'Not an assassin, an executioner. A Nokmim tribunal found Wolff guilty in absentia of crimes against humanity. Justice needed to be served. I was the one sent to administer Wolff's sentence.'

'You killed Johann Wolff?' Nolan moved up in his seat, his face now only a few inches from Cooper's.

Cooper nodded, a lump swelling in his throat. He closed his eyes for a moment to quell his emotions.

'I've killed a few men over the course of my life, Nolan, but none haunt me like Johann Wolff. As I said, the evidence against Wolff was thin and I did not feel it was conclusive. Regardless, a sentence of death was pronounced. When the time came for me to return to the States, I was given the task of bringing justice to Johann Wolff. Through my new job in the fledgling CIA, I was able to locate Wolff in Ann Arbor. In watching Wolff, I could not imagine how this man could have been the monster described in the documents that led to his conviction. He was living a quiet life. He was in love. I struggled with myself over these contradictions, but in the end my sense of duty overrode my desire for the truth. On the tenth of December 1948, I attacked Wolff just outside his office, murdered him, and concealed his body.'

Cooper flagged down the flight attendant for another drink. He waited until she was gone before resuming his story.

'After that, I went on with my life. I had a wife, children – all the things that I'd deprived Johann

Wolff of. I was haunted by him, because I wasn't sure that I'd done the right thing. This uncertain guilt was something I thought I'd take to my grave. When Wolff's body was found, I decided that for the sake of my soul, I needed to know the truth about him.'

'What did you find?'

'I found that Wolff wasn't what the Nokmim thought he was. I learned that he was a decent man, a brilliant scientist who had a great deal to offer. I found a man who put himself at great risk to prevent Germany from developing the atomic bomb. Wolff may have been the greatest hero of the war. And' – Cooper's voice cracked – 'I found that I had murdered this innocent man, in cold blood. Wolff wasn't guilty of any crimes against humanity, but by depriving the world of Wolff's potential genius, I am.'

Cooper sobbed quietly for a few minutes. Kilkenny was thankful that the darkened cabin provided at least some measure of privacy. In hearing this story, Kilkenny felt like a priest in a confessional, though there was no absolution he could give to ease Cooper's guilt.

'The debt I owe Wolff I can never repay.'

'Then why are you doing this?' Kilkenny asked.

'Because after more than fifty years, I have been given the opportunity to set a small part of this right. Wolff was a scientist, not a Nazi. He worked for the Germans because he simply had no choice in the matter. Lara Avvakum is in precisely the same position; she's working for Orlov because he has a gun to her head. The Allies freed Wolff, but who is going to free

281

Avvakum if we don't do it? People like her and Sandstrom are Wolff's heirs; they seek the truths that can change the world.'

Kilkenny nodded as the link between Cooper's past and the present became clear.

'I'm also doing this because I want to recover Wolff's notebooks. They are a record of this man's lifework, his legacy. If Wolff was as brilliant as you have come to believe, then these notebooks are proof of his genius and must be brought out into the open. In Orlov's hands, they might as well still be buried in the ground. That's why we have to get them back. I can't undo what I did to the man, but maybe I can do something for his memory.'

55

JULY 31

Saginaw Bay, Michigan

The *Sharon S* cruised effortlessly over the glassy waters of Saginaw Bay, the twin Detroit Diesel engines pulsing within the fifty-seven-foot Chris-Craft Constellation. The boat belonged to Harsen Smith, a shipbuilder from Algonac and a close friend of Martin Kilkenny's since the 1930s. While it appeared that the two friends were alone on board, Jack Dawson's SEALs were preparing for battle on the enclosed stern deck.

'I think we're getting pretty close,' Martin said.

'Almost,' Smith confirmed as he glanced down at the GPS receiver mounted next to the boat's compass.

Far overhead, a constellation of global positioning satellites girded the earth, each transmitting its signal down toward the surface. By receiving signals from at least three of the satellites, the GPS receiver was able to calculate, within a few inches, the boat's location anywhere on the surface of the planet.

Smith eased back on the throttles, and the *Sharon S* glided to a stop. The coordinates displayed on the GPS matched those given to Smith by Dawson.

'We're right where you wanted to be, Admiral,' Smith announced as he switched off the engines.

'Thank you, Mr Smith,' Dawson replied. Then he stepped over to the doorway between the bridge and the stern deck.

As Harsen Smith watched the SEALs prep for their mission, Martin walked over to his friend and draped an arm across his shoulder. 'With a little luck and some prayers, everyone might just get out of this mess unharmed.'

Smith had brought the *Sharon S* to a stop about a mile from shore, with her bow aimed at the point where the Rifle River emptied into the bay. From shore, the stern of the boat was hidden from view. The waters were calm, and they'd made good time cruising up the Saint Clair River from Algonac, into Lake Huron, around Michigan's Thumb, and into Saginaw Bay. It was now 8:30 in the morning on what promised to be a hot, sunny day.

On the way up from Algonac, the seven-man squad had reviewed specific segments of their mission plan. They had covered what they could expect during their underwater approach to the target area, including water conditions, currents, and underwater topography. Lieutenant Edwards had briefed the squad on the mission plan and each man's task assignments. Once the ideal plan was laid out, they had reviewed the contingency plan to deal with unknowns that might leave the ideal plan in ruins. Lastly, the SEALs had completed their check of weapons and equipment.

As this was a hostage-rescue mission, Dawson designated the squad Angel. The *Sharon S,* Dawson's flagship and base of operations, became Heaven. The hostages, Kelsey and Elli, were identified as Halos One and Two, respectively. By tradition, the hostage-takers were known as Tangos, and the SEAL sniper team as God.

The earpiece on Dawson's headset crackled with an incoming transmission. 'God to Heaven. Over.'

Dawson reached down to the unit clipped to his belt and flipped the SEND switch, allowing two-way communication. 'This is Heaven, God. Say status.'

'God is on station.'

'We read you, God. Heaven out.'

Dawson flipped the radio back into receive mode. 'Edwards, you copy that?'

'Aye, sir. God has found a perch near the target and is ready if we need him.'

'All right, men,' Gates boomed out, 'it's time to saddle up.'

The SEALs zipped into their formfitting, black Neotex wet suits to protect them from exposure during the mile-long swim to shore. Over their chests, the SEALS donned Draeger LAR V oxygen rebreathers – a type of closed-circuit scuba gear that left no telltale bubbles on the surface to give away their position. They then attached a variety of weapons and equipment to their backs, waists, and thighs, transforming each SEAL into a mobile arsenal.

Once the squad was suited up and equipped, Gates, the dive supervisor, checked each man to ensure that the dive gear was right and that the weapons and other equipment were secure. The squad then performed the predive purge, ridding their bodies of built-up nitrogen before switching to pure oxygen for the dive. This last step was done for safety, reducing the possibility that one of the divers might suffer from oxygen deprivation should exhaled nitrogen pass through the CO_2-absorbing crystals in the Draeger rebreather and take the place of life-sustaining oxygen.

Edwards checked his dive watch; it was time to go.

'Admiral, Angel will be on station at oh-nine-thirty and awaiting your signal.'

'Good hunting, Angel,' Dawson replied, loud enough for the entire squad to hear.

One by one, the SEALs stepped off the stern jump deck and into the water. Smith and Martin Kilkenny looked on. When all seven were in the water, Edwards flashed a thumbs-up at Dawson and the two elderly men. Then the SEALs disappeared into the lake.

56

JULY 31

Moscow, Russia

'*Zdrávstvuyte,* Bartholomew Georgievich,' a squat thickset man said as Kilkenny and Cooper entered their suite at the Metropol. 'How was your flight?'

'Fine, Iggy,' Cooper replied warmly. The two men embraced in a Russian bear hug. 'It's good to see you again.'

'*Da.* Like old times, but better.'

'Iggy, I'd like you to meet Nolan Kilkenny. He's the guy I told you about, the one who's helping me out on this. Nolan, this is Igor Sergeevich Fydorov of the FSB.'

'A pleasure,' Kilkenny said, offering his hand.

Fydorov grasped it firmly with his thick-fingered paw and squeezed, all the while grinning and looking Nolan in the eye. Kilkenny smiled and returned an equal amount of pressure in what was obviously a test of strength. The bushy mass of hair that formed a single brow over Fydorov's brown eyes furled as he bore down on Kilkenny's hand. Kilkenny matched him and

286

returned a tense smile.

'Enough, you two,' Cooper said, amused by the spectacle. 'Call it a draw.'

Fydorov and Kilkenny released simultaneously, both relieved that it was over.

'Your friend has quite a grip,' Fydorov said as he massaged the blood back into his reddened fingers.

'The same could be said for you, Mr Fydorov.'

In a friendly gesture, Fydorov slapped Kilkenny hard on the back. 'Call me Iggy.'

'Is everything set for our meeting with Orlov?' Cooper asked.

'*Da,* everything is as we discussed. When I get your signal, Alpha will move in.'

'Alpha?' Kilkenny asked.

'Alpha is a Special Forces unit, like your SEALs or Deltas. The KGB developed the Alphas for use in Afghanistan. I was part of the unit that attacked the presidential palace in Kabul,' Fydorov said proudly. 'We spearheaded the Russian invasion in 1979. When that first mission began to go badly and we came under heavy fire, Brezhnev ordered that we be abandoned and left to die.'

'Couldn't stomach the disappointment?' Kilkenny asked.

'Politicians,' Fydorov replied with disgust. 'We escaped from that betrayal and became the KGB's elite Special Forces unit. During the Battle for the Russian White House, when Yeltsin launched an eleven-day siege against Rutskoi and the Russian parliament, two Alphas entered the White House under a flag of truce and informed the rebels that they had thirty minutes to surrender, or Alpha would attack. The rebels surrendered immediately.'

'Politicians,' Kilkenny said.

'When the KGB was broken up,' Fydorov continued, the FSB inherited Alpha, and we use them as a counterterrorism assault unit. In their role as the government's enforcer, Alpha recently took it upon themselves to remove a Mafiya chieftain who boasted of being *untouchable* by the government. As he walked from the steambath to his armorplated Mercedes 600, surrounded by bodyguards, a sniper nestled in a fifth-story window put two bullets in his head and one in his heart.'

'Given that Orlov has surrounded himself with operators like Leskov,' Kilkenny remarked, 'it's nice to know the cavalry will be there when we need them.'

'Cavalry?' Fydorov questioned, not understanding Kilkenny's comment. 'Oh, like in cowboy movies. Yes, we are the cavalry. Is there anything you require?'

Kilkenny shook his head.

'No,' Cooper replied. 'I think we're all set here. Nolan and I just need to get ready for our meeting with Orlov.'

Fydorov checked his watch. 'It's time for me to go as well. I have a taxi waiting for you – one of our drivers. He'll make sure you get there. Good luck, to the both of you.'

'Thanks, Iggy,' Cooper replied.

'We'll see you when all of this is over,' Nolan promised.

57

JULY 31

Moscow, Russia

After a quick shower to wash off the twelve-plus hours of travel and wake him up, Kilkenny emerged from his room in khaki pants, an open-collared button-down shirt, and a tweed blazer.

'You look like a model for L. L. Bean,' Cooper said.

'Thanks, and judging by that old suit you're wearing, Mr GQ, I'd refrain from making any more fashion statements. Glass houses, you know.'

'Very funny, but we'll pass for *amerikanski biznesmeny*,' Cooper said with a wry smile. 'Let's get moving.'

At the main entrance of the hotel, the doorman escorted them to the curb and waved for one of the queued taxis to pull up. A battered yellow Lada stopped at the curb, and Cooper and Kilkenny got in.

'The FinProm building on Prospekt Mira, *da*?' the driver asked, confirming the instructions given him by Fydorov.

'*Da*,' Cooper replied.

The driver expertly negotiated the medieval maze of streets in Moscow's core out to the

Sadovoye Koltso. He followed the former garden beltway until it reached Prospekt Mira, where he turned and drove into Moscow's northern periphery. In the distance, Kilkenny saw a three-hundred-meter-tall obelisk of polished metal.

'What is that?' Kilkenny asked.

'What?' Cooper replied absently. 'Oh that's right. This is your first trip here. That tower commemorates Soviet achievements in space travel.'

'They're not much on subtle gestures, are they?'

'Not when it comes to bragging rights.'

A few minutes later the driver guided the Lada up against the curb in front of a stark, concrete-and-glass building. A westerly breeze pulled at the deep blue flag mounted near the roof, exposing the outstretched wings of a golden two-headed eagle. Beneath the flag, mounted to the face of the parapet, the building bore the name VIO FINPROM. Kilkenny noticed surveillance cameras discreetly mounted on the parapet and near the main entrance.

Cooper slipped the driver an American twenty, both as a courtesy, since the driver actually worked for the FSB, and to make the transaction appear ordinary, in case anyone inside was watching. Kilkenny grabbed his soft-sided briefcase and exited the taxi.

A giant of a man stuffed into an ill-fitting suit unlocked the vestibule door as they approached.

'Cooper and Kilkenny?' he asked, as if he'd memorized the line.

'*Da,*' Cooper replied.

The large man opened the door wide and

allowed them to enter; he then locked it once they were inside. In the lobby, Dmitri Leskov stood leaning against the reception desk. Leskov took scant notice of Cooper, focusing instead on Kilkenny with a venomous glare that would have looked more appropriate had he been aiming a pistol.

Kilkenny leaned close to Cooper and whispered, 'Looks like he remembers me.'

'What did you expect, flowers?' Cooper joked. 'Just remember, revenge is part of the Russian national psyche.'

'I get the picture.'

'Stop,' Leskov ordered.

Leskov straightened up and motioned for the doorman to frisk Cooper and Kilkenny. The man patted down Cooper thoroughly, showing no reluctance to investigate even the apex of Cooper's inseam in search of weapons or microphones.

'Search his bag,' Leskov ordered when the doorman approached Kilkenny. 'I'll search this one myself.'

Kilkenny handed his briefcase to the doorman. Leskov began searching Kilkenny as if he were probing for a physical weakness rather than a weapon. Kilkenny sensed he was being appraised as both an opponent and a target, knowing it was an effort to intimidate him. Leskov finished with his front and moved behind.

'I enjoyed doing this to your woman,' Leskov sneered, baiting Kilkenny.

Kilkenny slowly turned his head and looked over his left shoulder at Leskov, who smiled, amused by his taunt.

'Not half as much as you seem to be enjoying doing it to me.'

Leskov's smile vanished.

Kilkenny pursed his lips and made the sound of a kiss.

'*Yop t'voi yo mat!*' Leskov spat, his face flushing to deep red.

Leskov wound his right arm back, curling his hand into a fist. Pivoting on his left foot, Kilkenny turned his body ninety degrees to Leskov. As he spun, Kilkenny raised his left arm, blocking the incoming punch, and then wrapped his arm around Leskov's. Kilkenny snapped his arm like a whip, locking Leskov's elbow as he ground the knuckles of his fist into the soft flesh of the man's armpit. Leskov's arm went numb and was effectively immobilized, leaving his chest and abdomen open to attack.

Kilkenny snapped a quick punch into Leskov's solar plexus, knocking the wind out of him. Out of the corner of his eye, Kilkenny saw the over-size doorman drop the briefcase and begin moving to Leskov's aid. With a quick lunge, Kilkenny reached up and grabbed Leskov's throat, the tips of his fingers pressing deep into the flesh around the man's windpipe.

'Tell that trained grizzly of yours to back off, or I'm going to rip your fucking throat out.'

Kilkenny's fingers constricted just enough to let them both know this was no idle threat. Cooper hastily translated Kilkenny's demand for both Leskov and the doorman, hoping the situation wouldn't escalate further.

Leskov nodded and held up his hand; the mountain-sized man backed away.

'Dmitri,' a voice called out sternly from the doorway at the far end of the lobby. It was Victor Orlov. 'What is going on here?'

'I believe it's a cultural misunderstanding,' Kilkenny quipped, his eyes fixed on Leskov. 'But Leskov and I have worked out our differences, haven't we?'

Leskov stared straight back into Kilkenny's eyes, unwilling to give an inch. Had the choice been his, he would finish Kilkenny now or die trying.

'*Da,*' his voice croaked hoarsely.

Kilkenny loosened his grip on Leskov's arm and throat, then backed away with his hands held up at chest level. Leskov retreated as well, with one hand massaging his throat.

'Did they have anything on them?' Orlov asked.

'*Nyet,*' Leskov replied, his voice coming back. 'They're clean.'

'Very well, Mr Cooper, Mr Kilkenny, if you'll follow me, we can get down to business.'

Kilkenny picked up his briefcase from where the doorman had dropped it – checking to see that the laptop computer inside was still in one piece – then slung it over his shoulder and followed Cooper. Leskov trailed a few steps behind, nursing wounds to both his body and his pride.

'What the hell do you think you were doing back there?' Cooper whispered harshly.

'Recon, Bart.'

Orlov led them down a wide hallway that still held a faint aroma of fresh paint and new carpet.

Orlov led the group into his office suite, and Leskov closed the large, paneled wooden door behind them and took up station beside it.

'Gentlemen, before we begin,' Orlov said, assuming the role of gracious host, 'I would like to introduce Oksanna Zoshchenko, my scientific adviser.'

'Good evening, gentlemen,' Zoshchenko said with cool, professional detachment.

'Please, sit down.' Orlov gestured to a broad sofa.

They sat on the sofa with their backs to Leskov. Orlov and Zoshchenko seated themselves in a pair of upholstered chairs from the era of Louis XV.

Cooper coughed lightly to clear his throat. 'Our presence here is a sign of our good faith. Now it's time for a similar show from you.'

Orlov nodded and pulled a thin notebook from the inside breast pocket of his suit coat. He quickly thumbed through the pages until he found what he was looking for, then dialed a number into the speakerphone that sat on the hand-carved table beside him.

The sound of a distant phone purred from the speaker; after two rings it was answered.

'Yes?' a deep voice asked.

'This is Orlov. Put the women on.'

There was silence for a moment, then Kelsey Newton came on the line.

'Hello? Nolan?'

'I'm here, Kelsey. How are you and Elli?'

'We're okay. They haven't harmed us.'

'That's great. Hang in there, Kelsey, this will

soon be over. Can you put Elli on?'

'Sure.'

'Hello, Nolan,' Elli called out.

'Hi, Elli. It's good to hear your voice. I just wanted to make sure you were all right.'

'Other than it's too hot and humid, I'm fine.'

'Great, I'll see you both very soon.'

'Satisfied?' Orlov asked.

'What about their release?' Cooper asked.

'Once I'm satisfied that you can decode the notebooks, the women will be released.'

'Nolan, show the man.'

Kilkenny pulled his laptop out of the briefcase and set it on the polished oval top of the coffee table in front of him. The machine booted up quickly.

'I'm going to show you the algorithm that Wolff created to encode his research,' Kilkenny announced. 'He recorded it on the endpapers of each notebook.'

Kilkenny brought up a text file that displayed a complex mathematical formula, then turned the laptop to face Orlov and Zoshchenko. Both looked puzzled by what they saw.

'In case you're wondering, it's an algorithm designed to run on a quantum computer.'

'There's no such thing,' Zoshchenko said skeptically.

'No, not yet there isn't. Wolff's math is valid, though difficult to replicate in conventional terms. When he encoded his notebooks, he used this algorithm and did the work in his head. I've rewritten the algorithm to run on a conventional computer.'

Orlov scowled, looking for some deception in what he plainly didn't understand.

'What about the key?' Orlov asked. 'Where is the ring?'

'It's safely waiting for its owner. You don't need the ring anyway, only the inscription' – Kilkenny opened a text file and showed them Wolff's key –'which I've built into the decoding program.'

'Cooper said you decoded some of the notebooks.'

'Yes, I did,' Kilkenny replied.

'Show me.'

Kilkenny pulled six file folders from his brief-case and handed them to Orlov. 'Here's a few pages from the first notebook. Each folder contains a facsimile of the original notebook page, followed by our decoded version of the text.'

Orlov opened the first folder and saw a laser-printed version of a page from Wolff's notebooks. Turning the page, he discovered Kilkenny's plain-text version of Wolff's research.

'It's in German?' Orlov asked.

'Wolff's native tongue. We haven't had time to translate very much of it, just enough to know that it's not gibberish.'

'What do you think, Oksanna?' Orlov asked, handing the first folder over to her.

Zoshchenko studied the document, mentally translating from German to Russian. She spent ten silent minutes reading before she looked up from the page.

'Victor, I have to admit I don't understand this.'

'Then this is a fraud?'

'No, not necessarily,' she replied. 'It looks genuine, but the science is well beyond my ability. We need an expert in this field to make any meaningful determination.'

'Avvakum?'

'*Da.*'

Orlov thought for a moment. 'Dmitri, have Avvakum brought here.'

Leskov nodded and issued the order into his lip mike. A few minutes later Leskov opened the door. A woman with long, wavy black hair entered Orlov's office. Her clothes were rumpled, as if she'd slept in them. The dark circles beneath her eyes implied that, in recent days, she probably hadn't slept at all.

'Come here, Doctor,' Orlov demanded.

Avvakum walked toward Orlov numbly. When she drew near, Orlov indicated that she was to sit in the chair to his right. Avvakum complied.

'I would like your opinion on something, Doctor,' Orlov said.

Orlov then handed Avvakum one of the folders. She opened it and looked at the first page.

'This is a page from the notebooks,' she said.

'*Da.* Look at the next page and tell me what you think.'

Avvakum turned to the next page and began to read. She said nothing, but Kilkenny read her body language. Her eyes widened slightly, as if the larger aperture would somehow allow more of what she saw to enter her mind more quickly.

'*Boja moi,*' Avvakum said softly. 'Is there more?'

'Yes, there is,' Orlov replied. 'What do you

think? Do you believe it to be the true text of the notebooks?'

'*Da,*' Avvakum replied.

To Kilkenny, it was clear that reading the decoded page had brought some of the life back to this defeated woman.

'Would you like to see how I did it?' Kilkenny asked her directly.

'Please,' Avvakum replied.

Kilkenny showed her the original equation string, then briefly described how he and Grin reworked Wolff's quantum algorithm so it could be run on a conventional computer.

'How did you simulate the principle of super-position in your program?' Avvakum asked.

'We didn't,' Kilkenny admitted. 'We avoided it altogether. We translated Wolff's equation from a quantum language into something we could work with. It's certainly not as pretty as his code, and probably not as fast, but it gets the job done.'

'Can I see the rest?' she asked.

Orlov handed her the remaining files, which she eagerly pored over.

'Each page takes about half an hour to forty-five minutes to decode,' Kilkenny explained, 'depending on how much text there is on it.'

Orlov waited until Avvakum closed the sixth folder. 'What is your opinion, Lara?'

'These men can decode the notebooks.'

'Thank you. That will be all,' Orlov said. Then he looked over at Leskov. 'Dmitri, please have the doctor escorted back to her lab.'

After Avvakum was gone, Cooper leaned back and crossed his legs. 'Satisfied?' he asked.

'I am, Victor,' Zoshchenko offered.

'So am I.' Orlov leaned to the side and pressed the REDIAL button on the phone. This time the deep-voiced man answered after only one ring. 'Josef, release our guests.'

'*Da*, Victor Ivanovich,' the man replied.

Orlov pressed the button that ended the call. 'The women will be dropped off at a very public location within the hour.'

'Good,' Cooper replied. 'Now, let's work out the rest of this. In exchange for Kilkenny's decoding program, we want not only the release of the two women but your word that this is where all this ends.'

'What do you mean?' Orlov asked.

'I mean that your attacks are over. This shouldn't be a tough point for you to agree to; you've already got everything you want.'

'If your people watching Sandstrom have kept you up to date,' Kilkenny added, 'then you know that even if he survives, it'll be a long time before he'll be well enough to return to a laboratory again. There's nobody else in the world right now even close to catching up with you.'

Orlov smiled with satisfaction at Cooper and Kilkenny's appraisal of the situation.

'When Kilkenny and I walk out of here, that's the end of this whole affair. Agreed?'

Orlov thought about it for a moment, weighing it as he would any other decision. 'Agreed.'

'Great. Now, as a further sign of our good faith while we wait for the women to be released, I would like to offer Kilkenny's services in decoding more of Wolff's journal. If you like, he can

299

instruct Doctor' – Cooper hesitated, as if trying to recall a name – 'Avvakum in how to use the program.'

'That is acceptable,' Orlov said. 'Dmitri, have Kilkenny taken to Avvakum's lab.'

58

JULY 31

Moscow, Russia

Kilkenny followed the lean, muscular man into the deeper recesses of the building. Temporary walls of unfinished gypsum board blocked off large portions of the facility that were still under renovation, and mirrored half domes covering security cameras appeared in the corridors at regular intervals.

The security man led Kilkenny upstairs to an interior suite that was divided into a large laboratory space – which currently stood empty – and a row of offices. Several of the boxes stored along one side of the future lab space still bore the packing labels Sandstrom had placed on them back in June.

Kilkenny's escort pointed to the first door, then turned and departed. Avvakum's guard opened the office door, motioning for Kilkenny to step inside. Avvakum all but ignored his arrival.

'Hello,' Kilkenny said in a friendly voice as he

300

entered the office. The guard closed the door behind him. 'We weren't introduced earlier. My name is Nolan Kilkenny.'

'Kilkenny?' she questioned, looking up from the papers on her desk. 'You are the one I sent the message to?'

'Yes, and I wanted to thank you for that.'

'Why? It did no good, and now I am a prisoner here.'

'It helped me discover who was responsible for the attack on Sandstrom and, more recently, the kidnapping of two women, one of whom is very special to me.'

Avvakum smiled weakly at the thought that Kilkenny would travel halfway around the world in order to free the woman he loved. All her years of isolation had left Avvakum with no one to do the same for her.

'Why did Orlov send you here?'

'I'm supposed to teach you how to decode the notebooks his men stole from us.'

'I don't want to give him what's in those notebooks,' Avvakum said with a sigh. 'He doesn't deserve it.'

'I couldn't agree more, but I don't think either of us really has much choice in the matter.'

'Let me clear off some of this mess for you.'

Kilkenny gave Avvakum a hand in moving several piles of computer printouts onto the floor, then he moved a second chair around so that they both could sit on the same side of her long desk. He unzipped his briefcase, set his laptop on the desk near Avvakum's computer, and connected the two machines together with a gray cable. He then pressed the power switch and booted up the laptop.

'Are the image files from the notebooks on your computer?'

'No, they're kept on one of the network servers in the company's main building in Moscow.'

'Do you still have access?'

'Some. I'm restricted to areas specifically related to my project and have no outside access at all.'

'We won't need it. Are you logged in to the network?'

'*Da*.'

'Good, then I'll go to work.'

Using a mix of mouse clicks and keyed-in commands, Kilkenny opened up a window on the laptop's color active-matrix screen. The faint sound of a telephone being dialed pulsed out of the laptop's speakers before Kilkenny turned off the sound.

'What was that?' Avvakum asked.

'Nothing much, just a little communications program.'

In silence, the laptop completed dialing the preprogrammed sequence that Kilkenny had requested, initiating a satellite phone call from its internal modem to the network switchboard at MARC in Ann Arbor.

The MARC network answered, and the two machines electronically shook hands – exchanged communications protocols – verifying that they could trade information without difficulty. Once the two machines synchronized themselves, the window filled with the MARC network logo and requested Kilkenny's user name and password. He typed in both and logged on to the MARC network.

A message appeared across the top of the window.

NOLAN, YOU READY TO GO TO WORK?

Kilkenny smiled. YOU BET, he typed in reply.

Kilkenny knew that on the other side of the world, Grin had the Spyder primed and ready to attack Orlov's computer network. The window went blank. Kilkenny minimized it, making all but a small icon disappear from the screen. Now that the Spyder controlled the connection between the two computers, there was no reason to waste time displaying what it was doing.

'Well now that our computers are all talking to one another, I guess we could try and decode some more of Johann Wolff's notebooks.'

From a new window, Kilkenny tapped into Avvakum's computer and downloaded one of the scanned image files from Wolff's notebooks that had been stolen five days earlier. He brought up the decoding program and selected the image file for processing.

'That's all there is to it; you just pick the encrypted file and tell my program to translate it.'

Avvakum watched eagerly as the computer slowly, character by character, transformed the blocks of unintelligible characters back into the thoughts of the long-dead physicist.

Kilkenny sat back in his chair. 'Can I ask you a question?'

'Certainly.'

'Back in Orlov's office, when you read the pages I'd already decoded, what did you find?'

'You haven't read them?' she asked incredulously.

'Not really. I don't speak much German, and even less quantum physics. I assume you're fluent in both.'

Avvakum smiled and turned her head, embarrassed by the compliment and the attention.

'The work of your colleague, Ted Sandstrom, is brilliant. He has made remarkable strides with his experiments, and his discovery may well change how many things are done. From what little I've seen of the work of Johann Wolff, I believe he was developing theories that promise to open a new way of thinking about the physical universe.'

59

JULY 31

Ann Arbor, Michigan

'All right, we're in!' Grin announced as the Spyder took control of VIO FinProm's computer network.

Inside the MARC Computer Center, Mosley walked out of Grin's office, which was serving as his local base of operations, and over to the semicircular console where Grin sat surrounded by keyboards and computer screens.

'What's happening?' Mosley asked.

'Nolan just opened the door into Orlov's network. Our Spyder has latched on and taken control of network security. Right about now, it should begin issuing a series of new user log-ins and passwords to some friends of mine who are going to help us out today. These new log-ins will have unlimited access and control over pieces of Orlov's computer networks. Every other user's privileges on those networks will be knocked down to read-only status.'

The window displaying the Spyder's actions showed a series of new user identities being created and E-mail messages being sent by the owners of those new identities. One of the monitors on Grin's console announced, 'You've got mail.'

Grin opened the message and scribbled down his new user name and password. He then switched to a different window on the screen and keyed the information in to a waiting log-in prompt.

'Cal, I'm in FinProm's accounting system.'

The third monitor on Grin's console began filling with text as his closest friends in the hacker community began to report in. Grin turned to study his cohorts' progress.

'Jazz is in Orlov's petrochemical company, and Hemmy says he's digging into the television stuff. Way to go! Dredd, my man, has VIO shipping by the short and curlies. Oh my – Surfgrape, I bow before your greatness.'

'What did Surfgrape do?'

'Surfgrape, bless her heart, has just broken into Orlov's Swiss bank accounts and is downloading his transaction history for the past decade. She's freezing accounts as she finds them. VIO Fin-Prom is in a world of hurt.'

'It still scares me that there are people who can do this.'

'Yeah, but aren't you glad me and my crew are on your side? Fly, my pretties, fly!' Grin shouted excitedly as updates on the electronic assault on Orlov's business empire scrolled in.

60

JULY 31

Saginaw Bay, Michigan

Dawson pored over the collection of maps and satellite photos that were strewn across the chart table of the *Sharon S*. Notations made in water-based marker indicated the positions of his men near the remote hunting cabin.

Angel had reported 'feet dry' twenty minutes earlier, transitioning from the water phase of the mission to land. Their stealthy approach from the bay up the Rifle River had apparently gone undetected by the Tangos.

Once they'd reached the shore, the SEALs had disconnected their masks from the Draeger rebreathers. A rotary valve closed off the dual hoses, preventing any contamination of the rebreather's CO_2 scrubber. Angel approached the cabin in water that varied from knee to waist deep. From their last report, Angel was in position along the levee east of the cabin.

Dawson's satellite phone, which lay near the corner of the chart table, emitted a soft, pulsating sound.

'Dawson,' he answered.

'Admiral, it's Grin. Nolan is on-line.'

'Good. Everything going okay?'

'Yeah, the connection is clean, and we've got access to all the goodies. Does it look like they're going to release Kelsey and Elli?'

'No,' Dawson replied with near absolute certainty.

Grin said nothing for a moment, finding himself at a loss for words. 'Good luck, Admiral.'

'Thanks,' Dawson replied sympathetically before ending the call.

Dawson gazed down at the charts. The cabin was situated near the shore of the bay on an elevated patch of ground surrounded by an earthen levee. Water from the river flooded the surrounding area, creating lightly wooded wetlands ideal for hunting migrating ducks and geese.

God, the two-man sniper team, had worked their way on foot to the cabin from the adjacent Ogemaw State Forest. A knoll, approximately two thousand yards from the cabin across a wide expanse of cattails and marsh grass, provided the snipers with an unobstructed view of the northern and western sides of the rustic, one-story building.

'Heaven to God,' Dawson called out.

'This is God. I read you, Heaven.'

'Say status of Halos.'

'Halos are unchanged. Repeat, Halos are unchanged.'

From God's vantage point on the knoll, the snipers had a clear view of Kelsey and Elli. Both women were in the northwestern corner bedroom, and should any move be made against them, God was in a position to put an immediate stop to it. The 'unchanged' status of the hostages meant that no move had been made to harm or release the women. Enough time had passed, in Dawson's opinion, to determine that the hostages were not going to be released.

'Say status of Tangos, God.'

'Count is five – three plus two,' the sniper answered, identifying a total of five men; three inside with the hostages, and two outside on patrol.

'I read you, God,' Dawson replied. 'Heaven to Angel.'

'Angel here,' Edwards answered. 'I read you, Heaven.'

'Halos are unchanged. Confirmed Tango count is five. Tangos are three and two. You have a green light, Angel.'

'Green light acknowledged, Heaven. Angel out.'

Dawson looked up from the charts and out the bridge windscreen. Through the thick, moisture-laden air, the shore was a distant green-brown haze. Somewhere in that haze, his men were moving.

61

JULY 31

Pine River, Michigan

A few days ago, I was in the arms of a beautiful woman in Moscow, Dima thought as he spat on the ground near the cabin. *Now, I'm in a godforsaken swamp.*

Late Saturday night, he and another ex-soldier named Ilya had been flown halfway around the world to Canada, then driven across the Blue Water Bridge into Michigan. Now he was on patrol in a swamp while recovering from the combined effects of jet lag and a hangover.

Dima swatted another of the interminable parade of mosquitoes that had tormented him throughout the past day. As he rubbed the spot on his neck where the ferocious insect had bitten him, he noticed a flash of light from across the open marsh. He studied the small hill where he'd seen the bright flare of reflected sunlight, then there was another flash.

Dima crouched low alongside the levee. He'd seen light flares like that in Afghanistan and Chechnya, and they'd always been man-made.

'Josef,' he called into his lip mike.

'*Da,*' the Georgian answered.

'It's Dima. I saw a reflection flash on a nearby

hillock, northwest of camp. Request permission to investigate.'

'Granted. Hold position until I get someone out to replace you on patrol.'

Josef knew that the reflection Dima had seen was probably nothing, but to ignore even the most mundane observation on a mission like this invited disaster.

'Ilya, take Dima's post on patrol.'

Ilya got up from the ancient couch, slung a sub-machine gun over his shoulder, and walked out the cabin's front door. When he neared the northwestern corner, Dima threw a short wave at him and crawled over the levee.

'Hey, Gorski,' Ahsan said quietly, 'I think some-one might have spotted that scope of yours.'

From beneath the lightweight camouflage tarp that concealed his prone body, Gorski pulled his face away from the telescopic sight on his sniper rifle and surveyed the area in front of him. As a two-man unit, he and Ahsan were collectively known as God because they could strike down like a bolt of lightning out of the sky.

'I see him, about ten o'clock,' Gorski replied, the long barrel of his custom-built. 50-caliber rifle defining twelve o'clock relative to their position on the knoll.

'Yep, he called out a replacement, then moved into that patch of woods. I'll keep an eye on him; just wanted to give you a heads-up.'

'I appreciate that,' Gorski replied to his protector.

310

From the knoll, Gorski lined up a shot through the front window of the room where the two hostages were being kept. He rechecked the settings on his scope, making certain he had the distance and wind adjustments dialed in to his satisfaction.

Gorski's earpiece crackled. 'Angel to God, we're moving.'

'I read you, Angel,' Gorski replied.

Gorski pulled back on the set trigger until it clicked into place. This step expended most of the energy required to fire the weapon, thus removing the slight tug induced by a cold trigger pull. At this distance, even the smallest shudder of Gorski's rifle could easily throw a shot wide of the mark. If need be, death was now just a few ounces of pressure on the hair trigger away.

Using hand gestures, Edwards put Angel into action. The squad broke up into two fire teams – the first composed of Edwards, Rodriguez, Hepburn, and Gilgallon, and the second made up of Gates, Detmer, and Darvas.

As Edwards's team clambered over the earthen levee and began moving toward the cabin, Gates took aim on the Tango patrolling near his team's position. Two shots flashed in rapid succession from Gates's venerable, government-issued 1911 Colt .45; a double tap of 230-grain ball ammo drilled a hole the size of a half dollar in the Tango's forehead. The man's head snapped backward from the impact; the rest of his body followed, and he landed with a muffled thump on the ground.

A burst of automatic-weapons fire shattered the glass of a window in one of the cabin's back rooms. Detmer answered with a fusillade from his .50-caliber machine gun that splintered the aging clapboard siding and removed both sashes of the double-hung window.

Protected by Detmer's punishing cover fire, Edwards's team reached the cabin's back door. Rodriguez kicked it in with such force that the lockset ripped free of the wooden stile.

Edwards tossed a flash-bang grenade through the cabin door. The SEALs shielded their eyes as the grenade exploded inside with a nonlethal combination of a blinding flash of light and a sonic assault that knocked most victims senseless. The SEALs then poured into the smoke-filled cabin, each man training both his attention and the barrel of his weapon on a pie-shaped wedge of space that expanded in front of him. The overlapping wedges were each man's field of fire, and each was responsible for what happened in his lethal zone.

The main room was clear. Edwards motioned for Gilgallon and Hepburn to check the rooms on one side while he and Rodriguez cleared the room on the other.

Josef had just zipped up his pants after relieving himself when he heard Misha firing from the rear bedroom and the back door crashing open.

'Fuck!' Josef cursed, realizing that they were under attack.

He pulled the 9-mm pistol out of his shoulder holster and began counting slowly, waiting for the inevitable explosion of concussion grenade – a device he had used many times to immobilize people he'd been sent to capture rather than kill. Three slow seconds passed, then the wood-frame cabin shuddered from the grenade's sonic assault.

The noise was still echoing off the plaster walls when Josef bolted from the bathroom, across the short hall, and into the far bedroom, where the hostages were being kept. Both women were still tied to their chairs, frightened but apparently unaffected by the deafening blast. Josef swept the room, looking for any armed targets; it was clear. Then, without hesitation, he raised his pistol and took aim at Elli.

Gorski saw the bedroom door fly open as a swarthy black-haired Tango entered the room where the Halos were being kept. With his pistol held chest high in a two-handed grip, the man swept the room from left to right. Then he turned his pistol toward the Halos. Gorski gently squeezed the hair trigger. With a satisfying crack, the .50-caliber round erupted from the barrel in a blast of expanding superheated gas.

Most of what had been Josef's head splattered against the long wall of the room in thousands of tiny bits of bone fragments and gore. The pistol, which he had aimed directly at Elli's face at point-blank range, jerked upward as Gorski's round slammed home.

The bullet intended to end Elli's life lightly grazed the top of her head, scorching a narrow groove in the thin layer of skin on her skull. Elli fell back when Josef's pistol fired; the chair she was lashed to tipped against the twin bed. Josef's nearly headless body collapsed sideways as if flung toward the doorway by an unseen hand.

'Elli!' Kelsey screamed as the elderly woman slumped in the inclined chair. Blood seeped out of her wound, drenching her gray-white hair with a bright crimson sheen.

Rodriguez caught a blur of motion in the hallway; someone had run from a room on one side of the hall to the room on the opposite side, where the hostages were. He held up his hand to let Edwards know that he'd seen at least one Tango. With Rodriguez providing cover, Edwards moved down the hall, positioning himself to cover Rodriguez as the point man leapfrogged past him toward the bedroom door.

Edwards heard a thundering crack inside the room, then a bloody spray exploded out of the open doorway. 'God, was that you?' Edwards asked into his lip mike.

'Roger, Angel. Tango with Halos is down,' Gorski responded as he slid back the bolt and chambered another round.

The Tango who'd taken over perimeter patrol from his comrade was now running back to the cabin. Gorski lined up the crosshairs on the back of the man's head and fired. The view through the scope briefly went out of focus as a cloud of hot gas from the barrel floated across Gorski's line of sight. In the distance, he saw the Tango crumple to the ground, dead.

'Tango in front of cabin is down,' Gorski announced with the emotional detachment of a surgeon excising a tumor.

Rodriguez and Edwards filled the bedroom doorway, each quickly surveying the room. Edwards sidestepped with his back to the wall, moving toward the corner of the room, where he'd have a clear view of the concealed side of the bed.

'Clear,' Edwards shouted from the corner.

Rodriguez holstered his weapon, stepped over the dead Tango, and moved to Elli. He placed two fingers on the side of her neck.

'She's alive,' he told the other man.

'One Tango down. One Halo wounded,' Edwards announced.

'One Tango down back here. All clear,' Hepburn called back. 'Corpsman is on the way.'

Rodriguez was cutting Elli's bonds when Gilgallon entered the room. The two SEALs carefully lifted Elli off the chair and laid her unconscious form on the twin bed. Using his k-bar knife, Edwards freed Kelsey.

Gilgallon checked Elli's eyes; both were responsive to light. He then inspected the bloody wound near the crown of her head.

'Will she be all right?' Kelsey asked.

'The wound's superficial; it should heal up with minimal scarring. Looks worse than it really is.'

The corpsman then cracked open a small packet of smelling salts and held it under Elli's nose – her eyes immediately sprang open.

'*Vat?* I? Elli said, startled, grasping for words.

'Easy, ma'am,' Gilgallon said calmly. 'You've

315

got a nasty scratch, but you're going to be fine. Just relax and let me patch you up.'

'Four Tangos down,' Edwards reported. 'Anyone got a line on number five?'

Dima was slowly working his way through the ankle-deep mire of the wetlands when he heard the sounds of gunfire from both the cabin and the knoll. An explosion shattered several windows in the cabin's central room, followed by a cloud of thick, white smoke. Then he watched as Ilya's dash to the cabin ended when a single round fired by a very skilled sniper obliterated the man's skull.

'*Yop t'voi yo mat,*' Dima muttered, the all-purpose Russian profanity fitting both his mood and the situation.

As he watched the cabin, three men dressed head to toe in black scaled the levee and quickly cleared the front of the cabin for targets. Dima's remaining comrades appeared unable to offer any effective resistance to the assault team.

Dima crouched down into the swampy water.

If I can just keep out of sight, he thought, *maybe I'll get out of here alive.*

With his peripheral vision, he caught some movement to his right. He turned in time to see a lightly built man rise out of the water, leveling an HK MP5 assault rifle.

He turned, but before he could bring his weapon around, Ahsan perforated his chest with a pair of two-round bursts. Dima continued to rotate on his right foot, spiraling down into the water.

'Tango five is down,' Ahsan reported as he watched the man drop facedown into the shallow water.

Inside the cabin, Gates holstered his pistol and walked back to the bedroom where Kelsey and Elli had spent the past few days in captivity.

'Max?' Kelsey said when she saw him in the doorway. 'What are you doing here?'

'U.S. Navy SEALs at your service, ma'am,' Gates replied. 'Compliments of Rear Admiral Jack Dawson.'

'Is Nolan with you?'

'No, but not because he didn't want to be. All the guys here, except Lieutenant Edwards over there, served with Nolan. We promised him we'd get you and Miss Vital back safe and sound. You okay?'

'Other than a little rope burn around my wrists and ankles, I'm fine.'

'How's your friend?'

'Your medic says Elli will be fine, just a superficial wound on her head.'

'Chief,' Edwards called out, 'we got all five.'

'Hoo-yah!' Gates replied.

'Hepburn, give Heaven our sit rep,' Edwards ordered.

On the bridge of the *Sharon S,* Dawson took the news with a mixture of pride and relief.

'Bravo Zulu, Angel. Heaven out,' Dawson said, acknowledging the squad's situation report.

'What's the word, Admiral?' Martin asked anxiously.

'The news for the most part is good. Kelsey's fine, and Elli suffered only minor injuries. The corpsman is patching her up right now, and we'll get a doctor to look her over ASAP. Our men took out all the Tangos and came through without a scratch.'

'Do you want me to move us in closer to shore now?' Harsen Smith asked.

'That would be fine, sir,' Dawson answered.

Dawson then picked up his satellite phone and dialed Grin's direct line at MARC. Grin picked up before the first ring faded.

'Grin here.'

'Grin, it's Dawson. We freed the hostages. Pass the word.'

'Gladly, Admiral.'

'Mosley, they freed the hostages!' Grin shouted as he cradled the receiver. 'Kelsey and Elli are fine.'

'Great! I'll contact the Russians,' Mosley said. 'Let Nolan know.'

'I'm already typing.'

62

JULY 31

Moscow, Russia

Cooper sat patiently in Orlov's office. Once the deal had been struck and Kilkenny had left to instruct Avvakum on using the decoding program, there was little left to do but wait.

In the twenty minutes since Kilkenny had departed, Leskov remained at his post by the door, distracted from his watch over Cooper only by the status reports he received from the security teams posted around the building. Each time a report came in, Leskov cupped a hand over the earpiece and cocked his head slightly – a habit rooted in years of combat.

The phone on Orlov's desk rang, and he answered it. Cooper watched, hoping to pick up clues from Orlov as to what he was being told. The man's brow creased, as if some external pressure were trying to hold the thoughts inside his head. Whatever the news, the look on Orlov's face told Cooper that it was unexpected.

Orlov tilted his head, cradling the phone with his shoulder, and turned around to face the computer on the credenza behind his desk. He pressed down on the keyboard hard enough for Cooper to hear the impact.

'Oksanna,' he summoned without turning away from the video display.

Zoshchenko rose and quickly moved to his side. Orlov struck a few more keys, his growing anger becoming more evident.

Orlov looked up at Zoshchenko, puzzled; she shook her head in reply, offering no answer as to what they were seeing on the monitor.

'I don't care how you do it, just stop it!' Orlov shouted into the phone before slamming down the handset. 'Dmitri, we've been shut out of our computer networks. Have Avvakum's guard find out what Kilkenny is doing. Now!'

'*Da*,' Leskov said before calling out the order into the thin microphone that curved from his earpiece to the corner of his mouth.

'What is that?' Avvakum asked when a tiny animated blinking red light appeared in the lower-right corner of the screen on Kilkenny's laptop.

'A message.'

Kilkenny clicked on the blinking light, and a small window appeared in the center of his screen. Two lines of text scrolled up from the bottom of the window.

GOOD NEWS: BOTH HOSTAGES
RESCUED!
BAD NEWS: SOMEBODY HAS NOTICED
OUR HACK. HEADS UP!

Kilkenny smiled, relieved.

'What does this mean?' Avvakum asked, becoming anxious.

Kilkenny looked at her and saw the fear rendered plainly on her face. He reached over and grasped her hand.

'What this message means is that two good people are now safe and that Orlov's people have noticed something terribly wrong happening inside their computers.'

Kilkenny turned back to his laptop and closed the window. As the window disappeared from the screen, Avvakum's oversize guard opened the door to her office and shouted something in Russian at Kilkenny.

'I don't understand what he's saying,' Kilkenny said to Avvakum while keeping his eyes on the Russian.

'He wants to know what the fuck you are doing,' Avvakum said, translating the guard's demand literally.

'Tell him I'm decoding information for his boss.'

As Avvakum translated his response, Kilkenny waved the guard over, motioning with his open hands at the screen to emphasize that this is where he should look. The bulky guard moved around Avvakum's desk to get a better view. One half of the screen showed a matrix of Wolff's encrypted characters; the other displayed a slowly growing string of mathematical formulas and German text.

As the guard leaned close to inspect the laptop, Kilkenny reached up with both hands, grabbed two large clumps of the man's greasy brown hair, and pulled down. In the same motion, Kilkenny sprang up from his chair, swung his right leg back, and then drove his knee up into the guard's face. Driven in by Kilkenny's *hiza geri* knee kick, the guard's lip mike tore the corner of his mouth and dug a groove into his cheek before it snapped free of the ear-piece. Blood flowed freely from the man's battered nose and mouth.

The guard groaned, dazed, as Kilkenny tilted the man's head slightly, then quickly wrenched it as if he were unscrewing it from a socket. The stack of vertebrae that formed a shallow curve in the guard's neck collapsed, the twisting motion too quick for the neck muscles to counteract.

'You killed him?' Avvakum gasped out.

'It's not like I had much choice in the matter. Orlov wants us dead.'

Kilkenny laid the guard on the floor, then inspected the damage to his leg. Two of the man's teeth had ripped through his khakis and were now imbedded in his knee. Avvakum winced as he pulled the two incisors out and tossed them in the wastebasket.

'Don't worry, I'll be fine,' Kilkenny said as he inspected the two punctures in his skin. 'I just hope he had all his shots.'

Kilkenny then grabbed the guard's body underneath the arms, dragged it out of Avvakum's office, and laid it down in the center of the empty lab.

'Why did you put the body out here? Won't the others see what you've done?'

'I hope so. This guy is my scarecrow; if his comrades see him lying here lifeless, maybe they'll think twice before coming in here.'

Kilkenny stripped off the guard's shoulder holster, strapped it on himself, and quickly checked

322

the weapon. He then patted the guard down and found two more full clips of ammunition.

'Let's get back in your office,' Kilkenny said as he pocketed the extra clips.

Once inside, Kilkenny stood in front of his laptop computer. 'I guess I can shut this down now.'

He closed the translation program, powered his laptop down, and disconnected the cables. 'Can I ask you a question?' Kilkenny said as he shut the laptop and slipped it back into his briefcase.

'Certainly.'

'Why did you send me that fragment of Sandstrom's research?'

'I am a scientist, not a thief. I wanted to know the truth.'

'Sometimes the truth isn't pretty,' Kilkenny replied, turning to face her, 'and very soon it's gonna get downright ugly. Stay close to me, and just maybe we'll both get through this alive.'

63

JULY 31

Moscow, Russia

Out of the west, a matte gray Mil Mi-38 helicopter raced over Moscow's outer periphery. It roared over the VDNKh, as the All-Russian Exhibition Center was known, and crossed Prospekt Mira. The pilot changed the pitch on the

Mil's six rotating blades, adjusted the throttle on the twin TVD-300 turboshaft engines, and brought the ship into a thundering hover over the VIO FinProm building's flat roof. Ballast aggregate flew out in all directions, propelled by the downward thrust of the helicopter, and hailed onto the ground below.

The royal blue flag that so proudly bore Orlov's golden double eagle snapped crazily in the rotors' gale-force blast; the fabric around the flag's eyelets quickly tore free, and the shredded emblem fell into the street.

As soon as the Mil parked itself over the building, doors on both sides of the craft slid open and armed men in black ninja suits rappelled down onto the roof. The blue-and-white cars of the Moscow Militsia suddenly appeared, choking off Prospekt Mira and all secondary streets around Orlov's building. Two large black trucks pulled up, one at each end of the long slab of a building, and disgorged two additional elements of the Alpha assault force. Three coordinated, well-armed teams of fifteen men poured into the building, routing Orlov's perimeter security as they pressed their attack.

Orlov's office reverberated with a deep rumbling like a continuous explosion of thunder.

'Victor!' Zoshchenko screamed, afraid.

'Dmitri,' Orlov shouted over the noise, 'what is going on?'

'Government forces are attacking the building,' Victor Ivanovich Leskov replied, piecing together the jumble of reports flooding through his

324

earpiece. 'My men are moving into defensive positions. You should evacuate.'

Of all the people in the office, only Cooper seemed unaffected by the mounting chaos. The aging spy leaned back into the sofa and folded his hands over his stomach.

'I'd surrender if I were you,' Cooper said. 'It's your best chance of staying alive:

Orlov turned and saw Cooper sitting as serenely as a Buddha. Sporadic bursts of gunfire could now be heard.

'You are responsible for this!' Orlov shouted.

'I can't take all the credit. You have a lot of very powerful enemies.'

Pistol in hand, Leskov ran to Orlov. 'You must leave, immediately.'

'Give me that,' Orlov barked as he took the pistol from Leskov's hand.

Without a second's hesitation, Orlov raised the Glock and fired three shots into Cooper's chest.

Cooper slumped back on the sofa. Blood poured out of his chest with each beat of his heart. Though pained, Cooper managed to lock eyes with Orlov.

'Fuck your mother, Victor Ivanovich,' Cooper said, his voice beginning to fail. 'You're finished.'

Orlov shuddered at the pronouncement but said nothing. An explosion sent tremors through the building. Zoshchenko ran up to Orlov and grasped his shoulders.

'Victor, they're going to kill us!' Zoshchenko screamed. 'We *have* to surrender! You have money; you can make a deal to save us!'

Orlov looked into Zoshchenko's teary eyes with

disgust, then squeezed the Glock's trigger. Zoshchenko staggered back, and he fired again into her chest – she collapsed onto the floor. Orlov handed the pistol back to Leskov.

'How long can your men hold the building?'

'Ten, maybe fifteen minutes.'

'Long enough. Let's go,' Orlov said, leading the way out through the office's private exit.

Seven Alphas eliminated the two men guarding the main hallway and then entered Orlov's executive suite. They found Cooper slumped on the couch and Zoshchenko lying on the floor.

'Corpsman!' one of the Alphas called out.

The corpsman placed two fingers on Cooper's neck.

'This one's dead.'

He then moved over to the woman.

'Pulse is weak and she's lost a lot of blood, but she's still alive.'

64

JULY 31

Moscow, Russia

Near the center of the building, adjacent to the main vertical riser for electrical and communications wiring, Arkady Malik sat in front of a wall of small black-and-white video monitors, each displaying a feed from a closed-circuit camera mounted somewhere in or around the building. Malik watched nervously as several of the monitors relayed images of the battles taking place not far from where he sat.

Leskov punched in his access code and opened the door to the building's security center. He and Orlov jogged down the short hallway, past a flush steel door and frame, and turned into the room where Malik sat. 'Malik,' Leskov shouted, 'how's the perimeter holding?'

'Our men have fallen back from the main entry points on the first floor and from the roof access points.' Malik played the keypad in front of him like a piano, cycling manually through all the available cameras, both inside and outside the building. 'We've lost about a third of the first and fifth floors but still control all of floors two, three, and four.'

Several of the monitors showed some of Leskov's men exchanging gunfire with men dressed in black ninja suits.

'Fuck, it's Alpha,' Leskov cursed. 'Victor, my men will make them pay for every square meter of the building, but it's only a matter of time. We are outmanned and out-gunned.'

'What is the status of the tunnel?' Orlov asked.

Malik brought up different camera views on a bank of four monitors. The first displayed a large steel vault door mounted flush to a concrete wall. The second showed the back side of the door from a distance inside a concrete tunnel wide enough for three people to walk abreast. On the third and fourth, Orlov saw the far end of the tunnel, where it reached the Metro's Chelobitevo Line tunnel running beneath Prospekt Mira.

The workmen renovating Orlov's building had discovered the abandoned tunnel while replacing outdated utility feeders. Though not shown on any of their drawings, the tunnel had been used for material storage during the construction of the Metro line, then abandoned once the work was completed. Orlov had the tunnel extended beneath the building, where it terminated at the flush steel door.

'Tunnel is clear on both ends,' Malik responded. 'Show me Avvakum's lab,' Orlov demanded impatiently. Malik typed in another number. The static on the one large monitor was replaced by an image of an empty lab space. Using the thumb-dial controls for pan-tilt zoom operation, Malik swung the camera around and adjusted it to zoom in on the doorway that led to the lab's office suite. The body of Avvakum's guard lay prone on the floor near the center of the lab.

Leskov slammed his fist into the desktop with such force that Malik jumped back, startled.

'The incompetent fool! I told him Kilkenny was a dangerous man and that he shouldn't take his eyes off him. Now Kilkenny is armed.'

'Are Kilkenny and Avvakum still in the lab?' Orlov asked.

'*Da,* Victor Ivanovich,' Malik replied. 'I haven't seen anyone in the corridors.'

'Dmitri, take Malik and kill them both.'

'Gladly.'

'I'll wait for you here. When you get back, we'll

use the tunnel.'

'Malik, what's left in the armory?'

'A few pistols and a couple of Krinkovs.'

'Get them,' Leskov ordered. He then handed Orlov his pistol and a spare clip of ammunition. 'Take this. Keep an eye on these monitors. If Alpha breaches our defenses before I get back, go.'

'Good luck, Dmitri.'

'To us both, Victor Ivanovich.'

Malik handed Leskov one of the Krinkov AKS-74U submachine guns from the rack and two spare clips. Leskov quickly checked over the weapon and flipped off the safety.

'Let's go.'

65

JULY 31

Moscow, Russia

Kilkenny began rearranging the furniture in Avvakum's office to create a defensive nest. Already, he heard the sounds of gunfire and knew that he needed to keep Avvakum safe until the battle was over.

'Lara, whatever happens, don't come out of here until I tell you to. All right?'

'I understand,' she replied, curling herself down behind the protective wall of furniture.

Kilkenny went back into the lab and began looking through the pile of boxes and equipment that was stored in the far corner – most of which had been stolen from Sandstrom. It didn't take long to locate the three-inch-thick stainless-steel top of Sandstrom's vibration isolation table.

After removing the boxes that were stacked on top, Kilkenny grabbed two of the table's legs and dragged it back to the doorway that led to the suite of offices where Avvakum hid. He flipped the table onto its side, then pushed it until one edge touched the lab wall to form a defensive barrier.

Kilkenny crouched behind the makeshift barricade, peering over the top at the two doors that led from the lab into the hallway. From where he was positioned, he had a wide triangular field of fire. He pulled the spare clips from his pocket and set them within reach on the floor.

As they neared the lab, Leskov pressed himself against the wall to reduce his profile. Malik followed his lead. The two men slid along the wall until they reached the first of the two lab doors. Inching forward slowly, Leskov peered through the door's glass panel. He saw on the opposite side of the room a large metal table lying on its side in front of the suite entryway.

'Dmitri' – Orlov's voice filled Leskov's ear – 'Kilkenny has built a barricade in front of the lab's offices.'

'Understood,' Leskov replied. He then turned to Malik. 'Did you hear that?'

Malik nodded.

'I'm going to double back and move into the empty space on the other side of the lab. When I'm in position, I'll signal you to fire on that barricade. I'm going to attack from the rear.'

'There's no door back there?' Malik replied.

'Not yet, there isn't.'

Leskov slipped around Malik and headed toward the area of the second floor still under renovation.

Leskov worked his way through the poorly lit space behind the lab to where a wall framed in steel studs carved out a large chunk of the space. The wall that defined the perimeter of the lab was finished only on the lab side; the studs, wiring, and other services were still visible from where Leskov stood. He measured off the distance in his head, working his way around to what he believed was an empty office in the lab suite.

'Now, Malik!' he signaled.

In reply, Leskov heard an explosion of gunfire through the newly built walls.

The sudden burst of gunfire caught Kilkenny off guard. He hadn't noticed anyone moving in the hallway. In response, Kilkenny randomly fired a couple of shots at the door, just to keep the shooter pinned back in the hallway. A short burst of four rounds answered back, hammering into the slab of stainless steel. Malik fired again, this time high over the top of Kilkenny's barricade. The high-velocity rounds ripped through the wall behind him, grazing the top of Avvakum's desk and imbedding themselves in the back wall of her office. Avvakum screamed as the bullets flew all around her.

'You okay back there?' Kilkenny shouted after firing back at Malik.

'*Nyet! I* want this to stop!' Avvakum screamed back in tears.

'You and me both,' Kilkenny replied.

Leskov stood about two meters from the wall and emptied the entire clip of the Krinkov into it, drawing an elongated oval on the gypsum wallboard. He then popped the empty magazine out of the weapon, slipped in a fresh one, and kicked the wall in the center of the perforated oval. The wallboard snapped and clattered onto the floor of the empty office.

Kilkenny turned when he heard the burst of gunfire behind him, and saw several rounds ricochet into the suite's hallway.

'Shit!' he growled.

Another burst from the far door slammed into the steel barricade. When the firing paused, Kilkenny rose up, aimed at the wall beside the far door, and emptied the Glock. The tightly clustered rounds pounded through the wallboard like a hammer, opening a hole wide enough for the last of Kilkenny's shots to tear through with full force. A loud moan answered Kilkenny's barrage, followed by a brief glimpse, through the door's shattered glass, of someone collapsing in the hall.

'Keep down, Lara!' Kilkenny shouted as he discarded the empty clip, slammed one of the spares into the Glock, and leapt to the opposite side of the barricade.

Leskov stepped out of the office, firing wildly down the short corridor. He aimed low, and on full auto, the Krinkov was nearly empty before he realized that Kilkenny was in midair jumping over the protective slab of steel.

As he hurdled the table, Kilkenny turned and aimed the Glock at Leskov. A shock of fiery pain struck his right forearm like a blistering whip when he fired and the double tap intended for Leskov's chest flew wide of the mark. Struck numb, Kilkenny lost his grip on the pistol, which clattered to the floor on the opposite side of the tabletop.

Leskov cautiously advanced on Kilkenny's position, slipping his last magazine into the Krinkov. 'Malik,' he said into the lip mike, 'Kilkenny is on your side of the barricade.'

No answer. Leskov cautiously moved farther down the hall. On the floor near the table, he saw the Glock Kilkenny had taken from Avvakum's guard and a few droplets of blood. Leskov neared the barricade, the Krinkov cradled in his right arm, his left hand wrapped around the barrel grip for support.

The bullet that ricocheted off the steel tabletop dug a deep groove in the underside of Kilkenny's right forearm. The wound stung, but he ignored the pain and the bleeding. He crouched low as he scanned the edges of the table, his weight balanced on his tightly folded right leg. His left leg was extended full length parallel to the tabletop – in this position, he could easily shift from one leg to the other without lifting his head above the barricade. He cocked his left arm at eye level in front of him in preparation to block an attack from above.

Kilkenny caught sight of the Krinkov's short barrel near the top of the barricade. When six inches of the stocky assault rifle were visible, he sprang up and struck the barrel of the weapon with his left elbow, pushing it away from him. Rising up, he coiled his left arm around the Krinkov like a snake until he grasped Leskov's left wrist from below.

Leskov squeezed the trigger as Kilkenny trapped the Krinkov between his arm and torso. The barrel flared red hot, vibrating against Kilkenny's ribs as a rapid series of explosions blazed within its milled steel barrel.

Continuing with his upward momentum, Kilkenny twisted his torso counterclockwise, pulling the erupting weapon forward and Leskov off balance. Kilkenny's right arm swung fluidly with the rotation of his upper body, the palm of his hand held flat in search of a target.

He struck at Leskov's head, ramming the heel of his palm into Leskov's face with such force that the Russian's nose folded over against his right cheek. Still pulling Leskov forward, Kilkenny used his elbow to cave in Leskov's eye socket.

Leskov howled in pain. Coiled like a spring, Kilkenny snapped back in the other direction, yanking Leskov over the barricade and driving him headlong into the vinyl-tile floor.

Holding tight on the Krinkov, Leskov pulled

the weapon free as he fell. As soon as he hit the floor, Leskov pointed the barrel upward and drove it into the soft tissue of Kilkenny's left armpit. Kilkenny recoiled, a numbness like an electrical discharge racing from shoulder to fingertip. Leskov dug the barrel in deeper, wedging it in the underside of the shoulder joint, separating the bones of Kilkenny's shoulder. With his left arm now free, Leskov rolled clear as Kilkenny fell back, clutching his damaged limb.

Leskov clambered to his feet, keeping some distance between himself and Kilkenny, took aim with the weapon, and pulled the trigger.

Click.

Nothing. Furious, Leskov grasped the Krinkov, swung it up over his head like a club, and charged Kilkenny.

Kilkenny backed away, protecting his left shoulder. As Leskov charged, Kilkenny slipped to his right, moving out of Leskov's path and into his blind spot. Crouching with all his weight balanced on his right foot, he snapped a devastating kick with his left leg into Leskov's groin. Leskov doubled over, screaming an unintelligible epithet; the Krinkov clattered to the ground.

From the same position, Kilkenny folded his leg back, thigh against abdomen, and kicked again, this time snapping the outside edge of his foot straight into the side of Leskov's knee. The joint buckled, and Leskov lost his balance, toppling over in front of Kilkenny. As Leskov fell, Kilkenny reached out, grabbed a handful of his hair, and drove the Russian's head into the floor.

He reset his stance, ready to strike again as

Leskov lay motionless. In the corridor, the sound of gunfire drew closer; then, after a fierce exchange, it stopped. Two Alphas stepped over Malik's body in the corridor and entered the lab with weapons trained on Kilkenny. Kilkenny gingerly raised his arms in surrender.

'Kilkenny!' Fydorov shouted as he followed the Alphas into the lab.

Fydorov said something in Russian, and the Alphas turned their weapons away from Kilkenny. One of them quickly checked Leskov for a pulse, then turned to Fydorov and shook his head.

'So, at least you're still alive,' Fydorov said.

'Yeah, so's Avvakum. She's holed up in her office. How's Cooper?'

'Dead, I'm sorry to say. We found him with Orlov's mistress, Zoshchenko. She was shot as well but may yet live.'

'What about Orlov?' Kilkenny asked as he retrieved the Glock and set it in the holster.

Fydorov shook his head. 'Haven't found him yet.'

Kilkenny groaned as he rolled his head in a wide circle, stretching the tightened muscles in his neck. His shoulder ached. Then he noticed another of the mirrored half domes in the ceiling near the corner of the lab.

'Security camera. Have you taken the security office yet?'

'*Da,* just a moment ago.'

'There are cameras all over this building, inside and out. If he's still here, we should be able to spot him.'

336

66

JULY 31

Moscow, Russia

After pulling Avvakum free of the makeshift barricade in her office and placing her under the protection of the Alphas, Kilkenny and Fydorov worked their way down to the security office on the first floor. Though they still heard occasional bursts of gunfire, the assault on Orlov's building was nearly over.

Several corpses lay where they had fallen in the corridors. Visual evidence of the intense battle for the first floor – spent shell casings, bullet-scarred walls, and scorch marks left by flash-bang stun grenades – was strewn everywhere, and the air was heavy with the acrid scent of recent gunfire. Corpsmen were carefully removing the wounded Alphas, and a triage had been established at the building's loading dock. Gear removed from the injured Alphas lay in a pile by the wall.

'Here, put this on,' Fydorov said as he handed Kilkenny a black, Kevlar-plated vest from the pile. 'This way my people won't think you're one of Orlov's men and fuck with you.'

'Will do,' Kilkenny said as he carefully worked the vest around his injured shoulder.

They cut through the loading dock and made their way to the security office. Along the concrete wall, Kilkenny saw a flush stainless-steel door and frame. The door had no visible hardware except for a keypad mounted on the wall to the left.

'That a vault?' he asked.

Fydorov threw a quick glance at the door. 'Could be. We'll open it up later.'

Kilkenny and Fydorov passed the armory and entered the monitoring room. Banks of small, black-and-white closed-circuit video screens filled the wall above the operator console. Rows of numbered buttons lined the console, each tied to a remote camera, in addition to the joysticks and sliders that allowed the operator to pan, tilt, and zoom the cameras. Kilkenny studied the monitors – black figures passed across a few of them, but the rest showed empty corridors and offices.

An Alpha entered the security suite, walked up to Fydorov, and said something in Russian. Fydorov nodded and turned to Kilkenny.

'At the moment, I am needed elsewhere. Stay here, I'll be back in a minute.'

After Fydorov left with the Alpha, Kilkenny started punching the numbered buttons and cycling through a series of preprogrammed views. The first set of buttons covered the building's exterior, rooftop, and entry points. He left those on, as they were the only way in and out of the building, then began looking at the interior camera views on the remaining monitors.

He visually swept through the building –

section by section, floor by floor – but Orlov was nowhere to be seen.

'He's got to be hiding somewhere,' Kilkenny mused as he punched up the next camera series.

Four monitors flickered as linked cameras relayed images of their remote locations. The eerily lit images on two of the screens showed a long, narrow concrete passageway.

The fourth monitor showed a bright flash of light approaching the camera from a distance. The camera shuddered as the bright light quickly passed underneath, followed by a strobelike pattern of light and dark.

'That looks like a subway.' Kilkenny studied the image intently.

He turned his attention back to the previous series. Using the controls, he maneuvered the cameras and swept the length of the passageway. Zooming deep with the second camera, he detected some movement. A figure came into focus – Orlov, with a flashlight in one hand and a pistol in the other.

'Gotcha! But how'd you get in there?'

Kilkenny looked at the first monitor, which showed a corridor. He swiveled the camera and found that it provided an excellent view of the vault door just outside the security suite.

He ran to the loading dock, but Fydorov was nowhere in sight.

'Shit!'

Kilkenny searched through the pile of vests and assault gear until he found a coil of ribbon charge and a detonator, then ran back to the vault door. Carefully, he uncoiled the white ribbon of explosive and taped it over the seam between the door and frame where the locking bolts should be. He then set the detonator, activated it, and ran for cover in the security office.

The five-second detonator fired, igniting the linear explosive charge. The blast rang loudly off the concrete walls, and a cloud of smoke filled the short corridor. The blast compressed the edge of the door as it peeled the thick steel skin back and away from the rigid metal core.

Kilkenny found the door hanging ajar, its torn metal edges still hot. As he nudged it open, one of the actuated bolts fell out of the jamb and clattered onto the floor.

Beyond the door he found a narrow flight of stairs. Kilkenny drew out the Glock and carefully began his descent into the darkness below.

Orlov was three-quarters of the way down the hundred-meter tunnel when the eerie, subterranean silence was replaced with an ear-splitting roar of concussive energy. The blast knocked him to his knees, and he dropped both his flashlight and his pistol. His ears rang as if someone were boring through them with a drill into his skull.

He shook off the dizziness and groped around on the floor. He found the flashlight first and tested the switch. Nothing. He blindly twisted the screw fittings as tight as they would go and tried the switch again – a dim light shone. He aimed the faint beam on the floor and searched for the pistol.

Kilkenny reached the bottom of the stairs and, other than the glow of light from the doorway above, was enveloped in darkness. In the distance, about seventy-five meters ahead of him, he saw a faint illumination.

'Orlov!' he shouted, his voice echoing down the long concrete passageway.

The summons thundered around Orlov, breaking through the high-pitched ringing in his ears. He glanced back down the tunnel but saw nothing in the darkness.

'Orlov!' the voice boomed out again, getting closer. 'Surrender!'

Orlov reached down, picked up the Glock, and fired.

In the darkness, Kilkenny moved carefully in a crouch along the tunnel wall as Orlov fired recklessly down the darkened passageway. He focused his attention on the dark space between the dim light and the flashes of Orlov's pistol fire. His body ached, both arms throbbing.

'Fuck this!' Kilkenny cursed, and fired his weapon.

Orlov shrieked as the bullet ripped through the thin metal housing of the flashlight, shredding the device in his hands. Kilkenny then broke into an open sprint, screaming like a madman. Muzzle flashes from Kilkenny's Glock illuminated the tunnel like a strobe as he closed in on Orlov.

Orlov cowered under the sonic assault of gunfire and Kilkenny's deafening *kiai*, lying on the

341

floor as bullets flew over his head. Terror gripped him, and then he felt a warm, liquid sensation around his abdomen and thighs.

Kilkenny dove the last two meters headfirst, landing squarely on Orlov's back. The two men slid across the concrete floor before the friction of the rough surface brought them to a stop.

'Move, and I'll kill you,' Kilkenny warned, more a promise than a threat.

He propped himself up, grinding his knee into the center of Orlov's back. He then pulled the pistol from Orlov's quivering grip and tossed it down the tunnel.

'I have money,' Orlov said feebly.

'What?'

'Money. I have money, lots of it. I'll give you ten million dollars to let me go.'

'How the fuck are you going to get me ten million dollars?'

'I have accounts, in Switzerland. Personal accounts,' Orlov rambled nervously. 'I can wire the money anywhere you like, with a phone call.'

'You *had* Swiss accounts.'

'What?'

Kilkenny placed the barrel of his Glock at the base of Orlov's skull, then leaned close to the oligarch's ear.

'Everything you owned is gone. Your companies. Your investments. Your numbered Swiss accounts. Your real estate. Every fucking thing in your billion-dollar portfolio is gone, and I'm the guy who took it from you. Hell, the only thing I didn't get is the change in your pockets.'

Kilkenny pressed his pistol deeper into the flesh

of Orlov's neck.

'You're going to kill me?' Orlov shrieked.

'A coup de grâce *would* be appropriate, don't you think, considering what you did to Sandstrom and Paramo and a lot of other people who had the misfortune of coming into contact with a disgusting parasite like you.'

A bright flashlight flooded the tunnel.

'Kilkenny!' a voice shouted from the far end.

'The Alphas are coming, and they seem to want you alive. I guess I'd better finish this now.'

Kilkenny leaned back, the Glock still poised to blow Orlov's head open.

'Kilkenny!' Fydorov shouted, fast approaching – more footsteps behind him. 'Let us handle Orlov!'

As Kilkenny squeezed back on the trigger, he shifted the barrel of the Glock two inches to the right. A burning flash erupted from the pistol as Kilkenny's last round ripped through the top of Orlov's ear, struck the floor, and ricocheted into the black distance of the tunnel.

'You're in luck, Orlov. I missed.'

Orlov fainted, and a small pool of blood formed beside his head. Kilkenny stood as Fydorov and two Alphas arrived.

'Did you kill him?' Fydorov asked, looking down at the motionless form.

'Not my style. I'll let the courts deal with this scumbag. Do you still have gulags over here?'

'I'm certain an appropriate home can be found for him.' Fydorov turned to his men. 'Get him out of here.'

'I'm glad you figured out where I went,' Kilkenny said.

'That little explosion you set off left no doubt. Come on, let's get your injuries taken care of.'

67

AUGUST 1

Moscow, Russia

A young FSB officer led Kilkenny through the corridors of Lubyanka, as the former offices of the Rossiya Insurance Company had been known since Lenin's secret police commandeered the building in 1918. After the assault on Orlov's building, Kilkenny was taken to a private hospital for treatment of his injuries, then discharged and returned to his hotel for the night. The next morning after breakfast, he was escorted to Lubyanka for questioning regarding the Orlov affair. His interrogation was merely a matter of courtesy.

'You are finally here. Good, have a seat,' Fydorov said with a smile as Kilkenny entered his office. 'That will be all, Lieutenant.'

The officer snapped a crisp salute, turned on his heel, and departed down the corridor.

'How is your arm?' Fydorov asked.

'Fine. The docs say it's just a separation; I have to keep it in a sling for a couple of weeks. They say I might have some tendonitis in the joint.'

344

'I am relieved that your injuries weren't more severe.' Fydorov's manner grew more somber. 'I have received a message from our President. On behalf of the Russian people, he extends our gratitude to both you and Bart Cooper for your assistance in bringing Orlov and his associates to justice.'

'I guess the appropriate thing to say would be *pazhálsta*.' Kilkenny then laughed.

'What do you find amusing?'

'Nothing, really. It just struck me a little odd that, after everything that's happened, I can be thanked for my "assistance" in this matter. It sounds like I changed a flat tire for the guy.'

A toothy grin transformed Fydorov's stern face. 'Politicians. They have the unnatural ability to state things in such a way as to render the words utterly devoid of meaning.'

'I see some things are universal.'

'*Da*. Death, taxes, and politicians, who are often responsible for some of the former and all of the latter.'

Fydorov reached down and picked up a black, softsided briefcase, which he set on top of his wooden desk.

'This was retrieved from the lab; I believe it belongs to you.'

Kilkenny unzipped the briefcase; his laptop was inside.

'Our technicians were very impressed with your computer, particularly with the internal satellite modem.'

'It turned out to be quite useful in tackling Orlov's network. Did you get everything you need?'

'Da. Your associate Grinelli was most helpful in unlocking Orlov's secrets. I realize that we may not have as sophisticated computer equipment here as you do in the United States, but how did you take so much information out of Orlov's network in so short a time? It took hours for my people to download the information Grinelli sent them.'

Kilkenny sucked in a deep breath through his teeth. 'I'm afraid I'm not allowed to answer that.'

'State secret. I understand,' Fydorov replied, withdrawing the question. 'We have an entire team of people sifting through the information you and your associates siphoned out of Orlov's various businesses. This investigation will go on for years, and before it's done, a lot of very powerful individuals will have to explain their dealings with Orlov. This may result in some much-needed housecleaning in the executive and legislative areas of our government.'

'Sometimes, a little revolution is a good thing.'

'Oh, I have something else that I believe belongs to you.' Fydorov picked up a wooden box from his credenza and placed it on his desk. 'We found this in the vault at Orlov's bank.'

The side of the box bore a University of Michigan library bar code label. Kilkenny opened the lid and saw Johann Wolff's six notebooks.

'There is no need for these books to remain here as evidence. Cooper told me of their suspected importance, and I agree with him that they should be put back in the hands of their rightful owner.'

'What about all the lab equipment that was stolen by Leskov?'

'Dr Avvakum was most helpful in identifying those materials in her lab that she believes were stolen. These items have been packed and will be sent back to the United States.'

'Thank you,' Kilkenny said gratefully. 'This is a great help in getting Ted Sandstrom's research back on track.'

'Regarding this research project you are involved in, I have a favor to ask.'

'Oh,' Kilkenny said, wondering what possible conditions Fydorov might have in exchange for the equipment and the notebooks.

'Dr Avvakum has been completely cleared of any criminal involvement in this affair. Unfortunately, due to circumstances well beyond her control, she now finds herself unemployed. Cutbacks in the Academy of Sciences budget make it unlikely that she will be rehired there, not that I believe she wishes to return to her former posting in Siberia.'

'Are you saying she needs a job?'

'She has expressed an interest in continuing to work on this project. Do you think this Sandstrom might have an opening on his research staff for someone with her qualifications? I understand she's quite a gifted physicist.'

'I'll talk to Sandstrom about it,' Kilkenny replied. 'He's going to need someone who understands the work to help out while he's getting back on his feet.'

'Excellent. I've already spoken with officials at your embassy. There will be no problem with her visa or work permit. In fact, I've even made arrangements for her to fly back with you.'

'How convenient.'

'Yes, isn't it? When Cooper explained your plan to me, he said that two of the goals were the retrieval of the notebooks and the liberation of Dr Avvakum. I can think of no better way to honor my old friend than to see that Avvakum has the opportunity to choose what she will do with the rest of her life.'

Kilkenny recalled the conversation he had had with Cooper during the flight to Moscow, and nodded his head. 'I think he would be pleased.'

'There is one more thing. I've taken the liberty of making a small change in your flight back to the United States. Instead of Detroit, you will be arriving at Washington, D.C. I didn't want to send Cooper's body home unescorted.'

Kilkenny stood and extended a hand across Fydorov's desk. 'That's very thoughtful of you, Igor Sergeevich. Thank you.'

'You're welcome,' Fydorov replied, grasping Kilkenny's hand with firm respect.

68

AUGUST 2

Washington, D.C.

Upon their arrival at Dulles Airport, Kilkenny and Avvakum were met by a Customs official who whisked them through the border-entry process in near record time. Once their passports were stamped, they gathered up their carry-on baggage and entered the airport's main concourse, where CIA director Jackson Barnett and Cal Mosley stood waiting for them.

'I wondered who expedited our arrival paperwork,' Kilkenny said as he walked toward Barnett and Mosley.

'I heard you got a little banged up over there, Nolan,' Mosley said. 'How are you feeling?'

'Other than a few dings and some jet lag, I'm fine.'

'I'm glad to hear it.'

'It's good to see you again, Mr Kilkenny,' Barnett said.

Kilkenny reached out and shook Barnett's extended hand. 'And you, too, sir. If I may, Dr Lara Avvakum, I'd like to introduce you to Jackson Barnett and Cal Mosley. They were associates of Bart Cooper's.'

Avvakum smiled and offered her hand. 'A

349

pleasure to meet you, gentlemen. My condolences on your loss.'

'Thank you, Dr Avvakum, and welcome to the United States,' Barnett replied, his voice and manner rich with Southern warmth. 'Bart Cooper was a unique individual whom I, and many other people at the Agency, will dearly miss. On behalf of the CIA, I'd like to thank you both for escorting him home.'

'It was the least we could do,' Kilkenny acknowledged.

'I am certain that you want to get home as quickly as possible, Nolan, and I apologize for the layover that this stop has added to your journey. By way of compensation, I've made some dinner reservations for the four of us at an excellent restaurant not too far from here. I hope you don't mind.'

'I'm starved,' Avvakum said, appreciative of Barnett's gesture.

'It beats spending a couple of hours waiting here. Are we dressed appropriately?'

'You're both fine,' Barnett replied. 'Dr Avvakum, if you'd like to freshen up a bit, Cal and I need to have a word with Nolan in private.'

'Sounds like business,' she replied. 'I should be presentable in about ten minutes. Will that be enough time?'

'More than enough. Thank you.'

Avvakum picked up her overstuffed carry-on bag and walked toward the ladies' room. When she was out of earshot, Barnett turned to Kilkenny, his face serious.

'Nolan, from what Bart and Cal told me, the

concept for this operation was your idea.'

'In broad strokes, yes, it was. Cal, Bart, and my friend Grin can certainly take credit for fleshing out my idea and making it work.'

'He's being modest, sir,' Mosley said. 'This was his show from the beginning.'

'I was up to my neck in this, Cal. Vested interest.'

'I appreciate that,' Barnett said. 'I'm just pleased that you came back in one piece, more or less. Mosley painted a very bleak picture should Orlov have succeeded in acquiring ownership of this quantum technology.'

'In the long term, Orlov could have been in control of an industry with significant influence over the global economy – kind of like a one-man OPEC. Now that we got it back, quantum technology can evolve as it should in a free market.'

'When we first met, a little over a year ago, you were in the thick of a technological problem that was, in many ways, of the Agency's own making,' Barnett said. 'I am pleased to learn that my decision to leave that Spyder with you and your associate has proved to be a fruitful one. You've not only improved the device but applied it in a manner my operations planners hadn't yet contemplated.'

'The Spyder is very amenable to improvisation.'

'Yes. Now I find you involved in rescuing a technological advance of enormous magnitude that somehow slipped past all the analysts working for me.'

'Progress often comes from the most unexpected places.'

'True, but the Agency's job is to look for the unexpected and to protect the industries and technologies that underpin our economy. Industrial espionage is the most serious threat our nation has ever faced, and more and more the CIA is being drawn into cases involving technologies that few people have ever heard of. This is the second time you've risen to the challenge, Nolan. Twice now, you've proved to me that someone with your unique expertise would be of immense value to the Agency.'

'Are you offering me a job?' Kilkenny asked.

'In a manner of speaking.'

'Sir, I have the job I want at MARC and, frankly, I don't think I would make a very good spy.'

'I disagree, but I'm not asking you to be an agent. In fact, I'd prefer that you remain at MARC, where you will continue to be exposed to promising technological developments. You see, your value as an adviser to the Agency demands that you retain a level of professional objectivity.'

'Define *adviser*,' Kilkenny requested suspiciously. 'Do you want me to report on private-sector research? On who is working on what? There are both legal and ethical problems with that.'

'I understand your reluctance, but I believe your participation in this effort is crucial.' Barnett looked straight into Kilkenny's eyes. 'I have the authority to reinstate you in the navy and have you reassigned to the CIA.'

'I think I understand your motive, and I agree

with it, but this isn't the way to do it. You said it yourself, my value as an observer depends on my ability to work. If word ever got out about this relationship you're proposing, there wouldn't be one researcher in this country who'd even talk to me. Then there's the issue of nondisclosure agreements; reporting to you would be a violation that opens MARC, the CIA, and me to a lawsuit that we would, in all likelihood, lose.'

'There has to be some way that we can come to an agreement, Nolan. This is an issue with grave implications for national security, and it's not going away anytime in the foreseeable future.'

'I think there is a way. What if the CIA was to become a client of MARC's? In that kind of business relationship, I could provide you with assistance on technological issues on an as-need basis.'

'Much like our current arrangement involving the Spyder?'

'Exactly. We come to each other with specific issues, like the theft of Sandstrom's research by Orlov. If it ever got out that I was working with the CIA on something like that, the research community would probably hail me as a hero of intellectual-property rights.'

'As well they should. I think what you're proposing is workable, Nolan, and I'm sure we can come to some sort of arrangement.'

'I think so, too, sir.'

'If we're going to be working together, you're going to have to drop the *sir*. Call me Jackson.'

'All right, Jackson.'

'Welcome to the team, Nolan,' Mosley said.

69

AUGUST 3

Ann Arbor, Michigan

'Hello,' Kelsey called out from the base of the barn's spiral staircase. 'Is anybody home?'

'Morning, Kelsey,' Nolan answered. 'C'mon up. I'm in the kitchen.'

The loft smelled of bacon and brewing coffee. Nolan cracked the last egg into a bowl, dropped the shell into the sink, and then stopped to listen to the rhythmic patter of Kelsey's ascent up the metal stairs. He turned just as she reached the landing, backlit by the morning sun pouring through the east windows. She wore a light denim short-sleeved shirt over a white tank top and a pair of white cotton shorts. A waterfall of blond hair cascaded past her shoulders, shimmering as she walked. Though he'd spoken with her on the phone several times since her release, this was the first time they had seen each other.

'Aren't you going to meet me halfway?' Kelsey asked

'No. I'm just gonna stand here and watch you walk toward me, while I mentally undress you each step of the way.'

'Why do it all in your head?'

'Because I still have a couple of houseguests who'll be back from their morning run any minute now.'

Kelsey wrapped her arms around Nolan's neck, careful of his injured arm, and kissed him hungrily. 'More than enough time.'

'Kelsey, my love,' he said as his free hand roamed the length of her back, pressing her body into his, 'for what I have in mind, we'll need the rest of the day.'

'Oooo,' she purred. 'I like the sound of that.'

They kissed again, patiently savoring the sensation. The fears of the past few days evaporated with the reality that they were both back where they belonged.

Below, they heard the door to the stair tower open; Dawson and Gates were back from their five-mile run.

'Yo, Nolan,' Dawson shouted loudly from below. 'I see Kelsey's car out there. Is it safe for us to come up?'

'We're decent, Jack,' Nolan shouted back.

Dawson and Gates began thundering up the staircase.

'I don't know that I'd ever use the word *decent* in describing you, Nolan,' Gates said, his voice echoing up the stairwell, 'even if you are fully dressed.'

'Very funny, Max. You wanted that omelette burned, right?'

'Something smells good,' Dawson said appreciatively.

'Hit the showers, guys. I'll have my world-famous one-handed Mexican omelettes ready in five minutes.'

Both Dawson and Gates snagged a slice of bacon before heading off to clean up.

Kelsey glanced over at Nolan's table and saw five places set. 'Who else is dining with you and the guys?'

'My dad and Lara Avvakum, the physicist I brought back from Moscow. She bunked down in one of my dad's spare bedrooms last night. He called just before you arrived, and they should be over in a few minutes. You eat yet?'

'I had a bagel before I drove over. You don't have to make me anything, I'll just steal some of your omelette.'

'Fair enough, you can squeeze another chair in next to mine. Is Elli over at my grandparents'?'

'Yes, they're finalizing arrangements for the memorial service tomorrow. After all these years, she can finally lay Johann to rest knowing that he always loved her.'

'I'll bet that means more to her than the truth about what he did during the war, or even his notebooks.'

'It does. Speaking of the notebooks, your father negotiated a deal on Elli's behalf with the university. She's granted MARC development rights to the intellectual property, and the notebooks themselves will eventually go to the library.'

'What did my dad get for Elli in return?'

'MARC paid her a nominal amount, one dollar, for the development rights.'

'A buck? You're kidding.'

'No. Elli isn't rich, but she has enough to live

out the rest of her life in comfort, so she's not interested in money. She wanted something else.'

'What, then?'

'A building. If Wolff's notebooks turn out to be as valuable as we think they are, then the university stands to make a lot of money through the patents it'll hold jointly with MARC. If that happens, then the university is to erect a new physics building and name it in Wolff's honor.'

Following their late-morning breakfast, Sean Kilkenny and Lara volunteered to clear the dishes as Nolan and Kelsey walked Dawson and Gates out to their waiting cab.

'It's a shame you guys can't stick around longer,' Nolan said.

'That would be fun, but if Max and I don't report back in, we'll be listed as AWOL.'

'Can the navy really do that to an admiral?' Kelsey asked.

'It's not the navy we're worried about,' Gates answered. 'It's our wives.'

'Yeah, well, be sure to give Marcy and Julia my best.'

'Will do, Nolan.'

'And guys' – Nolan's voice tightened with emotion – 'thanks for everything.'

'Not necessary, Nolan,' Dawson replied, 'but you're welcome.'

'Anytime,' Gates said as he clasped Kilkenny's hand in his bearlike paw.

Kelsey gave both the admiral and the chief a warm embrace, knowing she owed them her life.

As the cab disappeared down the long gravel

drive, Avvakum and Nolan's father emerged from the barn.

'Thanks for breakfast, Nolan,' Sean said. 'Now, I think it's time you introduced Dr Avvakum to Ted Sandstrom.'

On their way to the hospital, they stopped by the MARC building, where Nolan retrieved the latest output from Grin's decoding program. Most of the first notebook was now deciphered, and Avvakum devoured each page as if it were a well-written novel.

'Hi, Kelsey,' Sandstrom said excitedly when she entered his room. 'Nolan, how's the shoulder?'

'Fine, Ted. It just went *pop*. We've brought along someone I'd like you to meet.' Nolan stepped away from the door. 'Come on in, Lara.'

Avvakum entered the sterile room nervously, her eyes aimed at the floor.

'Ted, I'd like to introduce Dr Lara Avvakum, formerly of the Russian Academy of Sciences.'

'Doctor,' Sandstrom said, 'pardon me if I don't rise, but it is truly a pleasure to finally meet you.'

Avvakum smiled slightly and looked up at Sandstrom. She didn't flinch when she saw his injuries.

'I don't know what to say,' Avvakum bubbled.

'Well, I do,' Sandstrom replied. 'I understand that you sent Nolan the message that helped him recover my research.'

'*Da.*'

Sandstrom stared directly into her eyes. 'Lara, in a sense you've saved my life. Thank you.'

'You're welcome.'

358

'I understand you've had a chance to review my work?' Sandstrom asked.

'Yes,' Avvakum replied.

'What do you think?'

'I think it's beautiful. Your work has taken you to the very threshold of creation; I could envision the delicate balance of order and chaos.'

'You see it the way I do,' Sandstrom said, pleased that he'd found a kindred spirit.

'Lara,' Kelsey spoke, 'why don't you show him what we picked up at MARC.'

Avvakum pulled out a thin sheaf of papers from her shoulder bag and handed them to Sandstrom. He studied the pages for a moment, baffled, then looked up at his visitors.

'Are these from Wolff's notebooks?'

'Yes,' Kilkenny replied. 'We're in the process of decrypting them.'

'It looks like they're in German. How soon before we can get a translation?'

Kilkenny leaned up against the windowsill. 'It's funny you should ask that. Not only is Dr Avvakum a very competent scientist with a strong interest in quantum physics, she also happens to be multilingual. Two of the foreign languages in her repertoire are German and English. While you're recuperating, MARC has hired Lara to translate the notebooks. She will, of course, pay you regular visits to report on what she's learned. If those first few pages are any indication of what's in the rest of the notebooks, you're both in for some very interesting reading. Once you're ready to restart your lab, I think you'll find Lara to be a very capable collaborator.'

Sandstrom looked at Kilkenny dubiously, knowing full well that he was being railroaded. Avvakum picked up on it immediately.

'Dr Sandstrom, I know how important it is to have the right people working in your lab. All I ask is that you give me a chance to prove my worth to you. After studying your research notes, I want to work on this project more than anything else in the world.'

'While she's here, you might as well give her a shot,' Nolan said.

Sandstrom nodded, disappointed at his momentary bout of selfishness. 'You're absolutely right. I can't do this alone; I'm going to need good help. You're on the team, Lara. Heck, you and I *are* the team. So, from now on, call me Ted.'

'Wonderful,' Avvakum replied. 'Would you like to know what is in the first notebook?'

'Yes!' Sandstrom said excitedly, handing her back the files.

'I skimmed through them on our way over to see you. You are, of course, familiar with Maldacena's work on M theory?'

'Of course.'

'I believe Wolff was pursuing a similar approach, and in the first notebook he's developed it quite extensively.'

'What do you mean by *extensively?*'

'I think his approach may successfully unify the four primary forces of nature.'

'Are you sure?' Kelsey asked.

'A workable theory of everything,' Sandstrom said slowly, his mind staggering with the

360

possibility that someone could attain the physicist's version of nirvana.

'That's what I am seeing in here,' Avvakum said. 'We won't know if he actually put it all together and made it work until the rest of the notebooks are decoded, but what I see of his approach so far is absolutely brilliant. If Wolff's theory works, he'll be hailed as one of the greatest minds of all time.'

70

AUGUST 4

Dexter, Michigan

On an unusually cool, clear summer morning, Elli Vital wept quietly as Reverend Bothe of the Dexter Lutheran Church said a final prayer. In addition to Johann Wolff's fiancée and the family of his friend Martin Kilkenny, the President of the University of Michigan and several members of the Department of Physics were present to pay their respects. Photographers and video crews kept a polite distance from the gravesite, their long telephoto lenses allowing them to get their pictures of the slain physicist's memorial service.

Bothe closed his prayer book and walked around to where Elli sat with Martin and Audrey Kilkenny. 'Ms Vital, I just wanted to express my deepest sympathies to you.'

Thank you,' Elli replied softly.

Martin drew Bothe aside. 'Reverend, you did a fine job. I appreciate your doing this for us, even though none of us are in your flock.'

'When Father Walsh called and explained that Johann Wolff was a Lutheran, well, how could I refuse?'

'Walsh's right. You're a good man, for a Lutheran.'

Bothe laughed, and pumped Martin's hand warmly, then walked back toward his car.

'Nolan,' Elli called out. 'Could you give me a hand?'

'Sure. I've still got one good one left.'

Elli stood and slipped her left arm through Nolan's right, bracing her elbow in his.

'Kelsey, you don't mind if I steal him away for a moment? I need to have a word with him.'

'Just as long as you return him.'

Elli led Nolan up to the headstone, where she paused for a moment. The marker bore both her name and Wolff's. When death finally came for her, this was where she wanted to be laid to rest.

'It's a strange thing to see your own name on a grave marker,' she said. 'But reassuring, in a way.'

They walked past a few more rows of headstones until they were well out of earshot of the small group of people milling around Wolff's grave. Elli pulled her arm free and turned to face Nolan.

'I wanted to thank you for everything you've done for me, and for Johann.'

'I'm just glad that both you and my grandparents lived to learn the truth.'

362

'It is a comfort.' Elli sighed, then held up her left hand. 'On the night before he was murdered, Johann proposed to me and gave me this ring. It was a symbol of his promise to love me always. As you know, Johann and I never married. Now I am an old woman. This is an engagement ring, and nothing would please me more than to see it used for its intended purpose. Unfortunately, I have no children of my own to pass it on to. Kelsey and I went through quite an ordeal together, one that I was uncertain we would survive. I would like her to have this ring – I believe she would appreciate it on many levels – but it's a gentleman's place to offer such a gift.'

Elli carefully slipped the ring from her finger and offered it to Nolan.

Nolan eyed the gold band carefully. 'Do you think Johann would mind?'

'If your heart, your mind, and your soul support the promise of that ring, then I know he would be pleased.'

Following dinner at Martin and Audrey's house, Nolan and Kelsey took a walk down by the small spring-fed lake. The evening sky burned with an orange-red glow, and the lake's surface mirrored the unearthly blaze. They walked side by side, each with an arm wrapped around the other's back.

'You know, Kelsey, I've been thinking about something.'

'Yes,' she said coyly.

When you and Elli were taken hostage, your kidnappers sent me a video clip to show that you both were unharmed.'

'I remember,' she replied, not at all sure where this was leading.

'In that clip, I saw that you were wearing what I assumed was Elli's ring.'

'I was hoping you'd notice.'

'I knew you were trying to send me a message. Actually, you sent two.'

'Two? What message did you get besides the obvious "I've got Elli's ring, please get us out of here" message?'

'This one.'

Nolan pulled away from Kelsey and turned to face her.

'Kelsey, will you marry me?'

'Are you serious?'

Nolan pulled the ring Elli had given him from his pocket and held it in his fingertips. Kelsey held out her left hand, and he carefully slipped the band onto her ring finger. Then he wrapped his hand around hers.

'When I saw this ring on your finger and thought about the very real possibility that I might lose you, I knew that when I got you back, I would ask you to marry me. I love you and want to spend the rest of my life with you. Will you marry me?'

Kelsey drew close and gently pressed her lips to his. She then withdrew, but only an inch.

'Yes.'